"WHERE THE DEVIL ARE YOU?"

Jemma called to Hunt as she jumped out of the car and switched on her flashlight. She stepped over the tire jack and peered down the embankment. "Hunt? Don't fool around. Where are you?"

"Jem?" Hunt cried out in a weak voice.

The tiny beam of her flashlight picked him out. He lay on his back, his eyes closed. Jemma scrambled down the embankment. "It's okay, Hunt. I'm here. Don't move." She bent over him and gently touched his face.

Hunt opened one eye. "I think every bone in my body is broken. I need doctoring. I may bleed to death."

Jemma reached over and tweaked his nose. "Charlatan! Imposter!"

"Desperate, that's all." Hunt grabbed her and pulled her to him. "Can't blame me for resorting to a groan or two to get your attention."

"Hunt, I swear—" His mouth came down on hers, hard and insistent, and she never finished the sentence....

ABOUT THE AUTHOR

In *One Hot Summer*, the writing team of Eve
Gladstone wanted to share with readers their love
for Upper New York State. The fictitious Ramsey
Falls is an amalgam of the best of small-town
Americana and the down-home values the authors
nostalgically remember. While both of these New
Yorkers love the glitz and glamour of their city,
they have a special place in their hearts for the
upstate paradise that so few people even know
exists.

Books by Eve Gladstone

HARLEQUIN SUPERROMANCE
297–ALL'S FAIR

HARLEQUIN INTRIGUE
23–A TASTE OF DECEPTION
49–CHECKPOINT
75–OPERATION S.N.A.R.E.

Don't miss any of our special offers. Write to us at the
following address for information on our newest releases.

Harlequin Reader Service
901 Fuhrmann Blvd., P.O. Box 1397, Buffalo, NY 14240
Canadian address: P.O. Box 603,
Fort Erie, Ont. L2A 5X3

Eve Gladstone

ONE HOT SUMMER

Harlequin Books

TORONTO • NEW YORK • LONDON
AMSTERDAM • PARIS • SYDNEY • HAMBURG
STOCKHOLM • ATHENS • TOKYO • MILAN

Published September 1988

First printing July 1988

ISBN 0-373-70324-4

To Joan Eckstein
Thanks for all those
magic moments of our friendship.

CHAPTER ONE

TOO HOT, Jemma Whiting thought as she crossed Main Street at an angle, and summer was a week away. The woolly caterpillar had arrived, or hadn't, or was it locusts that predicted weather, days, weeks, months in advance? Or neither, but something else with far too many feet. She had lived all her life in the Hudson Highlands and still couldn't get straight the tenets concerning long hot summers or long cold winters. Jemma knew one thing, though, Whiting Printing lay dead ahead, and it was air-conditioned.

Whiting Printing. The sign above the old-fashioned store on Main was brand new: gold letters on black in keeping with the turn-of-the-century reconstruction bug that had hit the town of Ramsey Falls like Elvis fever.

Jemma Whiting pushed the front door open and stepped into a sharp, pleasant cool. A cowbell above the door sent off its sonorous note announcing her arrival. She sucked in a proud sigh as she did every time she entered the shop. Inside, everything was polished oak, from the front counter to the reproduction roll-top desk piled with papers in her corner office. An old theatrical poster dominated the far wall, flanked by an assortment of eighteen-nineties calendars. The place smelled of fresh paint, ink, wax and success. Too bad the assortment of presses and duplicating machines had to be so prominent, but then this was the late twentieth century and one had to keep up with the times.

She stepped through the wooden gate that separated the reception and work areas, calling out, "Adriana." Turning right past the old oak library table stacked with printed materials, she stopped dead. "Who the devil are you?"

A dark-haired stranger was standing over the laser printing press with his back to her. He straightened up, and for a moment he stayed very still, as though he had been caught out and wasn't quite certain how to handle it. Jemma waited, curiosity beginning to drain some of her anger away. He was wearing creased chinos and a khaki shirt, and she thought perhaps he had come about the press. Except, of course, she hadn't called anyone and for a very simple reason. There was nothing wrong with it.

He turned suddenly, smiling, and flashed eyes of midnight black at her. "Hunt Gardner. I suppose you're the proprietor of the establishment." His voice was deep and resonant, the kind of voice that took command. She noted with appreciation his carelessly tossed hair and the evident wit in his dark, clever glance. He was handsome by anyone's standards.

"Where's Adriana?" she asked, catching a breath she wasn't even aware of holding.

He shrugged. "Said she wanted to have a bite, and I said go ahead, I'll mind the store."

"Oh, wonderful, I must have a word with her about talking to strangers." She came over and extended her hand. "I'm Jemma Whiting."

"Pleased to meet you, Jemma Whiting."

His touch was strong, warm and sure. For a long moment they regarded each other openly, and it was Jemma who had to pull her hand away.

"That's my shopper's guide on the press," she said, flushing slightly at his bemused smile.

"Is it? I was under the impression that it was a flyer for the new adult education center at Pack College."

"I'll kill Adriana if it is."

"I wouldn't do that if I were you. I paid hard money for my flyer." He nodded in the direction of the old-fashioned cash register on the counter.

"My shopper's guide," she said weakly. "My penny-saver crew is due in another hour. Oh, blankety-blank, stop the presses."

He threw his head back and laughed. "Stop the presses!"

At that moment the door burst open and Seth, her six-year-old son came tossing in, followed by his baby-sitter, Mrs. Lawson.

"Mr. Novak said I could have karate lessons starting next week," he announced. A towhead with a broad forehead and wide, intelligent eyes, he was dressed in full karate regalia, including a black belt. He took a brave stance once he came up to his mother, hitting the air a couple of times with balled fists, until he realized Hunt Gardner was watching him. He stopped in his tracks looking over at Jemma with a rueful, embarrassed expression.

"He's a black belt," Jemma explained to Gardner with a conspiratorial wink that asked him to keep secret from her son the improbability of a six-year-old obtaining a black belt in karate.

"A black belt. I'm impressed," Gardner said.

"This is my son, Seth. Seth, Mr. Gardner."

Seth advanced and allowed his hand to be encased in a man-sized shake. He stared at Gardner for a few seconds and then came to a decision. "Want to see me do karate?"

"Come on, Seth, time for lunch." Mrs. Lawson smiled apologetically at Jemma as she took him by the hand.

"I'd be interested," Hunt called as Seth was whisked away to a rear stairway that led to a rambling, five-room apartment over the shop. "The kid's good," he said to Jemma.

"Saw a movie and decided all he needed was the suit, and I haven't been able to stop him since. I guess I'll line him up for lessons, although I doubt his instructor will appreciate the black belt."

Hunt shook his head. "Enthusiasm is what counts, and I think your son has it in aces."

"Oh yes. The problem is going to be when he finds out he doesn't know the first thing about karate and what it takes to win a black belt."

"I suspect he's made of the right stuff."

"Oh, that he is, all right."

After taking in at a glance her brown hair and green eyes, Hunt said, "Seth looks like his father, I imagine."

"No." Jemma bridled, annoyed and yet oddly flattered by his scrutiny. "My side of the family all the way."

His eyes swept over her and in his half-grin she read too much curiosity, as if somehow he knew she was fudging the truth. And who in the world was he to have opinions about whom her son resembled and didn't?

"Wait a minute," she said, going to the press and reaching for the Off button. "We're standing here being very social and I've got a paper to get out."

"Uh-uh, bought and paid for." He put his hand on top of hers. "A paper to get out? Sounds like more of that 'Stop the presses' stuff. My order will be run off in another ten minutes, then it's yours to the end of time. What are we arguing about?"

"Stop the presses. Paper to get out." Jemma smiled. Far back in the pale reaches of time, a little more than a decade before, Jemma had been a journalism major at Pack College. She quit to send her husband through law school and didn't return until after the divorce. The *Ramsey Falls Shopper's Guide* was hardly journalism. It was an eight-page giveaway filled with advertisements, television and radio listings and the very short list of things to do weekly in Ramsey Falls. Lately she had, for a lark, added a column, "Jemma Says," which was turning out to be the most popular feature in the paper.

Hunt Gardner, catching her smile, took his hand away. The printer hurried obligingly on.

He was right, Jemma thought. What were they arguing about, she and this disturbingly attractive man? She picked up one of the flyers and began to read aloud. "'Marriage and Morés in the Twenty-first Century. A series of four public evening lectures conducted by Hunter Gardner, Ph.D., Ed.D, in July at Pack College, Merriman County, New York.'" She glanced at him. He was leaning against the oak counter, hands dug into his pockets. His grin was interested, as if he were waiting for a sigh of admiration. "Professor Gardner...marriage and morés in the twenty-first century. Tired of this century already, professor?''

''Until today, anyway.''

''And what do you think marriage will be like a dozen years from now?''

''You'll have to attend my lectures to learn.''

''Ah-ha, you have a crystal ball.''

''A solution,'' he said.

''A solution. Then you think marriage is a problem in search of a solution, which of course, you have.'' She was being aggressive and knew it. His dark, unfathomable eyes glistened slightly, as if he had arrived at some opinion about her that wasn't at all flattering.

''You don't think marriage is a problem, then,'' he said.

The press rolled efficiently on. Jemma glanced at the pile of printed flyers slipping smoothly out of it. He had ordered ten thousand, she guessed, far too many for little Ramsey Falls with its summer population that wanted to swim and picnic and most assuredly didn't want to listen to lectures on marriage at the local college. ''I think getting up in the morning is a problem sometimes,'' she remarked.

''Morning grouches,'' he said. ''Your husband, I hope, is quite cheerful.''

She hesitated before answering. His statement threw her off kilter, and she found herself not wanting to admit, for any number of reasons, to being divorced. ''An embarrassingly cheerful man,'' she said at last. ''And you?'' she asked, unable to avoid glancing at his left hand. Finding no wedding band, she added, ''And your wife?''

''I'm unfailingly good-tempered, although alas, no wife. Never had one, come to think of it.''

"No wife, pity. That should make you an expert on marriage."

"Ah, I understand, Mrs. Whiting. Signing a license and saying 'I do' is a guarantee of one's expertise in the matter."

She flushed and toyed with the idea of admitting that the embarrassingly cheerful Walt was now waking up in the arms of his current wife, and decided against it. That she did not wear a wedding ring but her school ring on her third finger left hand, had to do with covering what she thought of as an emptiness.

The press came to a smooth stop. The last page slipped out, clean and crisp. She glanced again at the flyer in her hand. "'Starting two weeks from now,'" she read. "'Subjects covered: Life in Micronesia, happy marriages, well-adjusted children.'" She smiled at him. "Slides?"

"It's not a travelogue, Mrs. Whiting."

The rear door opened and her baby-sitter peered out. "Seth said he doesn't want eggs."

"I'll be right there," Jemma said. "I could sack Adriana," she went on to Gardner, as she quickly wrapped the flyers for him and made out a bill. "Cash did you say?"

"Paid in full to your young assistant."

"I'll have to believe you, or have Adriana's head."

He took his package and shook her hand solemnly. "Don't. She's going to Pack in the fall, and she'll most assuredly need her head."

Jemma stared earnestly at him, not quite certain what to make of him. "Learned all about my assistant, have you?" she remarked at last.

He grinned, but she thought he looked faintly embarrassed. "It's my open face and guileless manner. You'd be surprised what people tell me voluntarily."

It was possible with his direct, interested gaze that he had the talent to make people confess their life stories and troubles to him. Well, she'd be on her guard against such incursions into her past. Jemma picked up the flyer she had attached to the bill. "You're not teaching full-time at Pack, are you?"

"No. As a matter of fact, Ramsey Falls is a stop between my lost vacation and Thailand. I'll be here until the end of July leading a seminar for doctoral candidates in adult education in third-world countries. The lecture series at night..." He stopped. "Tell you what, it's complicated. I could explain it all to you over coffee."

"I have to get my shopper's guide on the road," she said shaking her head. She wondered if he meant it and then decided that since he knew all about her deadline, he was merely being polite. "Sorry. Anyway, after the guide, I have to print some flyers on our tricentennial celebration."

"How about enclosing one of my flyers in each copy of your shopper's guide?" he asked.

"I charge for advertising, Professor Gardner."

He glanced quickly at the bill she handed him, marked paid in full. "Yes, of course you do."

"We get results."

"Well, I'll try the old methods," he said. "Handouts."

"You charge for the series, I note."

"The college charges. Don't forget to come to the evening lectures. Bring your husband."

They stood at the door of the shop for a moment, smiling at each other with a kind of aimlessness, as though they had all day. "Well," he said and opened the door. Then, after another slight hesitation, he left, closing the door gently behind him, the cowbell signaling his departure. Jemma marched quickly to the rear of the shop. Then, almost against her will, she turned and glanced out the window. He was crossing the street with a long stride, an easy, self-assured lope. Tall, broad-shouldered with a slender torso and narrow hips, he had the kind of physique that was hard to imagine out of chinos and in a business suit. Doctor of Philosophy, Doctor of Education. She wondered why the titles didn't quite square with the man. There was something disturbingly controlled about him, as though under the well-bred exterior were some wild, sexual, untamed animal.

"Mom?"

Her son's voice startled her for some reason. "Just give me a minute, Seth," she called. "Want to come help me set up the press?"

"Yeah." The response was a low, charming growl as he dashed up to her.

"Oh, hi, Mrs. Whiting." Adriana came in the front door with an ice-cream cone in her hand. She was a pretty redhead with guileless brown eyes and a face full of freckles. "Where's Professor Gardner?"

"Adriana," Jemma said with a sigh and then ran out of steam. Every time she saw the eighteen-year-old, she felt a sense of vexation. Perhaps because Adriana was young and without fear; perhaps because she made Jemma, at thirty-two, feel aged in a way Seth never did.

Adriana came over and handed Seth the ice-cream cone. "I saw you when I was in the ice-cream parlor," she said, talking to him in a fond, very grown-up way, "and I figured what you needed on a nice spring day was a double scoop of strawberry."

"Hey, neat," Seth said, taking the cone with a glance at his mother, waiting to be admonished.

"He hasn't had lunch, Adriana."

"Okay, come on, Seth. We'll put it in the freezer."

"Eggs," he groaned.

With a shrug of her shoulders, Jemma let them both go. Adriana was a darling. She meant to pay her for the extravagance of a very expensive ice-cream cone. And she had better stop daydreaming. The penny-saver kids were due, and once the guide was out, the four-color flyer for the tricentennial was scheduled.

No complaints, mind you. She had made a small profit this year of the Ramsey Falls tricentennial, and if juggling flighty freshmen college kids and her six-year-old son and every other damn thing were part of the cost, then so be it. Next year would be better. She might never have the time to relax, but then that was what kept the bogeyman away.

"CELIE, LOVE, how about slipping one of these in every issue of the *Times Herald*?"

Celie Decatur pushed her tinted aviator glasses high on her small, sharp nose. She took the flyer Hunt Gardner handed her and read it over quickly. "Who did your artwork?"

"Some kid in the Pack art department." He eased his lanky frame into the modern black leather and chrome chair that faced her desk in Ramsey Falls' tallest building, the four-story, pink brick, restored Decatur Towers that dated back one hundred years.

"Next time ask me."

"What's wrong with it?" The question was lazily asked. "Pay a college kid and you're going to get a college kid's ideas." Hunt was perfectly satisfied with the job.

"Not professional. Anyway, about distributing it with the paper, we don't offer free lunches at the *Times Herald*, Hunt, you ought to know that. I'd charge anyone else a goodly sum."

"Ramsey Falls is beginning to look like a backwater Wall Street," he told her, thinking of Jemma Whiting and her refusal for the same reason. With Celie Decatur, however, he was certain of more equable results. "This is adult education. I'm not in it for the profit, Celie."

"Really? You do like to eat, don't you?"

"Only my own words."

She pushed at her glasses again and read the notice. "Marriage in the twenty-first century. Where'd you come upon that title? You're going to get science-fiction freaks, you know that."

He laughed. "As long as they're interested in preserving the marriage bond, for all I care they can descend from the Crab Nebula and live on phony brick face. A flyer in each copy of the *Times Herald*, Celie. Your gift to education."

"How many do you have?"

"Ten thousand."

"Not enough, Hunt. I know you think our section of the Hudson River Valley is really Ruritania, but my newspaper covers the southeast corner of the county. That's fifteen thousand readers weekly guaranteed. You're five thousand short."

"Am I?" He grinned with satisfaction. "I'll just have to hie me over to the print shop and order some more."

"You know our little doyenne of Whiting Printing, then." Her remark was edged with ill-concealed annoyance. The *Ramsey Falls Shopper's Guide* was a free eight-page penny saver that paid its way with advertising revenues. As far as Celie was concerned, the guide cut heavily into *Times Herald* advertising and served no purpose except to pay Jemma's bills.

"Met the son, too," Hunt said. "The karate kid." Then added, although he couldn't say why, "But not the husband. He involved with the business, too?"

Celie didn't answer at once. She instinctively understood the quickened interest in his eyes, eyes so dark they lent a certain feral quality to his narrow, intelligent face.

Celie Decatur was a pretty woman in her late thirties, slim and well dressed, her blond hair short and carefully waved. She had been widowed three years before and wore a wedding ring on her right hand. Celie inherited the newspaper, the building it was housed in and important real estate along Main Street. It included Jemma Whiting's print shop.

"She's divorced," Celie said.

Hunt's smile turned into a crooked grin. "Is she really, now?"

"A bitter, acrimonious divorce."

"That the whole town is still talking about," he commented, surprised at how curious he was and yet how little he wanted Celie to know it.

"It happened three, four years ago, something like that. A few more interesting things have happened around town since. Walt's an overbearing, officious snob, and Jemma is well rid of him. Left her high and dry, too, with just the house, which she promptly sold to buy the print shop and that penny saver. I admit it took a lot of nerve for a housewife whose only business experience was waitressing, but she isn't out of the woods yet. Frankly, we were only too happy when Walt moved to the county seat. And married, incidentally. That's enough of Jemma Whiting. I'll enclose a flyer in each copy of this week's issue because I'd like to see more of our good citizens enrolled in Pack's adult ed program."

"Celie, you're to be congratulated. You're a model citizen." Hunt stood and said, "I've got the ten thousand sitting outside. Five thousand more delivered when?"

"Tomorrow."

"It's a deal." He stuck his hand out. Celie remained seated but grasped his hand in a strong shake. "I'll want you out at the house Saturday night. Dinner. The usual local muckamucks. The more people you meet and socialize with the better it's going to be for your program."

"I'll only be here until the end of July," he said and watched as a slight frown crossed her face. Jemma Whiting hadn't turned a hair when he mentioned the fact.

"You may want to come back," she said.

"Victor Bosworth only wanted a small slice of my life and ten quarts of blood, and that's all he's going to get. I'm on my way to fulfill my contract in Thailand. After that I've my sights set on Nepal."

She took her glasses and shifted them to her hair so that they sat like a crown on her head. "The well-traveled Mr. Gardner. Don't you ever think of settling down?''

He felt the familiar annoyance. Don't ask personal questions, don't close in. He liked the way he lived and needed no apologies. He was engaged in work of redeeming social value, and that was its own excuse.

Victor Bosworth had introduced him to Celie when Hunt first arrived in Ramsey Falls two weeks before. Celie was quick to move in. She was a forceful, forthright woman who held definite opinions about people. Hunt suspected that he had all the right credentials for piquing the interest of Celie Decatur: education, interesting work, a certain worldliness, and he was single. She was wasting her time, however, if she imagined him a permanent part of the Ramsey Falls social scene.

Still, Hunt liked a good time as well as the next man. "About your invitation," he said. "White tie and tails?"

She looked him over, as if aware of his refusal to discuss himself and smarting slightly. "A little better than what you're wearing now," she said, referring to his chinos and khaki shirt. "We, in the boondocks, do like to dress up in our Paris gowns and Saville Row suits every now and then. Six o'clock for cocktails.''

"Gotcha." As he went out into the warm, early-summer air he was whistling, and he wondered why he felt, for the first time since his arrival in Ramsey Falls, as if he was in a place he wanted to be—for the moment, anyway.

Ramsey Falls was a small town on the western side of the Hudson River, within three hours of New York City. The actual falls, which cascaded down a split of rock in the highlands above the river, were a local lovers' rendezvous. The area was filled with Gothic Revival houses, Federal houses, colonial houses and dozens of white Victorians, snug in amongst thick forests and rolling countryside. Once that corner of the county had been home to great apple orchards and dairy farms, but was now growing back to forest and a remarkable green revolution.

The towns along the river were old with active, enthusiastic historical preservation societies. The Ramsey Falls Preservation Society, in fact, was preparing for the town's tricentennial. The names of its citizens were as apt to be German as English, English as Dutch; its history as intertwined with the Indian Wars as with the Revolutionary War. From where Hunt stood, it seemed a microcosm of the best of America—stolid, self-sufficient, and in this its tricentennial year, self-congratulating. An America, he thought as he went back along Main Street to Whiting Printing, that had become a foreign country to him, in which he was just a tourist.

The bell jangled at Whiting Printing. Adriana was standing at the printing press, her expression suggesting she was staring into mindless space. Jemma Whiting was nowhere in sight. "Where's the boss?" Hunt called across to her.

Adriana smiled when she saw him. "Oh, hi, Professor Gardner." She came briskly over, a slight flush beneath her mask of freckles. "Everything okay?"

"More than. I figured on doubling this morning's order."

"Really? Wow. How come?"

Jemma came wandering out of her office, carrying a pamphlet in her hand. She stopped when she saw Hunt. Her face, which Hunt thought of as very expressive, underwent a remarkable change. Her eyes brightened. She tried to look stern, and he had the extraordinary feeling that she had been thinking of him.

"When do you need them?" Adriana asked, in a voice suddenly lowered a register and sounding very serious. "Mrs. Whiting, he needs ten thousand more flyers."

"First thing tomorrow. You have all day." Hunt looked at Jemma. "Got the shopper's guide out in time?"

"Managed, thank you." She checked the printing press, which operated silently at top speed.

"I could use a copy. I'm trying to find a second-hand desk chair. The one at Mrs. Duboise's charming retreat needs new caning."

"Mrs. Duboise. Is that where you're staying?" Jemma came over to the counter in short, almost dragging steps, knowing she shouldn't act curious. It was what he wanted her to be. Then she wondered why they had squared off so.

"Bed-sitter as they say in England. Very nice."

"You're very lucky. She's awfully fussy about her boarders." The Duboise place was a seventeenth-century stone house sitting on Cutter's Lane and was one of Ramsey Falls' treasures.

"She fusses about me all the time. The trouble with the chair is that its caning is as old as the house, what's left of it, the caning I mean, not the establishment."

"It's a venerable, noble cottage with an interesting history, and she's anxious to keep it authentic."

Adriana, who had been carefully making out a bill, said, "Ten thousand, right?"

"Right."

"Ready to be picked up tomorrow morning, right?"

"Right."

"Would you like to pay now?"

"If you'll take a check."

"We even take credit cards," Jemma put in. "Adriana, check the press, honey, and then work on those lists, okay?"

"See you later, Professor Gardner."

"I like your personnel," he commented to Jemma.

"We aim to please." She handed him the bill. "I'm amazed that you managed to unload ten thousand copies of your flyer already. Did you stand out on the highway and hand them to passing motorists?"

"I hadn't thought of that," he said. "Actually, I need five thousand more for the *Times Herald*. They're going out with the next issue. Courtesy of its owner."

Jemma regarded him steadily. She could see Celie's mind working. Something rare had floated into town and was teaching at the college, a genuine bachelor of a certain age, who was handsome, to boot. No, she decided immediately, that was stupid and unfair. Celie was really interested in seeing the adult education department at Pack succeed, and she had the good grace to do something Jemma hadn't—given him distribution for free.

"That's very nice of Celie," she said honestly.

"She'd like to see a few more of the town's citizens pulled away from television or bowling night to attend the college."

"In some ways, she underestimates the population of this town. It's full of working mothers with houses and kids to be taken care of after hours. It's a wonder they find time to breathe."

"Do you?" he asked, leaning across the desk and smiling at her.

"Not really."

"Mr. Whiting doesn't help with the housework."

"Never did."

"Mr. Whiting should be brought before the bar and sentenced to ten years penance. Washing kitchen floors day and night should do it."

They were close now, their faces inches apart. Jemma was aware of his rugged complexion, well-sculpted lips, strong narrow nose, and eyes that refused to be read. "I'm divorced," she said at last and then was surprised at the small breath of satisfaction that escaped from his lips. "You knew all the time, didn't you?" she said quietly.

"It depends upon how you define all the time." He picked a spanking fresh copy of the *Ramsey Falls Shopper's Guide* from a pile on the counter. "How about letting me make amends for using up your press time by distributing some up at the college. Service gratis."

"Already there, Professor Gardner. We don't let any grass grow under our feet."

He smiled and glanced at page one of the guide. "Ah, full-page ad for Cromers Corner Farmers Market. They give advanced degrees over at Pack in the pronunciation of that name. Let's see, early corn, six for ninety-nine cents. Too early for the local product. They must come from Mexico." He looked over the paper at Jemma and found her frowning at him. He opened the paper to the second page. "Ah, 'Jemma Says,'" he remarked. "You, I presume are the self-same Jemma."

She slammed the pamphlet down that she had been pretending to examine and went back to the press as it silently, slavishly dropped sheet after printed sheet.

Hunt resumed his reading out loud. "'Use is being made of the Falls Mall ...'" He stopped and smiled at Jemma, but all he had was an appreciative view of the snug fit of her jeans and her slender back, which stiffened slightly. He went on, certain she was listening to every word he said. "Falls Mall, Whiting Printing, Cromers Corner Farmers Market, the place is a hotbed of euphonics." He resumed reading, "'Use is being made of the Falls Mall by senior citizens who meet daily to hike the length of the mall. The shopping center is safe and our senior citizens get their daily exercise in charming surroundings. This is one case of function following form. I wonder,'" he continued reading, "'what the mall would look like if the architect had been told to design walks for senior citizens. Steps, dark corners, and the whole thing built uphill, I daresay.'"

Hunt gave Jemma an admiring smile, although she was still involved with the running of the press. Then the telephone rang before he could say anything. While she was on the phone, the door opened, the cowbell noted it obligingly, someone came in, then the door opened again, followed by three or four people in succession. Adriana rose from her seat at the computer keyboard and came over to the counter.

Hunt saw that he had quickly become excess baggage and glanced up at the old school clock on the wall. Damn, he had an appointment at Pack with the provost. He had walked into town, and it would take a brisk twenty minutes going back. "May I take this?" he asked Adriana, folding the shopper's guide in half.

"Sure, it's free."

"See you tomorrow, Adriana."

"Right, Professor Gardner." She gave him a harried grin.

At the door, before pulling it open Hunt turned back to Jemma. It was apparent she was still engrossed in her telephone call. At the same time she watched him curiously out of wide green eyes.

He'd been conned by Victor Bosworth of the Bosworth Foundation into coming to Ramsey Falls. But now he was here, and the landscape was suddenly beginning to look pretty good.

Hunt closed the door behind him and turned north toward the college. He was halfway up the street when he heard his name called. "Oh, Professor Gardner, could I talk to you for a minute?" It was Jemma Whiting, hurrying toward him.

"Anything wrong?"

"No, as a matter of fact," she said, a little out of breath. "I just wanted to do a solicitation."

He waited without saying anything.

"Why not take a full-page ad in next week's guide? It doesn't cost a bundle, and I'll bet you'll fill your class."

He felt genuinely contrite when he refused. "The college is tight-fisted when it comes to advertising funds."

"Well," she said, offering him a sunny smile, "I had to ask. I wouldn't be much of an advertising mogul if I hadn't. Anyway, here, let me show you." She reached for the guide that he was still holding and opened it to the second page.

"'Jemma Says,'" she remarked. "Halfway down the column are the following words: 'Congratulations to Pack College for offering a fascinating lecture series in its new adult education program. The program is a result of a full grant given by the Bosworth Fund and will consider all aspects of contemporary life. Of particular interest will be a month-long series of evening public lectures offered by Professor Hunt Gardner on the social structure of third-world countries.' You see," she continued, folding the paper and handing it back to him, "I do read the press releases."

"Then *you* knew all the time," he said, slipping the paper into his back pocket. He felt that he had been bested by her, and for once he wasn't quite certain that he wanted to talk his way out of it.

"Incidentally, our circulation is twenty thousand," she said. "That's five thousand over the *Times Herald*. Of course, we don't serve up late-breaking news."

"Mrs. Whiting." It was Adriana, calling her from the shop.

Jemma turned and flushed slightly. She had left some customers standing there while she had dashed out to make her point with Professor Hunt Gardner. Whatever had she been thinking? "Excuse me," she said and hurried up the street. The problem at hand prevented her from considering his reaction. She had time, however, to ponder why it was so important to her.

CHAPTER TWO

TWO O'CLOCK in the morning. A car rumbled past. The street lamp sent its fugitive cast through the window and along the bedroom ceiling. Jemma, lying awake in the dark, could hear the distinct click of the signal switch at the corner as the traffic light changed from red to green. Funny, but the sound was comforting. When she had first decided to rent the apartment over the shop, the bedroom window on Main Street worried her. Main Street, Ramsey Falls, not mean city streets; she'd cope she promised herself. Main, of course, wasn't in Manhattan, and except for a core of college kids given to riding noisily past on weekends at midnight, Ramsey Falls folded in upon itself early.

The important thing was that her son's room faced a back garden. In addition, the apartment contained commodious oak-floored rooms with fireplaces in both the living room and kitchen. The apartment easily swallowed the furniture she brought from her house when it was sold. What Jemma left behind, besides bitter memories of things gone wrong, was the quiet of the country, and she thought she would miss that most of all. But she hadn't. The country was left behind, and so was Mrs. Walter Whiting, the twenty-eight-year-old ex-wife of the successful lawyer practicing in the county seat.

Jemma had faced a tough decision when she rented the apartment. It was a little more than three years ago that she had signed on the dotted line for both the shop and the apartment over it. The money for the sale of her house—part of the divorce settlement—had been just enough to purchase the old *Ramsey Falls Shopper's Guide* and the only printing shop in Ramsey Falls.

Walt expressed his disapproval of the sale of the house, the purchase of the shopper's guide, of the shop, of the rented apartment. He seemed to think that as Seth's father, he still had a right to interfere in the way Jemma chose to live her life. "Jemma, you're a dreamer, you always were. That house was where Seth should be growing up. Good lord, don't you know anything?"

No, apparently she hadn't. She had thought they were in love. She had thought they had a life together. She thought they would produce a large, happy family and fulfill the only reality she thought worth having— home, hearth and continuity.

Another car rumbled past. Jemma turned on her bedside lamp and eased herself up against her pillow. Usually sleep came quickly. Her days were too hectic to fight the sandman when she managed to flop into bed each night.

Marriage and Morés in the Twenty-first Century. What had made her nose-dive so readily back into the past? Could it be the mocking, intelligent eyes of the professor from Pack? She shook her head. What was the use of contemplating the future when the here and now needed ever so many adjustments?

Her life, for instance. The professor could write a book about happy marriages turning sour like old milk

left out too long. You don't know you've left it out,
and by the time you discover it, you don't have yo-
gurt, and you certainly don't have cottage cheese. And
the trouble is, you realize you were never that crazy
about milk in the first place.

She reached over and flipped on the radio. The music came down from the state capitol, an all-night sta-
tion that played Bach in the early hours. She picked up
her yellow legal pad, on which only the words "Jemma
Says," were written. After a moment of empty contemplation, however, she put the pad back and leaned
against the pillow, her hands locked behind her head,
the smile playing about her lips that came over her each
time she thought of Professor Gardner.

He was a man who enjoyed repartee and tipped his
figurative hat when bested. But she'd had the last word
there on Main Street. She'd given his lecture series free
publicity, and before he could utter a word, she had
turned on her heels and gone back into her shop. Now
why, she wondered, did she feel such immense satisfaction from that encounter?

And why the devil couldn't she sleep?

She turned the radio off in the middle of a commercial, closed the light, snuggled down in bed, listened
automatically for the quiet emanating from her son's
room and tried to talk herself into sleep.

What would the professor say if he knew how Walt
had treated her? How a husband after six years of
marriage treated a wife. But it was all so complicated,
even if it had looked pretty simple a decade before. Fall
in love with a would-be lawyer while he was still in
graduate school. Help put him through school, and
when he graduated and took his first job, begin the
family she had always wanted. Smile with approval

when he joined a large law firm in Merriman, the county seat. It was thirty miles away, and because he often worked late, he eventually took a small apartment there, which he began to use more and more frequently.

Seth was three, and Jemma deep into apple pies and ruffled curtains, when the dream caved in.

Walt came home one evening and told her succinctly and without pity, that he had met the woman of *his* dreams and that he no longer loved Jemma. It helped that the woman of his dreams sat on the bench as a family court judge, giving Walt the cachet he felt he deserved. Oh, Walt was good at his profession, all right, as the divorce decree attested. He even convinced Jemma it was best for her to sign the papers quickly. Her own lawyer was lazy, distracted by his plans for retirement, used to making compromises, perhaps not even bright and certainly no match for Walt.

The house was hers, Walt proclaimed, proving how magnanimous he could be, aware of the gossip that would float around town otherwise. Seth would receive support and Jemma alimony as long as she didn't work. The alimony was frugal and forced her to make a few decisions.

The decree had an added feature, one Jemma virtually ignored at the time. It ordered perimeters around Jemma's social life or she could lose Seth.

It was summer at the time. It could have been winter. She could have been sent out into the snow to find her way in the dark. Suddenly she was Jemma, the unmarried lady with a small son and few skills to get on in the world.

Professor Gardner, she now thought with a faint little recollective sigh, *marriage will always be the same, today and in the twenty-first century, as long as men are men and women are fools.*

"How is the registration coming along for your lecture series?" Victor Bosworth gave Hunt an interested smile.

"Not bad." Hunt shoved the figures across Victor's modern teak desk.

"Not bad but not good, is that it?" Victor took up the list and read the tally. "Seventy-five so far. I'm impressed. We've been publicizing the lecture series for less than a month. The flyers went out with Celie's *Times Herald* two days ago, and the figure adds up very nicely. What did you expect?" He tapped the paper with a long, manicured finger.

"Considering I decided on the public evening lectures at the last minute, I'm not sure. The educational tastes of Americans haven't been my beat in a long time," Hunt said.

"Then it's a good thing I brought you back home."

Hunt laughed. "Kicking and screaming, cutting into my well-earned vacation. I'm still trying to figure out what happened."

"Promises of a Gardner-trained assistant, Maxwell J. Tam by name, paid for by the Bosworth Foundation, so that when you go to Thailand, you'll have the kind of field help you've always wanted," Victor said good-naturedly.

"Got me there." Hunt lounged back in his chair and stretched out his long legs in his characteristic way. "When every other grant available comes loaded down with enough stipulations to paper a path to the moon, you pull me into your web and then set me free on my terms. I thank you, and Max Tam also thanks you."

Victor Bosworth was a tall, scholarly man in his late forties, with a pale complexion and gray, serious eyes behind thick glasses. His thinning hair was of a nondescript brown, his clothes expensive and tweedy. He was poised, cool and had both exquisite manners and self-assurance.

His thousand-acre stud farm was located fifteen miles from Pack College. The colonial mansion, set high on rolling acres, overlooked half a dozen stables painted a pristine white and trimmed in navy blue, the Bosworth colors. Mares and their foals grazing in paddocks could be seen through the wide window of the library, where Hunt and Victor were having their conversation. A stallion, the color of sable and worth a million dollars, stood in lonely splendor behind an acre of white board fencing off to the right.

The Bosworth Foundation meant funding for a project dear to Hunt's heart, and as he glanced out the window, those rolling acres reminded him how bottomless that fund could be.

"The auditorium holds about a hundred fifty," Hunt continued, his full attention returning to his host, "and the registration shows we could have easily that many."

Victor smiled, revealing an unexpected sweetness. He was a bachelor, like Hunt. Unlike Hunt who grew up on a farm in the midst of a large, noisy family, Victor was the only son of a construction engineer who had made a great fortune building bridges in South America. Victor's inheritance was of sufficient size to endow the Bosworth Foundation, and as chairman, he

was able to back the serious educational projects he
was interested in.

Hunt had met Victor Bosworth the previous fall on
a ship bound from Singapore to a small island in Micronesia, where Victor would vacation and Hunt was
setting up an adult education program. Victor liked
Hunt's expertise and success rate, and it took him the
rest of that year and the beginning months of winter to
convince Hunt by telephone, telegraph and mail, that
he'd be welcome at Pack College if he wanted to train
recruits in the art of adult education in primitive third-
world countries.

Hunt wasn't buying. He had a contract to go to
Thailand in August. The idea of spending July in some
backwater community in the States was not part of his
plans.

Those plans, in fact, included a calorie-laden diet of
civilization. July in New York, museums, Broadway
plays, summer concerts in the park, and a tall, wil-
lowy blonde named Dara, who was pliable, willing,
free of encumbrances, and had a luxurious apartment
overlooking Central Park.

With his fortune, however, Victor Bosworth had
never learned the meaning of the word, "sorry," and
he was persuasive, indeed, offering the right medicine
at the right time. Hunt had always wanted to train an
assistant in the field, but there were never enough education funds from the government to cover it. He had
met Max Tam on a previous visit to Thailand. Hunt
caught up with him again in New York where the
young man was working on his doctoral dissertation.
The Bosworth Foundation would cover the cost of
Max's training as well as fund Hunt's project, Victor
promised. All Hunt had to do was give a month-long

seminar to a group of doctoral candidates at Pack, Victor's alma mater, and the grant was his.

Dara, disappointed, enplaned for the Riviera, and Hunt hitched up his jeans and came stalking into Ramsey Falls. The view, he was discovering daily, wasn't bad, it wasn't bad at all.

Hunt had volunteered to add a public evening lecture series to the summer adult-education program. A man of boundless energy, he saw the lectures as an interesting way to use his spare time. That he was attractive to women, Hunt would have been a fool not to know. Socializing in Ramsey Falls, however, wasn't on his agenda. He wasn't about to start something with Victor Bosworth breathing down his neck. It was a month or two in the country, and he meant to keep his nose clean and Victor impressed. So far his promise to himself had worked.

The telephone buzzed. "Excuse me," Victor said, reaching for the receiver. Hunt stood and ambled over to the window, his eyes on the playful foals and mares, one of which had begun to race around the edges of the paddock, stirring up the others.

"Jemma, good to hear from you. I know, don't tell me, it's not a social call."

Hunt started at the sound of Jemma's name and then shrugged, digging his hands into his pockets. An old-fashioned name. In a town rooted in history, there could be any number of Jemmas around. He moved restlessly away from the window, caught Victor's eye and the shake of Victor's head, which told him to listen in quite freely, without fear of embarrassment. The paintings on the walls were huge, modern abstractions, and Hunt stood in front of one, trying to make out the signature, while Victor talked eagerly on.

"Certainly, put Bosworth Stud down for a page. No, I don't know what kind of message. Tricentennial greetings—I'll leave it up to you, Jemma. How's Seth? Day camp and karate? That should keep him busy over the summer. Listen, have Mrs. Lawson bring him out here for riding lessons, why don't you?"

Hunt, listening, turned quickly and came back and sat down. Victor's face had reddened considerably and his gray eyes held a certain amount of sparkle. *Don't get involved,* Hunt told himself. *Don't even think about her, and above all, hold no opinions. One week to the end of June, then July, then you're out of there, taking no baggage with you. It's hot in Thailand. You don't need baggage, not even the kind that sticks to your memory.*

"Don't forget Saturday, Jemma," Victor added. He put the receiver down with a self-satisfied little sigh.

All the money in the world, Hunt thought, and it only took a green-eyed lass to bring the man to his knees. Love in the twentieth century. She was too young for him, dammit.

Victor gave an embarrassed laugh. "We have the tricentennial celebration coming up the end of July, if you haven't heard. Balloons, fireworks, posters, advertising. Bosworth Stud's on everybody's list."

Hunt offered him a smile of sympathy, which he didn't feel but was certain was expected. "Three hundred years old. Ramsey Falls is holding up well, under the circumstances. I suppose the very late Mr. Ramsey would approve," he said.

"I'm sure he would," Victor agreed. "Actually, we're descendants of Ramsey's on a distant cousin's side. Kit Ramsey was a farmer who emigrated north from Long Island with his bride. He was following in the footsteps of a brother who settled near Kingston. The site of the falls intrigued Ramsey, and he figured on building a mill for grinding flour, but it never happened.''

"Competition too tough?"

Bosworth shook his head. "He bought into the fur-trading business, which made him a far wealthier man. There's a handsome old stone house not far from where you're bedding down that he built for his bride. Museum now." Victor reached into his bottom desk drawer and extracted a small, hard-covered book. "Here," he said. "This is something I wrote a dozen years ago, tracing the history of Ramsey Falls. Had it privately published. The local historical society has ordered a couple of thousand to sell during the celebration.''

Hunt flipped through the pages, noting the watermarked paper it was printed on and the simple graphics. "Thanks," he said, and stood to take his leave. "I'll let you know as the returns on registration come in.''

Victor Bosworth walked him to the door, clapping a friendly hand on his shoulder. "Appreciate what you're doing, Hunt. I realize I moved in on your vacation plans, but I have the impression you think it's in a good cause.''

"It's a good cause, Vic. I'm also impressed that you've taken it on when there are plenty of charities waiting in line.''

"My father made his fortune building bridges in primitive countries. People were displaced and landscapes destroyed in the bargain. He wanted me to pay back what I could in education, and that's just what I'm doing.''

They shook hands, and when Hunt parted from his host at the front door, he had the odd feeling that something had been left unsaid, and the even odder notion that it concerned Jemma Whiting. All that history, all that money, all that power, and it was very possible Victor Bosworth needed a friend.

No friends, Hunt told himself as he stepped into his car. No friends, no attachments, no love affairs. So why the hell could the long reach of one woman threaten the tenuous relationship between the man with the message, and the man with the money?

"A DOG? No, Seth, no dog."

"Why?" Seth was sweaty, naggy and insistent, and Jemma was running late. He stood on one sneakered foot and then the other, a stubborn fist grasping the rubbery head of a model dinosaur. A hot June wind blew through the open kitchen window, caressing Jemma's freshly washed hair.

"No dog."

"Mommy, I'll walk him, I promise, I promise, I promise."

"Don't nag."

"Mr. Bosworth said he's an Australian shepherd."

"Seth, dinner's ready. Put the dinosaur down. Are your hands washed?" Jemma, in a cotton kimono, her thong sandals slapping on the linoleum floor, brought a plate of roast chicken, creamed spinach and potatoes to the kitchen table.

"Can I ask Daddy?"

"Your daddy's in Italy. I'm the officer in charge of this establishment—not your father. *And* whether you get a dog or not."

"When's he coming back?"

"I told you a dozen times, the end of the week. Sit down, Seth, and eat. Mrs. Lawson will be here any minute, and I'm late for my date with Mr. Bosworth, to whom I intend to give a piece of my mind."

"Huh?"

"Want milk or juice?"

"Why can't I have a dog?"

"I don't know why," she said impatiently. Satisfied that her son had at last picked up his knife and fork, she presented him with a glass of juice and stalked into her bedroom to dress.

Seth, as usual, with the fighting instinct of the very young, had the last word. "Spinach, yuk."

She laughed. Why not a dog, indeed? An Australian shepherd pup had wandered into the stables of Bosworth Stud, and Victor got it into his head that Seth should own the creature. She, of course, would have to walk it, feed it and love it. But there was no time, no *time*. She had pulled her son out of the country where he would have had a dog and a cat, a rabbit and geese, the whole gamut. She had stuck him over a shop through which the town winds blew a little dusty. She'd have to think about it. What in the world did an Australian shepherd look like, anyway?

Jemma sat down at her dressing table and began to brush her hair. Tonight she was being escorted by Victor Bosworth to Celie Decatur's grand white mansion in the hills overlooking the Hudson. As little as a year ago it was a scenario she'd never have dared dream. Well, she wouldn't have dreamed of Victor as a date under any circumstances. And Celie hadn't directly asked her to the dinner. She was coming as Victor's companion.

When Victor first invited her, Jemma had refused. "You know, Celie and I are on rather shaky terms. She's my landlord, which makes her a natural adversary, and she really believes I've taken advertising away from the *Times Herald*. I think I'll pass on this one."

"If she regarded you as competition, she'd squash you in a minute, Jemma."

Jemma's answer was quietly stated, "I don't think I can be stepped on that easily, Victor."

He gave a soft laugh. "No, of course you can't. Celie's parties are always interesting," he added.

"Let her know you've asked me, then."

"Certainly."

"Call me back and tell me her reaction."

Victor laughed once again, and when he spoke, it was in the same secure tone he used with Hunt Gardner. What he coveted was his, if not sooner, then later. "I'll call Celie, if that's what you want."

To Jemma, it wasn't a matter of what she wanted. It was more a desire not to rock any boats—particularly the boat belonging to Celie Decatur.

Celie hadn't minded, or so Victor reported back. Jemma agreed readily after that. It was not the first evening she had spent in Victor's company, and she knew nothing would develop between them. He was a confirmed bachelor, and she valued his friendship. Traveling in the rarefied circle of publishers, heads of family trusts, and the others that counted as Ramsey Falls' inner circle was an added boon that made Jemma feel good about herself and the distance she had come on her own. Walt, if he had been around and learned about it, would have given grudging approval.

Jemma took up her blow dryer and shaped her shoulder-length hair into a soft, natural fall. Then she checked on her son, who had carefully eaten around the spinach.

"Ice cream if you clean up your plate."

He made a half-hearted attempt, then tasting the spinach proceeded to finish it, frowning all the while.

Jemma served him the ice cream, savoring a tea-spoon herself and then taking another. She was a little too slender, had too little appetite. There was something about bringing up a son and running a business and a household that eliminated a lively interest in food.

Her baby-sitter, Mrs. Lawson, arrived on time, breathless as always from the climb up the flight of stairs. A friendly, overweight woman in her mid-sixties who had managed the local drugstore until her retirement the year before, she was a grandmother twice over. With her children living ninety miles downstate, she had taken on the care of Seth in a robust, happy way. Seth enjoyed her; she was the grandmother he needed.

"Hi, Seth."

"Hi," he said, ignoring her as he would anyone he liked and took for granted. "Mom, can I watch television?"

"Yes, you can." Jemma looked helplessly over at Mrs. Lawson. "I'm running late."

"I'm here now. You just do your stuff."

The black and white dress Jemma chose was short with a wide swing to the hem and a high, decorous neckline. Black high heel pumps added two inches to her height, and the stockings she wore were dark enough to give a smooth shapely sheen to her legs.

She came out into the living room, where Seth lounged on the couch watching television. Mrs. Law-

son was sitting in the armchair, working on a patch-
work comforter for her daughter-in-law. She beamed
at Jemma. "Well, you do look lovely. Nice change
from your jeans, I'll say that much."

"Thank you, Mrs. Lawson. That's a compliment I
prize."

Seth looked over at his mother with serious eyes.

The doorbell rang, and Jemma kissed the boy goodbye, hastening down the stairs and through the corridor to the door that led out to the street. Victor was
there, wearing a rather formal dark blue suit with the
eccentric addition of a bright red bow tie. He shook her
hand warmly. "You look very beautiful, my dear."

"Thank you." She felt a little apprehensive about
the invitation. She had never been to the Decatur estate, although the nineteenth-century Victorian mansion could be seen from the river below, as well as from
the tertiary road that curved around it. Decatur Hall
stood high and proud on a knoll of land, framed by
ancient sugar maples, with a wide skirt of green lawn.

"Celie will be delighted to have you," Victor said
once again in a kindly manner, as though he understood what she was feeling. "She likes having attractive people around her. Your son tell you about the
dog?"

"He did. I said no dog, not even something as exotic as an Australian shepherd."

"Pity."

"What will happen otherwise?"

"Oh, one of the horses will adopt it. They do that
sort of thing, you know."

"Victor, let me think about it." What she didn't like,
she realized, was his taking a proprietary interest in her
son, and she couldn't say exactly why. Seth was Walt's

son. Maybe she wasn't prepared to share him with anyone else, ever.

Celie, greeting them at the door, offered up her cheek for Jemma to kiss. "Delighted you could make it," she said, and Jemma breathed a sigh of relief. "Come out back. The day is too glorious to spend indoors." She wore a long silk dress of a mixed pattern that Jemma instinctively knew was extremely expensive and possibly one of a kind. Celie, in a subtle, feminine way, cast an appreciative eye over Jemma, as though thankful she had shorn her jeans and had come respectably dressed.

There was a scattering of people in the drawing room as Celie swept Jemma past. "Come along, everyone," she said. "We're going outside."

There were more people gathered on the broad flagstone terrace that faced the river. Others were lounging in white Victorian iron chairs under colorful umbrellas.

"Here we are," Celie cried. "Here's Jemma. Here's Victor."

Jemma, however, with Victor's arm tucked through hers, stopped short at the threshold, involuntarily catching her breath. At the terrace wall, completely ignoring her entrance, was Hunt Gardner. All the ease she was beginning to feel suddenly vanished into the soft summer night. She felt as though her evening had somehow been spoiled merely by his being there. Unfair, she wanted to cry. She'd successfully faced down Celie, and now here he was, looking so, so *splendid*. He was wearing a white tropical suit of great elegance, which emphasized his tanned complexion. He seemed very relaxed, casually seated on the low wall, a drink in his hand. His companion was a woman Jemma knew, the head of the tricentennial committee, who began to laugh heartily at something Hunt said.

Jemma was frozen to the spot, although something in her wanted to escape, wanted out of there. But why? She couldn't answer it. How could a comparative stranger with whom she'd had only a few words affect her in such a way?

"Come along," Victor whispered, tugging at her arm and drawing her onto the terrace. "Ah, there's Hunt," he remarked. "Celie said he'd be here. Our reluctant lecturer."

She looked at Victor, nonplussed. "Reluctant?"

Celie said, "You know everyone more or less, don't you, Jemma?"

Jemma managed a smile. "Yes, I suppose I do. I've visited them in their offices often enough." She was surprised at the brittle sound of Celie's laugh. The success of the shopper's guide still rankled Celie deep down, and her impeccable hostess, she realized now, had all she could do to hide it.

Jemma's glance strayed against her will over to Hunt and found him putting his glass on the terrace wall. He smiled at his companion, said a few words to her and stopped a waiter with a passing tray. He scooped up two glasses of champagne and came over to Jemma, handing her a glass and offering the other to Victor Bosworth.

"Now I know I'm traveling in power circles," he said to Victor, although his eyes did not stray from Jemma's. "Here we are with two publishers whose combined circulation covers all of the lower, southeastern part of the county. Heady stuff."

"Oh, get off it, Hunt," Celie said, coming over to him, and draping her arm over his shoulder. "The man spends the better part of his adult life in the far corners of the world," she said to the assembled party, "and passes himself off as an expert on civilization. I beg to differ, Hunt. You're a hillbilly."

Hunt grinned and said to Jemma, "Is that what you think, too, that I'm a hillbilly?"

"I haven't thought," Jemma said, "but give me time."

"Most sophisticated man I ever met," Victor grumbled. "I thought so when we met in the Pacific, and I think so now. Dealing with simple peoples, still relatively untouched by civilization, he's in a position to tell us where it's at and where it's coming from."

Hunt said smiling, but with a hint of veiled annoyance in his voice, "How in hell did I turn out the center of attention?"

"Maybe," Jemma said thoughtfully, "it's because you're the outsider, and we know we're being judged according to our tribal rites, and maybe that makes us a little uncomfortable."

"Clever," Celie cried, clapping her hands. "Cleverly put. You see, Hunt, you may serve a purpose in our lives, after all. The invited stranger who'll document all our foibles."

"Oh, I intend to," he said. "I'm the man who's here today and gone tomorrow. Gives me the opportunity to say what I think and then run."

"You believe we collectively need telling off," Jemma said. "Here we are, a tiny dot on the map about to celebrate three hundred years of peaceful living in our own little valley, and along you come to tell us we're doing it all wrong."

"Maybe," he said, his eyes dancing with light, "you can't see the termites for the trees."

"It sounds to me," Jemma said, aware of the quiet around them and the odd, personal, unexpected turn their words seemed to be taking, "you have an idealized idea of life that has nothing to do with reality. Trees live, trees die, and termites may hasten their death, but it's a long, slow, natural dying. Marriage and morés in the twenty-first century. You have long-term goals, Professor Gardner. I also hope they're not riddled with termites."

"I'm giving the present century a dozen years or so to get its act together. And call me Hunt," he added with a smile. "You're not my student, yet."

Jemma felt the warmth rise to her face, unnerved by the curious silence around them. Victor spoke up. "She just took her degree at Pack, Hunt. I'm trying to convince her to go for her Masters. Maybe she can fit in your seminar. How many credits can you give her?"

It took him a few moments to answer, all the time regarding Jemma out of his dark, hard-to-read eyes. "Oh, all the credit in the world," he said at last.

"Talk, talk, talk," Celie cried, "and my pâté is going to waste. Come along, Hunt, seriousness is for the classroom or for dinner talk. Let me freshen your drink."

Jemma breathed a sigh of relief, not realizing until that moment how vulnerable she felt, how drained, cut deep by the sharp laser light of Hunt's eyes. But why, she asked herself. Why was that?

At dinner, later, she found herself at the far end of the long, crisply set table, separated from Victor and seated between the editor of the *Times Herald* and the owner of the largest farm equipment dealership in the county. The conversation concerned real estate, and the loss of dairy land to housing development.

Hunt sat at Celie's right, with the mayor's plump wife opposite and the elderly owner of a local vineyard to his right. Jemma was at a diagonal at the opposite end of the table, and she spent what seemed an interminable time staring at her food and making a pretense of eating. When she dared to look up, she invariably found Hunt's eyes upon her, forcing her to turn away, to say something to her companions.

Over dessert, the mayor's wife said in her booming voice, "I'm thinking of sitting in on those public lectures you're going to give, Professor Gardner." With an unexpected, flirtatious titter, she added, "Although I doubt I can wait until the twenty-first century to put anything I might learn into practice."

"The idea of the series isn't to wait," Hunt said. "The idea is to implement change now so that Americans will go into marriage a dozen years away with the idea that it's a permanent arrangement."

"What kind of changes, Professor Gardner?"

"Attitudinal," he said with a brief look at Jemma. "Love isn't the whole thing."

"Isn't it?" Celie said. "That's the most interesting remark I've heard all day."

"Commitment," he added.

"You *have* been in the boondocks," Jemma threw in. "Love and commitment are two words that definitely don't go together."

"Oh, I've heard it, all right," Hunt said, smiling down the table at her. "Obviously the current, fashionable scuttlebutt is that both can go out the window at the first sign of disagreement. I'm talking about civilized people and civilized behavior."

"Professor Gardner," the mayor's wife said, "I consider myself civilized, and I've been married to the same man for forty years."

"Ah, there you are," Hunt said with a satisfied grin. "What held forty years ago has slipped away. I'm convinced it can come back here in the west, and I believe that the example of native peoples elsewhere can be our guide."

Jemma, looking carefully at Hunt, spoke up, trying to hide the irritation she felt over what she thought was his absolute self-possession on the subject. "Are we discussing native peoples who live on fish and breadfruit and aren't fixed on their careers?" She stopped short, aware of having given herself away.

"Coffee in the drawing room," Celie said before he could respond, unexpectedly coming to her rescue.

Afterward, as the long twilight progressed into a dark that never quite went black, the party moved into the drawing room for brandy. Jemma, however, wanted a breath of the fragrant night air and stepped through open French doors to the terrace. The night was swept clear of most insects, but for the on-again, off-again mating signals of lightning bugs. She went over to the terrace wall and stared down at the river traffic. Across the deep silvery Hudson were the shadowy foothills of the Berkshire Mountains. Along the river's edge a train skidded by, the faint sound reaching across the river.

"There isn't a more beautiful view in the world."

She turned. Hunt Gardner had come up to her, holding out a small brandy.

"I suppose you're in a position to know," she said shyly, taking the glass from him.

"My geographical knowledge is not what I came to talk to you about."

"I'd like you to know that I'm about worn out on the subject of marriage," she said, taking a little sip of the drink, which turned out to be orange brandy.

"Good. I was beginning to think you had a bee in your bonnet."

"I gave up bonnets a long time ago. Straw hats with big brims are more my style."

He reached out and touched her hair. "Big brims? Sounds like you want to keep away more than bees. How about Victor? He approve of your hats?"

The unexpected magic of the moment was gone. Jemma bridled, moving away from him, sensing the softness of his touch more than its actual feel. "Victor? What business is he of yours?"

"He's the man who took me away from my vacation and dragged me screaming to Ramsey Falls. He's a man who doesn't take rejection for an answer."

"I'm not interested in discussing him, Professor, and certainly not with you."

"Jemma doesn't say, in other words."

"You know, you're going to be in these parts for a very short time, Professor," she began.

"Hunt," he said.

"Hunt. I have the oddest feeling," she continued, striving to keep her voice cool, "that your name is a little too apt, and that when you leave, somehow, the wreckage will take until the year two thousand and one to clean up." She placed her untouched glass carefully on the terrace wall and turned on her heel. The air around them was disturbed with something not quite finished. She felt her heart beat erratically. She had no doubt Professor Hunt Gardner would be willing to

start something, that he was looking for an amusement to last him until it was time to leave. Let him find
it with his doctoral students, or with Celie, or one of
the women who'd attend his evening lectures. Jemma
had no time, no desire and no interest in being left
holding the emotional bag again, and especially not
with this man who knew precisely the effect he was
having on her.

CHAPTER THREE

A HIGH, CHILDISH GIGGLE floated up from the quiet street below. "Mom, I'm home."

Jemma glanced at the kitchen clock. Seven-thirty. She'd been so busy wading through her accounts receivable and payable, she hadn't even noticed the passage of time.

"Come on, Dad," Seth was shouting, "I'll beat you up the stairs."

She heard Walt's low grumble. Why in the devil was he coming up with Seth? Her ex-husband usually waited below until his son reached the landing, then left, his greeting to Jemma seldom more than a cold exchange of nods a staircase apart.

She got to her feet, flustered. The kitchen table was littered with invoices and checks, and Jemma thought about scooping them into a neat pile, then determinedly told herself no. Walt was the last person she'd tidy up for. She went quickly through the kitchen to the hall door and opened it wide. Even after three years she hadn't come to grips with parting with her son every other weekend. Seth would leave, and for two days the apartment seemed cold and abandoned. Now he hadn't even crossed the threshold and a feeling of peace drifted over her.

She found Seth scrambling up the narrow staircase, dragging a huge shopping bag that bumped against each step in his progress.

"Hi Seth, welcome home."

He looked up. "I'm winning," he told his mother.

Walt, several steps behind, carried Seth's overnight case. "Is everything all right?" she asked, her eyes on her son although her question was directed at her ex-husband.

"See for yourself," Walt said.

Seth came up to her grinning. "I won."

"Hi, honey."

"Hi." He submitted to her hug, squirming quickly out of her arms and running into the living room still dragging the shopping bag. "Wait till you see what I have. From Italy." The last was said with a certain amount of awe.

"All the way from Italy," she repeated, standing aside to let Walt through. "Evening, Walt, how was your trip?"

"Spectacular."

"And Priscilla?" she asked, referring to his wife.

"Had a good rest. We both did."

Seth was breathless as he fell to the floor spilling his treasures. "Look, Mom, a real laser gun, and a re-mote-control truck and a cowboy suit."

She peered down at the pile of gifts. "How quaint, a cowboy suit all the way from Italy."

"Yeah!"

Jemma tried to control the feeling of irritation over her husband's largesse. She had promised herself long before that she wouldn't react, at least not in front of Seth. Her son always returned from a weekend with his father sporting something new and expensive, while she was left saying no when the boy wanted a toy she couldn't afford. "Seth, how about a real, genuine, hi-Mommy-I'm-back kiss?" She scooped her son into her arms and hugged him.

He planted a wet chocolate-coated kiss on her cheek, then squirmed out of her arms once more. "A laser gun, zzzzzmmm, you're it." He was back on the floor picking up one toy and discarding it almost immediately for another. "Zzzzzmmmmm."

"How are things, Jemma?" Walt lowered the overnight case to the floor and stood regarding her.

He wore a blue, gold-buttoned blazer with light pants, every inch the carefully groomed lawyer. Without really meaning to, she took a breath to assure herself that he still wore the same expensive cologne. There it was, musky and a little too overpowering. She had once loved the scent but now wondered why. It struck her that he filled the room with his presence, a tall, sharp-featured man whose thick black hair was tinged with gray at the temples. It gave him a distinguished air she was certain wasn't lost on him.

He surveyed the living room before turning back to her. She had left the laundry unsorted on the couch and the Sunday papers scattered on the floor next to the fireplace. Not quite the ordered mansion he occupied with his wife in the county seat.

"I'm not used to your coming upstairs when you bring Seth home," she said lamely. "Is something wrong?"

"I figured it was time for a chat."

Usually their conversations were conducted over the telephone, with Walt treating Jemma as though she were Seth's nanny and in her ex-husband's employ. "Seth, take your toys and suitcase to your room and then get ready for bed." She gave the order without her usual softness of tone.

"Do I have to?"

"Yes, right now."

Seth reached for the truck, then turned to his father. "Can't I stay up for just a little while?"

"None of that, Seth," Jemma said with an edge to her voice.

"Listen to your mother," Walt said.

For a moment his conciliatory tone drew Jemma up short, and she threw him a grateful glance. They waited while Seth reluctantly collected his presents and retreated to his room.

"I'll come in to say goodbye before I leave," Walt called out.

"Would you like a cup of coffee?" Jemma asked.

"I could use a cup before heading back. We stopped for a hamburger on the way, but Seth got restless and I didn't have time for a cup." He followed her into the kitchen and she was acutely aware of the scattered papers on the table, the cup of half-finished cold coffee, the unwashed dishes in the sink. She had spent the day trying to catch up on her bookkeeping and a dozen odds and ends, and the apartment certainly looked it. After sending a quick glance over the open checkbook, Walt sat heavily down at the table.

"I'll, um, I'll just..." Jemma quickly pushed her papers into a pile, then carried them over to the counter. "Sunday's my catch-up day." She laughed and added before he could say a word, "and as you can see I've had trouble catching up." She reached for the coffeepot and began to rinse it at the sink.

"Seth tells me you're thinking of getting a dog."

She filled the coffeepot with water, carefully measured the coffee and then plugged it in. "Walt," she began, "we've talked before about this business of your plying Seth with big, expensive presents every time you see him. It makes things very difficult for me."

"I've asked you about the dog," he said calmly.

"Obviously something *I* can afford to give him," she responded, unable to keep the sarcasm out of her voice.

"Evidently it's a gift from Victor Bosworth." Walt made the remark stiffly, brushing some invisible crumbs from the table and then dusting his hands.

"Are we talking about a dog or the man who offered it to Seth?"

Walter Whiting had the goodness to flush. He stood and went over to the window, pulling the curtain aside to stare down at the street. "We're talking about my son," he said. "What a place to bring up a child, over a print shop and on a street full of traffic."

"Are we back to that?" she said coolly, then repeated the litany as she had before. "I sold the house because I had to, and as far as I'm concerned, the shop is the best investment I ever made in my life." Her remark was also a pointed reference to the years spent supporting Walter through graduate school.

"How does it look to people, living like this?"

"I haven't taken a survey of public opinion, but Seth seems happy enough."

"And the idea of getting him a dog is crazy. Where is a dog supposed to exercise around here? What if Seth is out with him and the dog pulls him right into traffic? Who stays here with Seth when you're out at midnight walking the animal?"

"I'll hire a dog walker," she retorted. No, she didn't want a dog, but she'd be damned if she'd let Walt talk her out of it.

"I had allergies as a child, and there's no telling whether or not Seth has inherited the tendency."

"He hasn't. He plays with the dog at Victor's farm." She stopped, aware of her gaffe, then noticed the change in Walt's expression. Why, she thought, with an inward laugh, he was impressed that she was acquainted with Victor Bosworth.

"Victor, is it? I'd no idea you were on such friendly terms."

He was baiting her. He knew, as did everyone in the area, that Victor was a bachelor, that he was easily the best catch in the county. Walt could be impressed, but at the same time he held a certain proprietary interest in whom she saw, whom she dated. In the three years since Walt had left her, there had been no serious men in Jemma's life. The divorce decree had made her wary, to begin with. Under the terms of her agreement, while she was bringing up their son, Walt had to be assured she was living a morally upright life, as he defined it. So far he'd had nothing to worry about on that score.

"Dad?" Seth was at the door, his pajamas on inside out. Jemma felt her heart lurch at his forlorn expression.

"Why aren't you in bed," Walt asked.

"Can't I have a dog?"

"Your mother and I will decide what's best for you."

Seth put his head down, sniffling a bit and pressing his bare toes against the floor.

"Come here, son," Walt said more softly as he reached out his hand. Seth came running over and buried his head in his father's arms. Walt kissed the top of the boy's head and then said, "Now, get ready for bed. Did you brush your teeth?"

Seth shook his head in a motion that meant yes and no at the same time. Jemma softened at the interaction between son and father. No matter what she felt about Walt, he loved his son, and it was apparent Seth returned the feeling.

"Kiss your mother good-night. I'll come in to see you before I go."

Seth came over to Jemma and nuzzled against her. She put her hands on the boy's soft hair. "We both love you, you know that, Seth, don't you?" She bent down and kissed him. Seth nodded and then slowly dragged himself from the room, looking back once more at his parents with a pleading expression.

"He's going to pull all our strings," Walt said with a tight smile. "About the dog," he went on, but Jemma lost track of what he was saying. She had a sudden vision of Hunt Gardner, the bachelor expert on marriage. How nice to know all about life from the vantage point of an ivory tower. How wonderful to think that if you laid down the rules of behavior, everything would work out fine. How wonderful to believe that love and respect lasted forever and that little boys weren't the victims of failed marriages.

She sighed. Walt lectured on. She was scarcely aware of him. Hunt had been at the back of her mind all week, and it had nothing to do with broken marriages and the end of dreams. Her thoughts had been of his blatant masculinity and the quickened look of interest in his eye. Forbidden thoughts, thoughts she hadn't allowed herself before. But then no one in Ramsey Falls had struck her with such force as the visiting professor.

The scent of brewed coffee filled the air, and she moved with a start. She heard Victor Bosworth's name intoned once again. "I'll get you some coffee," she said and went over to the cupboard and took out a mug. "Victor offered Seth a dog. If I decide to accept, it's because he should have a dog. As for walking it, you needn't have any fears on that account."

"All this because you had to set up as an independent woman. My son should be out in the country, running free."

She handed him the steaming coffee, black, the way he liked it. "I really don't want to discuss it, Walt." She understood what underlay his argument. Somehow the idea of her independence annoyed him. And he really didn't care about the dog. Appearances meant everything to him. How do you explain to your country club cronies that your ex-wife and son lived above a shop on a busy street? Ice for a heart, arrogant and worried about his image, that about summed up Walter Whiting. He had thrown her over, given her just enough alimony to exist on but wanted a say in how she picked herself up and dusted herself off.

"You don't want to talk about it." He slammed the mug down on the table. "Damn you, Jemma, haven't you heard a word I've said?"

"I think it's time you left," she stated.

"I never could talk to you." He went out of the kitchen, his long stride echoing on the floor as he headed for Seth's room.

Jemma took his mug to the sink and carefully poured the contents down the drain. She heard his voice and Seth's but couldn't make out the words. Then Walt left her son's room and walked heavily to the front door. He turned the knob, opened the door and closed it carefully behind him. She heard his footsteps down the wooden stairs, then heard the street door slam shut. She'd have to go down and lock up, but not until Walt was safely gone. He still had the ability to disconcert her, make her feel as though she were doing everything wrong from rearing their son to operating her *Ramsey Falls Shopper's Guide*. The door opened on the BMW and then slammed shut. The motor was engaged and the car moved smoothly up Main Street.

What had just happened? she asked herself. *"We have to talk, Jemma,"* he'd said. But about what? A dog? Victor Bosworth? This apartment? Her independence?

Control. That's what it was all about. She had let go, and in some way, Walt was offended by the notion. She turned off the coffee and then poured herself a cup, which she brought over to the table.

"Mom?" Seth called from his room.

"Be right with you, honey."

There was no reason why Seth couldn't have a pet. The love of an animal was more important than the problems entailed. The animal would be a big responsibility, but what was one more mouth to feed? She'd call Victor in the morning and tell him she and Seth were ordering up one Australian shepherd. They'd have to think up a name. Walt would be furious. She smiled as if she had just won first prize in a contest she hadn't even known she'd entered.

"Hi, Mrs. Whiting."

"Adriana, you're the last person I expected to see here."

"Oh you know me, always where the action is."

"So I see." Jemma handed her ticket over to the girl at the entrance to the Bosworth Lecture Hall at Pack College. "I'd no idea you were moonlighting."

The crush to get into the lecture hall surprised her, and she barely caught Adriana's answer before she was pushed inside. "It's just a way to make a little extra money for the summer, Mrs. Whiting."

Jemma smiled. An entrepreneur, that girl, or else Professor Gardner had a way with her. She suspected Hunt's smile had everything to do with it, and not the subject of his lecture, or the couple of dollars Adriana might earn as a ticket taker.

The pale, oak-paneled lecture hall had been built with Bosworth funds. A small, arenalike space, it was light, airy, modern and contained several large abstract paintings loaned from the Bosworth collection. An Alexander Calder mobile dangled on slender wires from the center ceiling just above the sight line of those sitting in the topmost row. There were no seats allotted, and Jemma had to climb halfway up the side aisle to find one.

She saw Victor enter the hall with Celie Decatur and the mayor's wife. That the series was beginning to have the air of a major event puzzled her. She hadn't expected the esoteric subject to be of much interest to the population of Ramsey Falls or its surrounding communities. But then again there wasn't that much going on nights, and the publicity had apparently paid off.

"He's gorgeous." The word was whispered behind Jemma by a young, breathless voice. "I mean gor-gee-us."

"I heard but seeing is believing," replied another voice, slightly skeptical and just as breathlessly young.

Jemma found herself shamelessly listening in. She had absolutely no doubt they were talking about Hunt Gardner.

"He isn't married, either. Sin-gul."

"He's too old for you, crazy."

"I like older men."

"He's thirty-five. That's pretty old."

The dean of the summer school came out and stood at the lectern for a moment adjusting the microphone. The sound in the hall died down, and by the time she spoke, she had the audience's attention. "I had no idea marriage was such a popular subject," she said, and added, "to such a wide variety of people. It's a splendid start to our new adult education program. I'm also very happy to see the heterogeneous makeup of our audience, young, old, and in-between."

There was a scattering of applause. "We have one man to thank for giving us this hall, for his generosity to Pack College and now for opening education to everyone with a yearning to listen and to learn. Victor Bosworth."

The applause was generous. Victor came up to the lectern and began speaking into the microphone in his clear, assertive voice. "The idea for this particular lecture series," he began, "belongs to Professor Hunt Gardner, who's in Ramsey Falls for a short time only, I'm sorry to say. I don't know what we can do to keep him here for a longer period, but if anybody has an idea, there's a suggestion box in the hall."

There was laughter and more applause, and Victor went on talking in his pleasant, offhand way about Hunt's expertise, about his experiences in primitive societies and how he and Hunt had met.

Jemma gave up listening. That Hunt Gardner had come among them and would then be gone forever raised in her an unexpected melancholy, an emptiness she could scarcely explain, a notion that the future would hold no surprises once he was gone. She shivered slightly, drawing her jacket close. Even though it was a mild summer evening, the hall was cool.

She directed her gaze hard at Victor Bosworth. What in the world was happening? Hunt Gardner meant nothing to her. They had met on three occasions, and that was all. They had met socially only once, at Celie's party a week before, and Jemma hadn't seen him since. He was a stranger with whom she had nothing in common. He was in Ramsey Falls until the end of July, and then he'd be on his way. Here today, spreading his charm amongst them, and gone tomorrow to the farthest corner of the world.

"And now," Victor was saying, "without further ado, may I introduce Dr. Hunter Gardner."

Hunt came striding out with a friendly smile and a bend of his head in acknowledgement of the applause. He looked tanned and relaxed in a cotton summer suit, blue shirt and red tie. He shook hands with Victor and then positioned himself in front of the lectern, ignoring the microphone. With a swift movement, he unbuttoned his jacket, loosened his tie and opened his shirt collar. Then he leaned back against the lectern, jammed his hands into his pockets and surveyed the room.

"See," the young voice whispered behind her. "I told you he was the living end."

"Okay, okay, shhh."

Hunt looked out at the sea of faces for a long moment, scanning the audience and at last settling on the side aisle seat in which Jemma sat. For a second their eyes held, then a young voice whispered behind her.

"He's looking at me."

"He is not. Boy, are you conceited."

Jemma smiled. She knew her cheeks were burning and she was the first to look away, settling on the Calder mobile moving in the slight breeze from the air vents. Hunt Gardner commanded attention without saying a word, and in the electric silence, Jemma could hear the thrumming of her heart.

Then he spoke. "Happy?"

Jemma glanced quickly back, but his question was general, asked of the audience in a soft tone that, even without benefit of the microphone, easily reached the last row. There was a slight shifting sound as people moved uncomfortably in their seats.

No one answered and after another long moment, in which he smiled hopefully at his audience, Hunt said, "Not such a difficult question, is it? Is everybody happy? Happy with your lives, happy in love, glad to be alive and looking forward to tomorrow, that kind of happy?" His voice was sonorous and deep with a touch of humor. Jemma could feel the crowd responding to him, as if their reaction were physical. His hair appeared to have been hastily brushed back; a recalcitrant lock fell over his forehead. He pushed at it, running his fingers through in a gesture Jemma found disarming. "I'm waiting for one hand, please, just one hand to show me that someone in this audience can't sit still for happiness."

A young man down front raised a tentative hand.

"Aaahh," Hunt said beaming, "at long last our search has yielded a happy man. Can you explain your happiness, sir, in half a dozen words or less?"

"Sure. I'm engaged."

The audience laughed, a light popping sound as though some nervous energy had been released. The young man put his arm around the golden-haired girl on his right, who immediately buried her face in her hands. "This is Peggy."

"Young love," Hunt said. "Congratulations, Peggy and her young man. That's happy."

The audience applauded, Jemma joining in. Someone shouted, "Right on."

Hunt waited until the applause died down, then said, "Wait until they tackle their wedding plans." There was general laughter. He reached into his pocket, pulled out a small piece of paper, carefully unfolded it and waved it at the audience. "No magic, just a message. When in doubt, look it up. My old, well-worn, beloved dictionary defines happy as follows: 'favored by circumstances, lucky, fortunate... having, showing, or causing a feeling of great pleasure, contentment, joy, etcetera, etcetera, etcetera.'" He smiled at his audience. "Lucky, fortunate, pleasure, contentment, joy, the very sound of those words makes us feel good. They're 'feel-good' words. Too bad we can't bottle them like perfume and tap into them anytime we're sad. Note that the dictionary says *causing* a feeling of. Happiness isn't something we experience alone. We share it with others. According to the dictionary, anyway. We give happiness, we receive happiness. In other words, it takes two or more to perform the happiness tango."

Jemma thought how she gave happiness to her son and received it. Perhaps it wasn't perfect happiness, however; there was always the bitterness of her divorce to take the edge off it.

"People everywhere want the same things—a decent place to live, good health, peace. They want to be happy, give happiness, receive happiness. Decades ago life was a 'no frills' trip for most of us. We stayed put, scratching for things from one end of life to the other—the way it still is in most parts of the world. But life in civilized society has changed. Oh, how it's changed. We give, we receive, and suddenly something goes wrong. The opposite of happy is unhappy. Two little letters, but what a world of difference in definition."

He paused, crumpled the little slip of paper and chucked it behind him. "The hell with definitions." The wadded paper landed on the lectern, then rolled to the floor. "Apologies," he said, smiling at Victor Bosworth. "I usually don't litter, but I'll do anything to make a point. And the point," he went on, surveying his listeners, "is, that even when we *are* happy, we don't seem to be able to sustain it for very long. Why is that? We've the richest society in the world. Rich in consumer goods, rich in education, rich in the choices that even the poorest of us can make. We go to school, to work, we fall in love, we become engaged, we marry, we produce children, we pay taxes and observe traffic laws, and then what do we do?"

Hunt stopped once more, his eyes ranging the audience as if expecting an answer in unison. "What we do in ever increasing numbers is *separate*. Fifty percent of marriages split because the partners admit to a mistake."

Jemma shook her head. He was on his soap box again. Hunt Gardner was the last person in the world to talk about marriage, a man of no fixed abode, no ties to anyone. He was a man without luggage, except maybe for his well-worn dictionary, coming and going as he pleased, traveling light and never saying good-bye. And forming opinions while he was at it.

"Whatever happened to those bonds that tied people together, to their homes, to their past and to their futures?" Hunt asked. "A fifty percent divorce rate, joint custody, the elderly packed off to nursing homes, rampant teenage pregnancies, school dropouts, adult illiteracy, loneliness, alienation, the detritus of civilization, and we're living with it and accepting it as the norm. What's wrong? What the hell's *wrong*?"

He held his hand up. "It's a rhetorical question, but if anyone has an answer, I'm willing to hear it." He waited a second for a response, then continued. "Our young engaged couple is going to be married according to the rites of society. Big wedding plans?" he asked, smiling down at the couple.

Peggy nodded her head vigorously. "Pretty big," she called.

"Nervous?"

"Uh-huh." Another vigorous nod of the head.

"Don't be. From the smile on your face, I can tell you're going to be in the fifty percentile that stays married forever."

The audience applauded, Hunt along with it. "Intact marriages are worthy of a lot more than applause," he said.

He doesn't know, Jemma thought, *he simply doesn't realize the sudden wrong turns that marriages can take, even when both parties are in love.* Jemma shook her head once again, surprised to find Hunt looking at her as if that slight movement caught him off balance.

Was Seth suffering, or was she providing him with all the love he'd ever need? In a primitive society, if a marriage broke down, there was family all around and plenty of love and support. Hunt didn't have to spell it out. She was alone, her mother living on the West Coast near her older sister. She had tied herself to Walt, and when Seth arrived, Jemma had drawn up the drawbridge, the three of them against the world. And even with the divorce she was tied to Ramsey Falls, not only because of the divorce decree, but because she genuinely wanted her son to be near his father. Her mother had once offered to return to help, but the cold winter climate was unsuitable to her health and Jemma had declined. Seth was happy, a normal little boy who understood his parents loved him, even though they were apart.

"Two people fall in love," Hunt said after a long pause. "They decide to marry. In this society, they decide. In others the decision is made for them, whether they're in love or not. In every society, the requisite fuss will begin over how much to spend, whom to invite or not invite, whose Aunt Bessie and Uncle Charlie will threaten not to show up because their in-laws weren't invited, and what kind of music the band will play. Then the wedding, followed by the party, followed by gifts, all laid down according to the way one's ancestors did it. In primitive societies, the gifts might be fattened pigs or a covey of fowl, the only members of the wedding party, incidentally, who won't be having a good time. In less primitive societies, of course, cash in the form of checks or crisp new bills, take the place of food on the hoof or claw, so to speak. So far, very much alike, what happens in Timbuktu and Ramsey Falls."

Hunt glanced quickly at his watch. "Before I go on, there's a movie I want you to see about life on a South

Sea Island, but why don't we take a fifteen-minute break while my assistant sets it up?"

"Professor?"

Hunt pointed out a big, broad-shouldered kid near the center aisle. He wore a gold earring in his left ear, and when he was singled out, the kid turned and gave the rest of the audience the benefit of his lopsided grin.

"Go ahead," Hunt prompted.

"How are the women on the islands?"

"Good question," Hunt said without smiling. "I'm glad to see you're interested in sociology. That your major?"

"I'm not in college at present."

"Pity," Hunt said after a pregnant moment. It was obvious the kid had wandered in with the hope of disrupting the lecture just because he was bored. "You strike me as good educational material. As for your question, stick around and take a look for yourself."

"Yessir, right, I will."

"Fifteen minutes," Hunt reminded him. Then, after a quick glance around the audience, he jumped off the platform and went directly over to Celie Decatur and Victor Bosworth.

There was a general creaking of chairs and limbs while the audience stood and stretched, some members milling around, others heading for the lobby. Jemma, unable to resist a peek at the two young women behind her, waited until they passed, then followed them down. Slender, pretty, with good profiles, they chatted and laughed, and once they reached the lobby, headed directly for Hunt.

"Mrs. Whiting?" Jemma turned in the crowded lobby to find Adriana smiling at her. "Neat, huh? I mean, I'm not sure what Professor Hunt's getting at.

I feel as if he's bawling me out for breathing, but still he's right and all.''

"Oh, absolutely," Jemma said, smiling in return.

"I mean I think Seth is an excruciatingly happy kid," Adriana said, "so Professor Gardner is making *some* mistakes when he talks about divorce and all.''

"I'm making some mistakes? Impossible." It was Hunt, coming up to them and putting an arm around Adriana's shoulder. "Hello, mutt, thanks for filling in at the door.''

Adriana cast a shy glance at Jemma. "The regular usher was sick so I filled in.''

"I know," Jemma said softly. "The money."

"Could you excuse me," Adriana added with a little shrug of apology. "My boyfriend's over there.''

"Not the fellow with the earring, I hope," Hunt said.

She giggled and shook her head and was at once swallowed up by the crowd.

Because of the movement around them, Hunt took Jemma's arm and drew her over to a quiet corner. "You look as if you want to come out swinging," he said at once.

"You're right. I said it before, and I haven't changed my mind. Only I'll couch my words differently this time. You've a bird's eye view of marriage, Hunt, a pretty myopic bird.''

"Myopic? You've got the wrong bird. I can see you quite well and the view looks damn good from here.''

She laughed and took a step back, remembering that silent exchange of glances in the auditorium. No, he wasn't myopic, at least not that way, and for a moment she was at a loss how to answer him.

He took it out of her hands, though, saying, "Listen, Celie has big plans for a late dinner with Victor and half a dozen other people at one of the local restaurants after the lecture. That should be around ten. I never said yes, I never said no. How about rescuing me? I'd like to buy you a cup of coffee."

"Sorry," Jemma said evenly. "I'm not in the rescuing business. Anyway, I promised my baby-sitter I'd be home right after the lecture. And I've a ton of work."

"Call your baby-sitter. Tell her you'll be late."

"Can't do, we have an excellent relationship built on the fact that I offer her no surprises and always show up as advertised."

"I'm out of luck, then."

"Plumb out of it. It's dinner at Fonda's, I imagine, with Celie and Victor." It was obviously Celie's party and not Victor's, but she felt no rancor at being left out, rather relief. "Fonda's is the only place open and still serving after ten," she added. "I hope you won't have to pick up the tab. It's ferocious. Incidentally, they serve a lot of pork and fowl, even when there aren't any weddings."

He gazed solemnly at her before speaking. "I felt you in the audience," he said at last, "right from the very first. Quiet, judgmental, ready to tear into anything I, the bachelor with opinions about married life, might say. You made me a mighty worried man."

"I wonder why I don't believe a word you're saying."

Jemma realized that they stood in a quiet corner of the lobby in a cocoon of their own making. She was even aware of someone standing a few feet away, as if trying to find an opening to approach Hunt. She was aware of the chatter all around them as friends met and talked, the sound a little distant, a necessary background to a small confrontation between two people who were veritable strangers. She was aware of Hunt's direct, deep gaze and thought that she might try forever but could never plumb his soul.

He reached out and grasped her arm. "I'm a mighty worried man. I asked a question back there," he said motioning toward the lecture hall, "and your lack of enthusiasm over responding made me think the whole evening was a bust."

"Really? And what question was that?"

He smiled, but the question when it came was a challenge. "Happy?"

CHAPTER FOUR

JEMMA BRIDLED. She had come to his lecture out of curiosity and didn't consider herself a candidate for instant analysis, not even from the worldly, attractive Hunt Gardner. She glanced down at his hand still gripping her arm. Hunt caught her frown and released her.

"Simple enough question," he remarked. "Wonder why it's so difficult to get an answer."

"Happy all the time," she stated evenly. "Divinely so."

"Now why don't I believe that?"

"Ah, you ask a question and want a preordained answer," Jemma responded. "You're very rigid about your opinions, aren't you? The natives of your islands aren't restless, but the natives of Ramsey Falls are, and you fault them for it. Or are you shaking us up just for the fun of it."

"Fun?" His eyes ranged over her.

She had an uncomfortable sense of having been on his mind all week, that he wasn't quite certain what to make of her.

"I'm having fun, you could say that," he went on, "and I think the good citizens need a bit of shaking up, but I'm not playing it for laughs, Jemma. I have something to say about a society falling apart at its collective seams, and I'm going to keep on saying it."

"You might answer your own question, Professor. Are *you* happy?"

They stood for a long moment regarding each other, Jemma's eyes dancing with the challenge. She wasn't fated to receive his answer, however. The mayor's wife came rushing up to them with Celie Decatur. "Oh, Professor Gardner," she called gaily, "here you are, hiding."

Jemma, glancing at Hunt, noticed his frown, which he quickly erased.

"Things aren't so bad in these parts," the mayor's wife declared. "I told you at Celie's party that I was a happily married woman. I was just a little shy when you asked that question during the lecture, I mean about raising my hand. Everybody knows—"

"And I believe," Hunt said with a slight bow, "that we've agreed there are always exceptions that prove the rule."

Celie, wearing black and a long necklace of baroque pearls, looked directly at Jemma. "He'll have us in grass skirts dancing the hula if we're not careful, don't you think so, Jemma? I wish Hunt felt life in the West was as good as I think it is, here and now."

"Ah," Hunt said, "but you're a wonderfully fulfilled woman, Celie. The world's your oyster. I'd say a couple of dozen oysters by the look of that necklace."

She laughed and was about to say something when Victor Bosworth came up to them, a distant cousin of his in tow.

"Here's Sarah, up from the city," Victor said.

"Hi, Jemma," Sarah said in her soft, breathy voice. "I was going to call you."

"Hi, love." Jemma was genuinely happy to see her friend and kissed her on the cheek. "I was wondering when you were going to show up in these parts."

"Sarah Crewes, Hunt Gardner, you know everybody else," Victor said, completing the introductions.

Sarah, Jemma thought, was looking more beautiful than ever with her luxuriant brown hair, wide eyes, translucent complexion and beautiful figure. She found herself glancing involuntarily at Hunt, and yet as he took Sarah's hand, he smiled at Jemma. She had the extraordinary feeling that he wanted to continue their private conversation, that all the chatter in the noisy lobby was inconsequential to him.

Sarah was saying in her warm voice with its light, enchanting catch, "You've wrapped the audience around your little finger, Professor Gardner, but I don't think we're so bad as you make out."

"I merely want to stir the pot, improve the taste of life, that's all."

Victor said enthusiastically, "Hunt, Sarah knows more about the history of Merriman County than anyone alive."

"Tell me things were better in the old days," Hunt remarked.

"I can't, as a matter of fact," Sarah said with a shake of her head. "I know a lot of general history and have a good idea of the county's 'begats,' but I'm a little short on the matter of the permanence of marriage vows." She turned to Celie. "The county archives are in a mess, and I really don't have the time to go through them. What they need is a full-time archivist, although you couldn't pay me for the job. Maybe an article in the *Times Herald* can get through to the powers that be."

"It's a well-known fact," Celie said, "that the condition the archives are in will land us in a mess sooner or later. We've covered it a dozen times in the paper, Sarah. You're just not up on home county news."

Sarah wasn't in the least perturbed. "You're absolutely right, Celie," she said in a conciliatory manner.

"Maybe we'll mount a campaign if you could just give me a good 'for instance.'"

Sarah smiled mischievously. "Great. I will, even if I have to invent one."

Victor put his arm through Jemma's. "Niko's waiting," he said. "He's been to the vet and been declared perfectly healthy. Approve of his name?"

"Absolutely," Jemma said. "Niko, I like that."

"Fifteen minutes," Hunt said, looking at his watch.

As they trooped back into the lecture hall, Jemma asked Sarah if she was on vacation.

"I've taken July off."

"How about coming over to the shop? I'd love to learn what's going on in your life."

"Great, we can have lunch."

When Sarah left to find her seat, Jemma turned to Victor and asked him a question that had been long on her mind. "What has Hunt Gardner's background in adult education in underdeveloped nations got to do with Ramsey Falls in the here and now? He's really socking it to us, and I can't say I'm happy about it. He's not an anthropologist, is he?"

"An educator, pure and simple, with a specialty in bringing adult education to third-world countries. He's thoughtful, brilliant and caring. I read a paper of his in which he outlined family connectedness in remote areas. It was fascinating, touching and has everything to do with our own roots, especially in this year of our tricentennial. He has something to teach us, Jemma, don't sell him short.''

''I don't want to, but I don't like being lectured about my failure in my marriage.''

''You're not taking it personally, are you?''

He looked worried, but all Jemma could do was shake her head over the irony of the two most eligible bachelors in Ramsey Falls preaching the virtues of family life. ''Well, it's nice to know his fervor is catching,'' she said.

Celie came up to them. ''I'm tremendously enthusiastic about our charming professor. Nothing like making the local population sit up and think.''

''Or throw tomatoes,'' Jemma said.

Celie frowned at her. ''Throwing tomatoes just because someone is telling us the truth as he perceives it? I think you were the one who said at my party last week that it's the stranger who can tell us what we're really like.''

''Yes,'' Jemma agreed. ''I suppose I did.''

A screen had been set up, and the lights were lowered when Jemma got to her seat. She took out her pad and pencil. It wasn't dark enough, however, to prevent her from writing a couple of quick, clear sentences that came to mind.

Not an anthropologist, not a psychologist, not even a student of American morés, a man floating loose without encumbrances, Professor Hunt Gardner has arrived at Pack College in time to tell us who we are and how we've gone wrong compared to our peers far away on an island in the South Pacific. If you'd like to have your wrist slapped in a charming way, I'd recommend his lectures. There are still a few empty seats at Bosworth Hall for anyone who hasn't signed up. I suggest you attend. Leave tomatoes at home.

The last was written in the near dark, and then she turned her attention to the picture coming on screen and the voice of Hunt Gardner in the background.

"I can't see him," the young woman complained behind her.

Jemma closed her eyes briefly. She had no doubt now that Hunt Gardner had singled her out. Given the differences in their opinions and in their life-styles, the question to which she could find no answer was why.

HAPPY. The word haunted her through that night and through the days that followed. More than once Jemma found herself engaging in imaginary conversations with Hunt, explaining that happiness meant fulfillment, accomplishment, a sense of self and she had all those. Happiness was Seth.

Happiness wasn't midnight-black eyes watching, waiting, almost haunting her. Happiness also meant being in love and she'd have none of it, none of the curious game she was certain Hunt Gardner was playing.

Are you happy, Professor? She found herself silently asking him the question over and over again, but the Hunt Gardner of her imagination never responded. He didn't have to. He was a visitor to Ramsey Falls, and it evidently mattered little to him what shards of broken hearts he might leave behind.

Early Friday evening the air-conditioning in the shop broke down. The heat was intense, business slow and Jemma closed up at six. When her son came back from his karate lesson, he was excited, sweaty and exhausted. Jemma had to poke him awake at the dinner table. Her son gave in and at seven o'clock went to bed, an hour earlier than usual.

A shaft of long summer twilight struggled through the bamboo blinds and illuminated the cotton print curtains of Seth's room. Jemma reached over and pushed the curtains aside and raised the blind to let in a faint breeze. Although Ramsey Falls sat high above the Hudson River, a hot July night was the same there as any other place in the world. She stared out over the back garden and tried to picture Seth romping on the grass with his dog. Well, the dog would become a reality soon enough. She had promised Victor to come for the animal on the weekend.

"Mommy, can I have my bear?" Seth's small voice showed he was nearly asleep.

"Of course, honey." Her son's eyes were already closed when Jemma pressed the raggedy, well-worn and beloved furry animal into her son's hand. She bent over and placed a light kiss on his forehead and drew a cotton blanket over him. She remained at the side of his bed, gazing down at him as she often did when he was asleep. Hot days, hot nights and a lot of activity in between. Awake he was often a savage, willful creature catching her off guard with his capacity to surprise. Asleep his soft, aching vulnerability and tender need never failed to move her.

Her son. She put her fingers to her lips, then touched them to Seth's warm forehead. After another moment she quietly left the room, closing the door softly on his sleeping figure.

She was moody, unable to say what was bothering her. Not the usual money problems or the backup of things left undone. It was something less tangible, something fleeting, skittering around the edges of her mind to disappear just when she was about to pounce on it.

It was the time of day that was always longest to Jemma, when she wanted to kick off her shoes and forget about bills to be sent, checks to be made out, telephone calls to return. Faced with the lingering twilight and utter silence of a town given over to dinner and family, she missed the *idea* of a family, the picture postcard view of life. Hunt Gardner's view, she supposed. Kids asleep, Mom and Dad in the living room, he with the papers, she with busywork. The scent of cookies and coffee emanating from the kitchen and the air reeking with love. Yes indeed, the Hunt Gardner view, and the trouble was it was a view she once shared, but no longer believed in.

She wandered into the living room, then plunked down on the couch and tucked her feet under her. She reached for a magazine and began thumbing through it, but put it down after staring blankly at the pages. She stretched, stood and pushed up the sleeves of the roomy, oversized sweatshirt she was wearing. She thought about taking a cool shower. Instead she checked Seth, left the doors to his room and the apartment ajar and went downstairs with the intention of working in her office for a while. The shop was still hot, and she opened the street door to let in the night air. It had cooled down some, and she stood in the doorway, watching the early-evening traffic and the nearly empty street.

The upholsterer, whose shop was two doors away, stepped out into the street and greeted her before locking up. "Nice evening."

"I never thought it would cool off like this," Jemma said. "The air-conditioning went and never came back on."

He nodded. "Here, too. I got Celie Decatur on the phone and gave her a good tongue-lashing. 'It's not enough to be a landlord,' I told her. 'You have to keep things moving.' She said it'll be okay by morning."

Jemma laughed. "I thought about calling her but never got around to it. Glad you did."

"Well, good night, Jemma. Sleep well."

"Good night, Art. Stay cool."

She went back indoors and stretched. She'd need a pot of coffee if she expected to stay awake and work.

HUNT GARDNER was about to tear the *Ramsey Falls Shopper's Guide* to shreds when he thought better of it. It was a rag, a penny saver, a throwaway, one woman's method of supplementing her income, that was all. "Jemma Says." Jemma says entirely too much. What the devil could she have been thinking of, reviewing his lecture series as though he were giving it at Carnegie Hall to the accompaniment of violins?

He went over to the bedroom window and gazed down on his landlady's herb garden and its delicate patterning. The heat of the day had dissipated, but all that the coolness brought on was a fresh bout of restlessness, something which had been dogging him all week, and which he didn't even try to analyze.

In the early-evening light, some of the low, mounded bushes had taken on a silvery appearance. Beyond the herb garden lay a border of freshly planted flowers, begonias Mrs. Duboise had told him proudly. Small, shiny pink heads with yellow stamens, they would wither with the first breath of winter. He thought of

how everything in that tender, nervous climate had to
be nurtured and cared for or it might wither, from
plants to relationships. He thought of the prolific,
flamboyant flowers of the South Pacific, frangipani
and bougainvillea and orchids, and the simplicity and
continuity of life in a benign, predictable climate.

He went back to his desk, picked up the *Ramsey
Falls Shopper's Guide*, and once again went through
the "Jemma Says" column until he hit the words.

Not an anthropologist, not a psychologist, not
even a student of American morés, a man floating loose without encumbrances, Professor Hunt
Gardner has arrived at Pack College in time to tell
us who we are, and how we've gone wrong compared to our peers far away on an island in the
South Pacific. If you'd like to have your wrist
slapped in a charming way, I'd recommend his
lectures. There are still a few empty seats at Bosworth Hall for anyone who hasn't signed up. I
suggest you attend. Leave tomatoes at home.

He slapped the paper down on the desk once again
and left his room, closing his door quietly behind him.
He hurried down the narrow staircase into the low-
ceilinged hall. Duboise House was old and venerable,
but to a man of his height, it was like living inside a
small sports car. He stepped outside, turned right and
went up the lane in the direction of Main Street. He
knew just where he was going and why. Common sense
told him to turn back, to borrow a car and drive up into
the mountains where he might cool off. But the matter
of Jemma Whiting was simmering, and Hunt Gardner
was never a man to avoid conflict.

JEMMA HAD BEEN DOZING over her work and now she awoke with a start. She checked her desk clock but no more than fifteen or twenty minutes had passed since she had closed her eyes. She listened acutely for a moment. The silence from above was profound, which meant Seth was still asleep. Her coffee was cold, but she took a sip nevertheless, then picked up her pen. The work at hand had never looked less inviting.

She put the pen down and went over to the drafting table in the corner of her office and stared at the mockups for a couple of ads for her next shopper's guide. While Jemma did most of the work herself, she had been training Adriana in the techniques of paste-up. She had recently purchased a computer program with simple typesetting and design capabilities, and while it made work easier, pasting up all the elements of the guide was still laborious.

The current week's issue was scarcely hot on the stands when the next week's was due. She'd have to think seriously about hiring permanent personnel. The idea was exciting, yet Jemma sometimes longed to have someone to discuss it with.

Still feeling restless, she wandered out of her office and through the semidarkened shop to the front door. She opened the door wide and stepped outside. The old-fashioned street lamps each cast a self-contained yellow glow into the late dusk. Main Street was quiet, most of the shops shuttered for the night. It was the time she liked best, when she could imagine Ramsey Falls the way it was in the nineteenth century.

The antique shop across the way was softly and dramatically lit with one small frosted lamp focusing on a display of old toys. Gazing intently at it were two young people, arm in arm. She was regarding them in

a curious yet dispassionate way, when the voice spoke
quietly in her ear.

"Waiting for me?"

Startled, she turned. Hunt Gardner was standing
there as though he had materialized out of the deepest
part of her thoughts. "What are you doing here?" she
stammered.

"I got your message."

"Message?"

"You really went out after me," he remarked in a
voice devoid of anger.

"I'm sorry," she stammered, "I don't know what
you're talking about." A car came slowly down the
road. Someone called out her name, and it took a few
seconds for her to realize it was the local doctor. She
waved in greeting.

"It isn't theater and I don't expect any reviews, not
from you and not from the arts and leisure section of
the *New York Times*."

"I still don't know what you're talking about," she
began, then stopped. He couldn't mean that paltry little remark in her weekly column. But apparently he
did.

"Oh." She put her hands to her lips, although her
eyes danced with humor. "You can't be angry, Hunt."

"Not angry," he said, pulling a copy of her shopper's guide out of his jacket pocket. "At least not
enough to kill."

She took the guide out of his hands and in the soft
light glanced quickly over her words. Damn, she had
lifted them hurriedly out of her notebook and set them
in type without really thinking further about them. A
filler, true, but her opinion, as well. She supposed she

should have thought twice about taking on Hunt Gardner in print.

"You have a friend in Victor Bosworth," Hunt said. "The vibes I've been getting are that Vic thinks a lot of you and your opinion."

"He's a nice man and I haven't any idea what he has to do with anything."

"Funding, you know, money, that thing we all work so hard for? I'm not paid by private industry to ply my trade, Jemma. Instead of teaching in the field full-time as I should, I have to spend a lot of time finding funds to back my work. Work of redeeming social value, as we in the teaching trade put it."

"And Victor's your passage to funding freedom. Okay," she said, "I understand, but you're crazy if you think he reads my column and is influenced by anything I say."

"If you care about a lady, you take in what she has to say."

She wasn't certain whether to be angry or flattered. "Hunt, don't give it another thought. Victor and I are friends, that's all. I'm sorry if you're offended over what I said, but I won't take it back. I enjoyed your lecture," she went on, "every minute of it, really I did. I love being told that everything in my beloved country is wrong, especially in this sleepy town just about ready to celebrate three hundred years of continuity. Especially by a man who isn't going to love us, and is certainly going to leave us. The fact that you should be tarred and feathered and run out of town for reminding us we're human and have frailties is something else entirely."

He laughed and relaxed visibly, coming up a step and leaning against the door frame. "The lady waxes eloquent," he said, "and if I weren't so damn mad, I'd tell her she looks very beautiful in the moonlight."

"If you're damn mad, then you can't be so very sure of yourself or your opinions. Come on." She stood back and beckoned him in. "I'm about ready for a fresh cup of coffee. How about it?"

"Buying me off with a cup of coffee won't quite solve our problem, Mrs. Whiting."

"Our problem?" She smiled. "I'll up the ante with a couple of donuts."

"Appealing to my sweet tooth will get you nowhere." Nevertheless he obligingly followed her into the shop.

She went over to the open stairwell and listened again for any sound of noise from her apartment. "My son's asleep," she said to Hunt who had joined her.

"Hard day at karate?"

"Hard day at being six years old. Look," she said, "I didn't mean to take off after you so much as advise my readers the preacher's come into town to tell us who we are and how we're going down the path to hell and damnation. And to be prepared, that's all."

"The coffee," he said softly.

"Right." She laughed, the air suddenly cleared of all argument, and she wasn't even certain why. She took him around to her office. "Have a seat," she told him, offering him a Windsor chair that stood before her desk. She thought of her ex-husband. If Walt had come fishing around for information about Victor Bosworth, what would he think of Hunt Gardner? Well, she was grown up, and one day soon she had every intention of fighting Walt on his regressive divorce decree.

Hunt didn't take the chair, however, but wandered around her office, looking at her posters and the bits of artwork that covered every available surface. "So this is where the damage is done."

"Yes, but it's become a bit overwhelming, frankly. I've got to think about hiring some permanent personnel." He turned to her, looking interested. She shook her head almost imperceptibly. No, he was the last person on earth she'd discuss her problems with. "Sugar?" she asked testily. "Milk?"

"The works. Two sugars. And the donuts you bribed me with. What you're trying not to tell me is that you can't make up your mind to go forward and that you need a strong arm to lean upon."

"You're so wrong." She went over to a small, antique wooden icebox and pulled out a box of packaged donuts. "Very four-star from the corner bakery. Help yourself. Napkins on that shelf over there."

"Wrong, am I," he said, picking up a donut and biting into it. "You're a great subject-changer, Jemma. I came here ready to throttle you, and instead here I am knee-deep in donuts."

There was a touch of sugar powder in the corner of his mouth. Jemma, handing him the cup of coffee, had to fight an unexpected but overwhelming desire to put her tongue to his lips and lick that powder away. Instead, she reached up and carefully, with one finger, brushed the powder away.

He smiled. "What the hell was that all about?"

"Sloppy eater. Is that what they taught you in the South Pacific?"

"That and a lot more."

"Really." She backed away and poured herself a cup of coffee. Her hand was shaking. She realized she had deliberately taken them down a dangerous pathway and the notion frightened her.

Hunt came up behind her and said in a quiet voice. "They taught me something about closed societies."

She turned and faced him, using her coffee cup as an effective barrier between them, but feeling unsure of herself, unsure of her reaction to him. "Really. What did you learn?"

"Never to start something you can't finish."

"You didn't have to travel ten thousand miles for that lesson. You could have learned it right here. Incidentally, we're a closed society, too. We're not really so far apart, Ramsey Falls and your South Sea island."

He took her cup and put it down. "No, we're not at all apart," he said. "As I'm learning every day."

She was aware with absolute clarity of the empty meaning of their words, that they were speaking merely to fill in the spaces, to give them time to breathe, to contemplate the outcome of their next move.

"I came here to ream you out," he said. "Instead, all I want to do is take you in my arms."

"No." The word burst out as he reached for her. She was aware of the light in her office, the huge window on the street, the fact that every move they made was visible to passersby. She was aware of a shadow in the corner of her mind that could only belong to Walt, Walt who always held the key to her future. But more than that, she was aware of how much she wanted to throw caution to the winds for once in her life, and how she never could.

He drew his hands away and contemplated her silently for a long moment. Then he turned abruptly and walked to her office door. "Goodbye, Mrs. Whiting," he said, "of Ramsey Falls."

CHAPTER FIVE

THE CRAMPED, ground-floor office assigned to Hunt Gardner in the administration building at Pack College had one good thing going for it—a clear, enticing view of the campus through an accommodatingly large window. The lush green lawn held a few enormous statues donated by the Bosworth Foundation—modern circles and totems in iron or bronze. They were soothing to the eye against a silvery backdrop of mountains, huge old oaks and maples and low-lying buildings. Summer students lolled about the lawn even though it was a hot Saturday afternoon and they had no classes. He had a sudden desire to let all that afternoon into his office. In spite of the air-conditioning he got up and pushed the window open. From somewhere off to the right, the sound of a pop signalled a run in a baseball game that was taking place out of his line of sight. There were some shouts of encouragement that soon turned to groans.

Hunt returned to his desk, sat down, picked up his pen and stared hard at the yellow-ruled pad on his desk. He was making a poor pretense at work. He threw his pen down. He had long since given up trying to concentrate.

He had to keep reminding himself that this little interlude in Ramsey Falls with its bucolic air and serene landscape was someone else's world, not his. Someone else's world. That required a wry smile. He had, in fact, been in someone else's world from the time he left his family's Minnesota farm for college. Why was this place different, then, except for a pair of green eyes? It wasn't. He picked up the pen again and made a stab at writing. He had work to do, a timetable to fill, and a wanderlust that was as natural to him as breathing.

As for Jemma Whiting, she was independent, stiff-necked, frigid and bent upon showing the world, and probably her ex-husband, just how far she could go without anyone else's help. Too bad. There were a couple of instances in which he'd like to come to her aid.

"Daydreaming, professor?"

Hunt looked up to find his assistant peering in at the door. "Hey, Max, come on in, pull up a chair." He gave him a genuinely welcome smile.

"I knew I'd find you here," Maxwell J. Tam said.

Hunt grinned. "Predictable as all that, am I?"

Max sauntered in, grabbed a chair and straddled it. He was a stocky, good-looking Chinese American in his late twenties, close to his doctorate in education. He had a young wife in Thailand and a new-born baby. When Thai and American funds were in danger of drying up, the Bosworth Foundation had offered to rescue the program, which was why Hunt was in Ramsey Falls and why Max was with him.

"Pretty predictable," he told Hunt. "Although the way I figured it out when we first came here, you'd consider Ramsey Falls a piece of packaged cake and would spend most of your time on the tennis courts. Instead you loaded your schedule with an extra series of lectures, and you're filling in the empty spaces sweating over an article. What gives? Not in hiding, are you? I mean from the tax collectors or something.''

Hunt stared at him for a moment, stung by the unexpected truth in his words.

Max, surprised by Hunt's reaction, raised both hands in apology. ''Hey, I wouldn't have said it, if I thought you hadn't figured it out for yourself.''

''Hiding? I'm the Ugly American visible as hell to natives everywhere. Where'd you pick up that notion?''

''Think about it, professor. If the local sachems in Thailand or Malaysia romanced you, you'd be right out there enjoying yourself. Here, well.'' He shrugged, letting the meaning dangle.

''You've been working overtime on my behalf,'' Hunt remarked, furious at how close Max had come to the truth.

''Yeah, you're hiding out,'' Max said with a grin.

''That obvious, is it?''

''You don't like being lionized by the local *hunt* club, if you'll pardon the pun.''

''It's unpardonable, but you get high marks for hitting the nail on its proverbial head.''

''Anyway,'' Max said, ''the truth is, I just came by to let you know I'm going into New York until Monday to visit some of my wife's relatives. Anything I can do for you while I'm there?''

Hunt laughed and shook his head. ''Nothing at all. What I wanted to do earlier this summer and to whom no longer signifies.''

''Don't know what you mean but should I be sorry?''

''No. Although you might ask me that question again in another three weeks.''

After Max left, Hunt sat for a long time at his desk, mulling over his assistant's words. His plans for July had been neatly skewed by one patrician American with an interest in education and the ways and means to get things done. Hunt would have been enjoying himself in a much less predictable way if it weren't for Victor Bosworth.

July should have been spent high in a penthouse in Manhattan with a beautiful, willing blonde named Dara. It was her penthouse, but then Hunt had made sacrifices before. Dara left for Europe with a shrug of pretty shoulders. Hunt had been disappointed but not devastated. Theirs had been a desultory affair, picked up in Hong Kong or Brazil, and even once in Appalachia. They enjoyed each other's bodies, but when it was time to pack up and go on alone, neither made a fuss. It was the way Hunt liked it, and so apparently did she.

She was undoubtedly in Cannes, baring her bosom on the beach. He, on the other hand, found himself reaching for the fully clothed, beautiful and thoroughly self-possessed Jemma Whiting. Must be the heat. It was getting to him.

His telephone rang just when he was about to surrender and close the window. Hunt picked up the receiver quickly, glad of the distraction. His first thought was that, incongruously, his caller would be Jemma Whiting. The voice that greeted him, however, was the one he should have predicted.

"Auction tonight, Hunt, remember I told you about it?"

He frowned. He suddenly felt like Gulliver in the land of the Lilliputians. If he didn't put a stop to it and soon, Celie and her minions would have him tied down unable to move.

"You'll like it," Celie went on. "The whole town turns out for this one. Especially as it's going to benefit the tricentennial celebration."

The whole town. Predictability, unpredictability. His mind slid to Jemma Whiting and he said, "You're on."

"MOMMY, when are we going to the auction?"

"Cool it, Seth, as soon as I finish."

"When?" Seth stalked over to the printing press and stared at it for a while. "They're giving rides on the fire engine, too."

"Wonderful."

"We eating at the auction?"

"We always do. Let Mommy work."

"Hot dogs, yum yum, I'm going to have two."

Jemma sighed and hit the Save button on her spreadsheet program. "You win, Seth, by a landslide. Let's go to the auction."

"Yay!"

It was nearly seven when they arrived at the firehouse, which was in a brand new building just outside of town. A banner strung across the highway announced that the auction would begin at 7:30 sharp, and that the proceeds were for the tricentennial celebration. Lined up on the common were three fire engines decorated with crepe ribbons, balloons and small multicolored lights. One of the trucks was filled with shoving, squealing, squirming kids sporting miniature firemen's helmets.

"There's your fire engine," Jemma told her son.

"I'm hungry."

"Fire engine first, then the hot dog. You know what happens if you eat and then have too much excitement."

He caught sight of a friend being helped up and ran over to him shouting joyously.

"Seth," Jemma called.

Her son stopped and turned around.

"Be careful, honey. I don't want you acting up. You'll behave yourself, won't you?"

"Uh-huh."

"Oh, and Seth, I'm going into the firehouse, okay? If you want me, you'll find me at the back."

"Uh-huh."

"See you later, honey." She waited while the fire chief scooped the boy into his arms and deposited him alongside his friend.

"Hey, Jemma, how's it goin'?" The owner of the area's biggest insurance agency tapped her arm in a friendly way.

"Fine, Bud. How's the family?"

"Can't complain. Oldest daughter's out in Colorado riding the rapids. Everything okay with you?"

"Great. Seth's into karate. Right now he's on the fire engine pretending to be a fire chief."

They parted with smiles, and Jemma headed into the firehouse, which was already crowded and noisy. Thick-foliaged hanging plants donated by a local nursery were strung from the rafters, giving the barn-like structure a friendly, festive air. A stage with a microphone and lectern stood at the front end. The firehouse was nearly filled, and Jemma saw that if she wanted a seat, she'd have to move fast to find one. Donated furniture, household items, boxes of books and cartons of early vegetables lined the side opposite the huge bay doors.

Jemma slowly checked the display, eyeing several practical items to bid on. That's what Ramsey Falls was about, she thought. Sally Cruthers donates a butter dish and Mattie Johnson buys it. Chances were that Sally would buy the pair of candlesticks that Mattie donated. Small-town stuff and dear to Jemma's heart. She easily found the large carton she donated, holding toys Seth had grown out of, including several very expensive ones Walt had given him. When she was married, she had accumulated all sorts of possessions, useful and otherwise, gewgaws that had seemed essential to her life. And then there was the divorce and the inevitable garage sale, her precious hoard wrapped in newspapers and carried off by strangers. It would be a long time before she became attached to things again.

Among the crowd she spied the owner of the local bed-and-breakfast, an expensive inn often featured in magazines, and the manager of the largest vineyard in Merriman County, as well as the butcher, the baker and the candlestick maker. The yearly firehouse auction was a great leveler; everyone came. Everyone had a stake in their firehouse, which also served as a focal point for dozens of community activities throughout the year.

"Biggest turnout ever." It was Mrs. Lawson, her son's baby-sitter, bearing a pie in her arms.

"Biggest," Jemma echoed. "Is that the pie you baked?"

"It is. Fresh raspberries. They're putting up a stand right inside the back door. The baked goods go fast, you know. Better come along and pick out something before they're all bought up."

Jemma reached for her wallet. "Mrs. Lawson, save me that raspberry pie. How much do I owe you?"

"I'll take care of it. We'll settle later."

"Deal."

"Okay everybody." It was the auctioneer, a distinguished-looking man in his sixties who donated his services to the firehouse auction every year. "Shall we begin?"

Jemma, standing on the sidelines, looked hastily around for a seat, but discovered they were all taken.

"Come on, Jemma, you can have mine." She found the doctor waving at her from his seat in the middle row.

"No, I'll stand, Doc, thanks, anyway." She was about to turn away and head for the back when she saw Hunt Gardner.

"Oh, damn." The word escaped her lips softly, and she was certain no one heard her. He stood across the way under the wide open bay door. He was with Celie Decatur, his arm draped casually across her shoulder. He held a can of beer. If he saw Jemma, he did not show it but rather directed his attention to Celie.

His words of the evening before still stung Jemma. *"Goodbye, Mrs. Whiting of Ramsey Falls."* Simple enough words and yet they'd had the curious effect of a slap in the face. They had haunted her through the day, words of admonition telling her she was cool, unresponsive, unapproachable—in fact, not worth the effort. He was the last person in the world she wanted to meet at the auction and it had the effect of dampening her spirit.

"Goodbye, Mrs. Whiting of Ramsey Falls," said with all the disdain he could muster, as though wanting a woman in his arms was an offer she shouldn't re-

sist. Well, she had and she would and the professor be damned.

The auctioneer cleared his throat into the mike. "Everybody? Let the auction begin." After a few seconds of shuffling, the crowd became quiet. "I'm supposed to ask if you all bought raffle tickets," he said in opening. "Raffle tickets? Here's your last chance to buy a raffle ticket. Remember, first price is a VCR from the Pinebush Supermarket. Second prize is dinner for two at Cobble Inn."

Local college kids wearing straw hats with red, white and blue bands on them, fanned out down the aisles selling tickets. No, Jemma thought, hailing one of the kids and buying a couple, she wasn't going to let Hunt Gardner's presence bother her in the least.

He was bored, he wanted to start something with one of the locals to while away the month of July, and Celie Decatur was welcome to him. *"I'd like to take you in my arms."* He expected her to be flattered because he had selected her like a prize yearling at an auction. She wasn't flattered.

The divorcée, in fact, had been picked out by several Ramsey Falls bachelors when she received her decree. They thought she was lonely. They thought they'd give her what she was missing. They thought any number of things, all wrong. She had set them straight, but the experience had left her cautious.

Jemma tucked the raffle tickets into her bag and then, like an insect drawn to a spider's web, couldn't resist a glance in Hunt's direction once more. This time she found him watching her. When their eyes caught, he raised his beer can and saluted her. She felt an unexpected rush of heat to her face, and with an imperceptible shake of her head, turned and headed quickly toward the rear of the firehouse. Damn again, he had the talent of disconcerting her, and she didn't like the feeling at all.

She was so bent upon escape that she almost crashed into Sarah Crewes who put a hand out to steady her. "Where are you going in such a rush? I was just looking for you."

Jemma's greeting was a little confused. "Oh, just, um, going to check on Seth. He's out on the fire engine."

"Great, I'll come along. I have to talk to you."

Jemma greeted her remark with intense relief. "Sure, what's up?"

Once they were clear of the firehouse and the auctioneer's booming voice, Sarah said, "I found out the weirdest thing, and if I don't tell somebody I'll burst."

"Not bad news, I hope."

"It's according to what you think is bad news."

Dusk had fallen, and Jemma glanced over at the engine where her son was playing happily with his friends. "There's Seth," she said. "See him?"

"He's grown," Sarah said admiringly.

"A handful."

"A handsome handful. Shall we sit over here and be cozy while we're at it?" Sarah pointed to a large, soft couch covered in plaid, which incongruously sat in the grass unclaimed. "Welcome to my house," she added plopping down. "Not in bad condition," she said of the couch. "Wonder why somebody wanted to get rid of it?"

Jemma shrugged. "Broken dreams."

"Didn't match the wallpaper, more like." They settled back into the couch, each in a corner.

"Okay," Jemma said, "shoot. What's up?"

"I feel like shouting stop the auction, folks, you have it all wrong. And then bolting for the hills before the arrows fly."

"Have all *what* wrong? Sarah, you're not making any sense."

"Oh, I'm going to make sense, all right, Jemma. You also know what I've been doing for the past couple of years, trying to get a history together of the Crewes in Merriman County. You know what a disaster the files are at the county courthouse."

"I see Celie took your advice," Jemma said, "and has done an editorial about it in the *Times Herald*."

"Bless Celie. She's all bark and has a heart the size of Rhode Island. Jemma," she added, turning serious, "I *did* find something in the files that I wasn't looking for."

"Dynamite?"

"Dynamite with the charge ready to be set off. There's a file cabinet in the basement of the county hall. It's a big, flat thing meant to hold surveyor's maps. It's very old."

Jemma glanced toward the firehouse and the bright lights within. She heard the children's cries from the fire engine and the faint sound of the auctioneer's voice. The evening was mild, beautiful, all of a piece, and she found herself wondering why she'd let Hunt Gardner intrude upon all of this, her warm, ordered friendly world.

"The cabinet is a mess and decaying," Sarah was saying. "Somewhere along the line I suspect it was rained upon and nobody wanted to touch the resulting goop. That could have been a century ago. It was consigned to the basement, and that same nobody never counted upon a descendant of the Crewes trying to pick her way through it. I came across something." Sarah paused, frowning as though she might change her mind and not tell Jemma after all.

"You're not going to hold back now, are you?"

"The original surveyor's map was there attached to the articles of incorporation for the town of Ramsey Falls."

"Wonderful," Jemma whooped. "Where are they? We can frame them and exhibit them at the town hall. You darling, you, and to think you had me worried."

"Jemma, I'm not worried, but you should be. Hold on to your hat."

Sarah's remark was quietly stated and Jemma felt herself pale. "Sarah, spill it right this minute."

"I'm going to and I feel unaccountably like laughing. Here goes." Sarah took a deep breath, then let out her words in quick succession. "Ramsey Falls was incorporated exactly two hundred ninety-nine years ago. You're celebrating the tricentennial twelve months too soon."

"What?" Jemma shouted the word so clearly that her son called her from his perch on the fire engine. "It's okay, Seth." She waved at him, then turned back to Sarah. "Mind running that by me again?"

"Ramsey Falls is not three hundred years old, Jemma."

"Have you told anyone else?"

"No."

"Not even your cousin Victor?"

"Definitely not Victor. I hate to see a grown man cry. Jemma, I haven't told anyone except you. I figured you're deeply involved with the celebration and you're levelheaded. My advice is to forget it. I can keep quiet at my end. In fact, if you want, I'll lay low."

"Why didn't you keep this to yourself in the first place, bury it even deeper than it is?"

Sarah shook her head, her brown eyes wide with surprise. "Jemma, it isn't mine to keep."

Jemma reached over and took her friend's hands in hers. "No, of course not, but sometimes it's expedient..." She stopped, leaving the sentence unfinished. She was preaching and had no right to.

"Maybe I should have buried it, but I couldn't, I just had to share it with someone. You."

Jemma laughed. "Thanks for your faith. I guess. Nothing like laying the problem on big sister."

"You're the big sister I never had."

They sat for a long moment contemplating each other with smiles on their faces. Jemma and Sarah had met in college, and although there was a couple of years difference in their ages, they remained friends— even when Jemma quit to support Walt through graduate school. They met rarely, but their feelings for each other were mutually warm.

At last Jemma said, "Sarah, if you laugh at any time between now and the tricentennial, I'll never talk to you again. It's terrible. The truth is bound to come out sooner or later. Do you know what we've planned, the money we've spent, the printing we've done? My shop has been going full blast for half the year making up material for the big day."

"The celebration's three weeks away," Sarah pointed out.

"Who else has access to the files?"

"I'm sure I'm the first person to look into them in this century."

Jemma thought of Celie Decatur and the projected history of Ramsey Falls her newspaper was planning to run in its weekend editions. Surely a reporter would make his way to the basement of the courthouse and discover it on his own.

"I stumbled across it," Sarah said, as if she read Jemma's thoughts. "No one's going to bother."

"Celie's planning a big story on the history of Ramsey Falls," Jemma said.

"They haven't done their homework, or they'd know about it by now."

"I suppose so. Look, let me think about it." Jemma glanced over at the firehouse. "Come on, I have to bid on a couple of things. It's my civic duty."

Once in the firehouse they separated, Sarah to look over some items she wanted and Jemma to make certain the ones she'd chosen hadn't been auctioned off. Hunt, Jemma saw with a feeling of relief, was nowhere in sight, although Celie Decatur had taken a seat down front with Victor Bosworth.

Jemma spotted the items she wanted, but stayed well to the rear of the firehouse, even when Sarah found a couple of seats and motioned to Jemma to join her. The bidding was lively when a basket of Siamese kittens came up for auction. The kittens were quickly taken. As half a dozen kids collected the tiny balls of fur, Jemma had successfully tucked the business of the tricentennial to the back of her mind.

"Funny, I could have sworn you'd bid for a kitten."

She turned and found Hunt, his grin lopsided and engaging. He smelled faintly of beer, and she had to resist the desire to raise her hand and push back the lock of hair that fell over his forehead. "A kitten! I'm going to have my hands full with a dog."

"What's a home and hearth without a kitten curled up in your favorite wing chair?"

"Fortunately I don't have a wing chair." She laughed, all feelings of animosity gone. When he wanted, she understood quite clearly, he could be the most charming man in the world. "Are you here for something special," she asked, "or to catch the locals in their annual tribal rites?"

"Strictly a voyeur, Jemma, the visitor from another planet watching the natives disport themselves."

"And planning, I've no doubt, on writing a paper for one of the more esoteric journals."

"Good idea. I was wondering what project I could take up in my spare time."

"An auction's as good a place to start as any. You see us with our insides out, so to speak, all our old dishes and chairs and television sets. If we don't know whom they once belonged to at least we know who's going to own them next."

"What happens to the stuff people don't buy?"

"Like what?"

Hunt draped an arm around her shoulder and turned her gently toward the side wall where a huge-antlered moose head had been hung high about the crowd. "That moose head, for instance. I've no idea how it got separated from its body," Hunt went on, waving expansively toward the object, "but I fail to comprehend why it's up for auction and why anyone would want to own it."

The auctioneer's voice could be heard intoning over the mike. "Twenty-one? Twenty, do I hear more? Nothing? Twenty-one? Twenty, twenty-one. Then twenty it is to that gentleman at the rear. Professor Gardner of Pack College, if I'm correct?"

Hunt snapped to attention. "What the devil," he began, then laughed. "I think I just bought something."

"You're lucky if it isn't the moose head."

They waited while a blond youth came rushing down the aisle toward them carrying a small carton. "That's twenty dollars, Professor Gardner."

Hunt dug into his pocket and came up with the money. "Here you go, Jimmy," he said.

"Enjoy it, professor."

"Is there anyone in this town you don't know?" Jemma asked.

"Played a game of touch football with him and his friends the other day," Hunt told her.

"You're fitting right in with the culture."

"Evidently I am," he said, examining the small carton.

"For a good cause, Professor," Jemma pointed out. "The tricentennial." She stopped, remembering her conversation with Sarah.

Hunt lifted the top flaps carefully. "I hope it doesn't turn out to belong to a lady named Pandora."

Jemma poked her hand into the carton. "What do you suppose is in there?"

"Might be a mousetrap. I'd be careful if I were you." He lifted out an old tattered velvet box.

"A jewelry box," Jemma said.

He struggled with the rusty catch and the top flew open. "Ah, the riches of the Orient."

"Serendipity," Jemma said. They found it filled with costume jewelry caught into a jumble of chains and pins, loose beads and old buttons, rhinestones without settings and settings without rhinestones.

"You might call it serendipity. I'd call it Captain Kidd's treasure chest, and he wasn't kidding, either. Let's see what we have here."

To Jemma's surprise, Hunt began to rummage gleefully through the jewelry. He discarded one piece, then picked up another. "Wonder whom it all belonged to?" she asked.

"Definitely not the Queen of England."

"You're enjoying yourself, aren't you?"

He smiled and tucked the box under his arm. "Come on, let's go outside and find some place to park so we can go through this at a proper pace."

"I wouldn't miss your treasure hunt for the world."

They found a wooden bench at the back of the firehouse with enough light from a window. Hunt began his search at once.

"Trinkets, gewgaws and gimcracks," Jemma said.

"The detritus of somebody's sad history."

"Maybe things have improved and she's into diamonds and rubies."

"Ah, what's this," he stated after a few minutes of picking his way through the jumble. "Pay dirt." He found a round object and tugged at it until it came loose from its moorings, dragging a chain with it. Hunt took out a handkerchief and began to rub at the metal.

"Decidedly not dross, more likely gold and eighteen karats at that." He held it to the light.

"A gold locket," Jemma said, excited. "Open it up."

"Beware of spirits flying loose." He pried it apart and showed the open locket to Jemma. It contained two yellowed photographs, one of a young woman with a sweet, shy smile, and the other of an equally young man in a high collar, his expression severe and direct.

"I wonder who they are," Jemma said.

"There are some initials on the back. B.W. forever, M.S."

"I wonder how long forever was," Jemma remarked, finding herself deeply moved.

"Long enough for it to end up lost in a box of misbegotten jewelry."

"Cynic."

"On the contrary. A believer, like you, in serendipity."

"An unexpected coming upon of a treasure."

"Madame." He held up the locket and before she could say anything, Hunt had placed it around her neck. "There. I can't think of a more beautiful forever." She turned, feeling the warmth ride to her cheeks. He fumbled with the closing, then said, "Done."

For a long moment he allowed his fingers to rest lightly against her skin.

Jemma turned to face him, her hand touching the locket. It had a cool, silken feel to it. "I'm not sure I should be wearing someone else's forever around my neck," she stated carefully.

"Whoever they were," he remarked in a softened tone, "they'd approve."

"Would they? You know that to a certainty."

The silence between them held while they gazed at each other. "Jemma," he began, but whatever he was going to say to her was lost in a sudden commotion emanating from the front of the firehouse.

Jemma got quickly to her feet, her hand fluttering unconsciously to the locket. "What's that?"

She heard her name called several times as she began to run. "Seth," she cried. "Is it Seth?"

CHAPTER SIX

JEMMA TRIED to still the tremor she felt starting in the pit of her stomach. "Seth." The word burst from her again and it was only when she reached the fire truck that she came to her senses. Lying in the grass was her son, a tiny figure surrounded by a hushed crowd. The fire chief bent over him, gently holding the boy's hand. He looked up at Jemma as she approached and shook his head reassuringly.

"What is it, what happened? Seth, darling, it's Mommy." There was a bruise on Seth's forehead but at the sound of his mother's voice his eyelids fluttered and he whimpered slightly.

"Seth, it's all right, I'm here." Jemma was on her knees. With tentative fingers she touched the bruise. His skin was scraped but there was no blood, although she could feel a lump beginning to form. She turned to the fire chief. "What happened?"

"It doesn't look serious, Jemma, relax, he's all of a piece. Nothing's broken. A lump on his forehead and a couple of bruises."

"For God's sake, what happened?"

"He was fooling around with the kids on the truck and lost his footing and fell."

"Fell." She echoed his words.

"Jemma, nothing like this has ever happened before, you know that as well as I."

"Where are the paramedics, dammit, I thought you had an ambulance here. And where's the doctor? He was at the auction, I saw him."

"We had another emergency, Jemma. The doc went with the ambulance to the hospital. Take it easy, now. I've had as much experience as a dozen paramedics, you know that. I'm taking him to the hospital right now."

"Jemma." Hunt crouched down beside her. "Take it easy. Your getting hysterical won't help."

"Do we dare move him?" she asked, feeling helpless, as though she'd never had to deal with an emergency before.

Hunt turned to Seth, bending close. "Son, my name is Hunt, and I'm a friend of your mother's. Can you open your eyes?"

Jemma waited, holding her breath as Seth slowly opened his eyes. "I fell down," he said in a voice so soft and low that Jemma had to lean forward to hear it.

"You're okay," Hunt said as he ran his hands deftly down the boy's body. "The only thing we have to worry about is concussion. Jemma, give me your car keys. Let's get him to a hospital for X rays."

"We're doing just that," the fire chief interposed.

"I'll handle it," Hunt said.

The fire chief looked over at Jemma.

"I know what has to be done, Jemma," Hunt told her grimly. "Got a blanket to cover him with?"

"I'll get one," the fire chief said.

Jemma shook her head. "No, it's okay, there's one in the car."

"Okay, then," Hunt said, "Let's go."

Jemma silently nodded her approval. She was aware of his strength and determination and instinctively trusted it. He picked the boy up, cradling his head and holding him close.

"I'm driving," he told Jemma. "You sit in the back with Seth."

"Do you know the way?"

"On the highway. You can't miss it. Jemma, he's okay, don't show your panic. It won't do any of us any good. Get that blanket over him."

She found it on the floor of the car, her son's favorite blanket that he towed everywhere. "It's dirty," she said inanely as she tucked the edges around him.

Her car was an old standard shift model, and she could hear that Hunt was having trouble with the gears.

"I don't think your son minds a dirty blanket," Hunt said as the engine engaged. "When did this car have a tune-up last?"

"That bad?"

"It'll never win the Indy 500."

Seth moaned a bit.

"What darling?"

"I fell off the truck."

"It's okay, everything's going to be all right."

"We going home?"

"Just as soon as we have this bump checked out, okay?"

"Okay." He closed his eyes.

Jemma lightly brushed the bruise. It seemed to her that it had grown a bit. She looked up and found Hunt watching her through the rearview mirror.

"Hurry, would you?"

"Ten minutes at most. How is he?"

"He told me he fell off the truck. He's okay, I guess. When Seth talks, then everything's fine." She gave a quick laugh and glanced out the window. As she stroked her son's hair she uttered a silent prayer that there was nothing seriously wrong with the boy. Under a dusky evening sky, they sped past houses tucked demurely behind well-trimmed hedges. The world seemed to exude a storybook calm, as though nothing could ever go wrong. And yet how suddenly her whole world had changed.

"Are you holding up?" Hunt's soft words broke through and she caught his eyes once again in the rearview mirror.

"Yes, it isn't the first time he's taken some lumps." But she wasn't holding up, wasn't able to stop the shivers of worry that coursed through her. It was just that years of handling the emergencies of childhood seemed to have dulled her ability to share anxiety. "How do you know so much about broken bones and bruises?"

"I've had to be doctor as well as nurse in many a backward village in the third world. I've learned how to bandage wounds, give penicillin and repair water pumps, all in the same breath. There it is, Bosworth Hospital. Bosworth, where have I heard that name before?"

The lights of the hospital came up on the left. Hunt turned in and stopped at the emergency entrance. "I'll park later. Come on." He carried Seth into the nearly empty waiting room, and with the boy still in his arms, explained the situation to the nurse at the front desk.

Jemma rummaged in her bag for her medical insurance card, and then, when Hunt nodded, signed her name to a piece of paper without reading it.

A gurney was wheeled out and her son placed on it by two aides. "Can I go with him?" she asked.

"He's going into X ray right now," the nurse told her.

"Mommy." Her son said the word, then yawned and closed his eyes.

"Why can't I go with him?" she asked plaintively.

"Come on, Jemma." Hunt took her arm and led her over to a corner seat near a large picture window. A woman sitting nearby fidgeted with her purse and gave Jemma a nervous little smile. A youngster sat all alone just opposite the nurse's desk, swinging his legs back and forth. The hospital was eerily quiet with only an occasional bell going off unexpectedly. Someone was paging a Dr. Roerem on the loudspeaker. Jemma sat wearily on a yellow Naugahyde sofa.

Hunt frowned down at her. "You're too pale. I don't like your color," he said. "I'm going out to park the car and rustle up some coffee for you. A shot of brandy might be better, but I doubt I'll find any. Stay put, Jemma. He'll be all right." For a moment his hand rested on her shoulder. Then he turned and was halfway across the waiting room when Jemma called out.

"Hunt."

"Yes?"

She released a deep sigh. "Thank you."

For the length of a heartbeat, their eyes held. Then Hunt turned and went rapidly through the door.

Jemma leaned back on the sofa and closed her eyes, surprised at the emptiness she felt. It was as if there were no past, no present, no future, as if everything in life focused on the door through which the gurney had rolled, carrying her son.

She had no idea how much time had passed or how she could have remained so foolishly still, but suddenly she felt the touch of a hand on her hair. She opened her eyes. It was Hunt carrying a container of coffee for her.

"Not a shot of brandy to be found in the neighborhood. I figured you for a lady who takes her coffee black, but I sweetened this one up for you."

"Thanks. How long does an X ray take, anyway?"

"Relax, Jemma. I have a feeling they don't let any grass grow under their feet. Drink up while it's hot."

"Why weren't they watching him?" she said. She took a sip of coffee. It was hot and tasted of too much sugar, but she drank thirstily at it nonetheless.

"On the fire engine? Unless they restrained the kids with harness belts, an accident was possible. I've no doubt he was showing his friends what a black belt terror he was."

"Oh, Hunt," she said, smiling and shaking her head, "you must think me absolutely incompetent. It's just that usually I handle everything myself and I don't have the luxury of paling out. He's all I have."

Hunt sat down next to her, took the cup out of her hand and placed it on the window ledge. "Jemma, I believe you're a paragon of motherhood, but I like you better this way, when you're vulnerable."

"Right now I'm a jellyfish. Keep me entertained, Hunt. I feel so damn helpless."

"Kids are always banging themselves up."

"Tell me something I don't know."

"That would have to be my life history, then. For instance, when I was twelve, I fell off a train trestle."

It was several seconds before Jemma caught up with his remark. "Did you say you fell off a train trestle?

With the train speeding down the track at a hundred miles an hour, I suppose. Go on."

"You're right. I could hear the whistle racing down the tracks ahead of the train and the ground rumbling under the trestle. I heard the screech of the brakes and then—Shall I go on?" His dark eyes were flecked with amusement.

"Only if the story has a happy ending. I'm into happy endings at the moment."

"Oh, it has the requisite one all right."

"Did the train hit you or not?" she asked, feigning impatience.

"Missed me by a hair's breadth, but I broke my leg in three places. Spent the whole summer in a cast looking out my bedroom window."

"And where was that bedroom window?"

"Minnesota. Small farming village called River's Edge. My view was of waving fields of wheat."

"Minnesota? Small farming village? Called River's Edge? Well, somehow I'm surprised, Professor Gardner."

"At what? My roots?"

"Precisely." She looked over at the reception desk. A young man had come limping in, leaning on the arm of a small, pretty woman. She could hear his voice, although she couldn't quite make out the words.

"Tripped getting out of her bed, no doubt," Hunt said in her ear.

In spite of herself, Jemma laughed out loud. "Really, Hunt, and you the man who touts old-fashioned virtues."

"All in the face of realities. I wasn't born yesterday."

They were interrupted by the appearance of a doctor asking at the desk for Jemma Whiting. Jemma stood, bracing herself and feeling Hunt's arm move protectively around her shoulder.

"Mrs. Whiting? Mr. Whiting?" The doctor came over to them smiling. "Your son's doing fine. I'm Dr. Roerem. I've just finished checking his X rays. We see no evidence of broken bones, and we're pretty certain he has no concussion. To be on the safe side, however, we'd like to keep him here overnight."

Jemma breathed a sigh of relief and yet she felt so shaken, she was certain her legs would buckle under her. It was only Hunt's holding her that kept her steady. "I'm so relieved," she managed. "Is it possible I could see him?"

"Fine, if you and Mr. Whiting—"

"This is Hunt Gardner," Jemma said, pulling away from Hunt. "A friend. If you would like to talk to Seth's father..."

The doctor shook his head. "Come on, you can visit your son for a couple of minutes, reassure him that he'll be all right, and then you can go home."

"I'd like to stay overnight," Jemma said, "in his room."

The doctor smiled. "Your son's okay, Mrs. Whiting. I'll be on duty. Seth's going to sleep through the night, believe me, and when you pick him up in the morning, I want you bright-eyed. You'll need all your energy to keep him quiet."

"Doctor's orders," Hunt said. "Come on, I'll go with you."

They followed the doctor down a long hallway into a small room with two beds in it, although Seth was the only occupant. A nurse stood over him, adjusting his covers.

"Two minutes," the doctor said, after peering down into Seth's face and then checking his pulse. He went out with the nurse, closing the door behind him.

"Seth," Jemma whispered. Her son's face had been washed and his hair slicked back. The bump on his forehead was hidden by a thin ice pack held down with tape. He had the beginnings of a shiner under his left eye. She touched his shoulder gently. "Baby, are you awake?" He seemed so small and helpless tears started to her eyes.

"I'm not a baby." He opened his eyes and looked around, finally settling on Hunt who had remained standing at the door. "Daddy?"

"No, honey, not Daddy. You remember Mr. Gardner?"

He shook his head, then winced. "My head hurts."

"I'll call Daddy, and he'll come to see you."

"Can I go home?"

"You're staying here overnight, Seth, so that the doctor can be sure the bump on your forehead goes down. I'll come for you in the morning, okay?"

"Can we get Niko tomorrow?"

"I hope so."

"I can't sleep without my bear," he said as he closed his eyes and drifted off.

Jemma sat for a while watching him, reluctant to leave. Then at last she felt Hunt's gentle touch on her arm. "Jemma."

"Right." She kissed her son, and after another lingering look, left him in the care of the nurse. Once outside, she said to Hunt, "I think I'd better call Walt."

"Phone's down the hall. I've got some change."

She accepted the coins gratefully. "I think perhaps you ought to forget that lecture series and offer one on lifesaving instead."

"Give me time." He grinned and took her arm.

"I didn't think you had any to spare, time, I mean."

"And I'm beginning to be sorry I don't."

She realized as they walked down the corridor that she was dragging her feet. Explaining the accident to Walt wasn't going to be easy.

Hunt picked up on her reluctance almost immediately. "I gather it's a call you don't want to make."

"I'm not quite sure how to explain what happened."

"He'll blame you, I take it."

"Of course."

Walt's reaction when she caught him on the fourth ring, was on target. "Dammit, can't you keep an eye on that kid?" His tone was the infuriating one he used with her. "What the hell was he doing on a fire engine anyway?"

"Having a good time," she said, trying to keep her voice neutral. "I don't recall your asking how he is."

"Your voice told me."

"They're keeping him in the hospital overnight just to be on the safe side. He asked for you." She heard Walt's breathing. A quick in and out. He was weighing his options. He really didn't want to make the trip from Merriman to Ramsey Falls at that time of night, not if Seth was all right.

"I've a case coming up in the morning that could mean a great deal of money," he began. "I'm knee-deep in papers right now."

"Look," she threw in quickly, "they expect Seth to sleep right through the night. I'll tell him when I pick him up in the morning that you came to see him but didn't want to wake him."

"Ah," Walt said, "the model mother. I'm touched at your thoughtfulness. Too bad you didn't use some of it when your son was on the fire engine."

Jemma glanced over at Hunt, leaning against the wall, his hands dug into his pockets. He was engaged in conversation with a young nurse who was waiting to use the phone. "Is that all you have to say, Walt, because if it is, then goodbye." She hung up, cutting off his next remark.

It was when Hunt scooped up her bag from the floor and handed it to her, that Jemma managed to shake herself free of the phone call. "Hey, pal, what's going on?" he said. He drew her away. The nurse slid into the booth.

"Let's go," she said.

He pulled up the collar of her linen jacket and touched her hair with light fingers. "If a talk with your husband gets that kind of reaction from you, I'd say legislating a ban on phone calls between you is in order."

"That's one bit of legislation I'd lobby for."

He tucked his arm through hers and directed her toward the door. "I'm willing to buy you that shot of brandy," he said. "You still look as if you could use it."

She cast a glance back at the reception desk. There were a few more people in the waiting room. She closed her eyes briefly, resisting the inclination to run back to her son.

"Come on," he urged gently.

"Right. I suppose I ought to let the fire chief know, too."

"You can call from the bar."

"Let's go back to my apartment," Jemma said, once they were in the car, Hunt at the wheel. "I'd like to be home, just in case the doctor might call. Unless you like fancier fare, I can whip us up a couple of omelets," Jemma said.

"Suits me." He maneuvered the car out of the parking lot and turned left on the highway for the short drive to the center of town.

At his quick agreement, Jemma felt a moment of apprehension, then erased it from her mind. The truth was, she didn't want to be alone, not quite yet. Walt's words still rankled; it had been a long day and she was nowhere near sleep. She glanced at the lighted hospital building as they drove past, wondering which window was her son's. "Poor Seth. He wanted a hot dog, no two, and I was being the supercareful mother. Didn't want him to upset his stomach with all the excitement. I told him he could play first and eat later."

"Jemma, stop beating up on yourself."

"You're right. That's precisely what I'm doing. Dammit, he's so fragile."

"He's a tough little kid, and he'll take a lot more bumps before he reaches ninety."

She leaned back against the seat and closed her eyes. Hunt put the car into gear, and the silence between them lengthened. It was only when Jemma opened the door to her apartment and stepped into its familiar scent of lemon polish and potpourri that she spoke again. "Welcome to Whiting Manor."

She smiled awkwardly at him, however, once the door was closed and they stood alone in the foyer. They were no longer on neutral ground. But Hunt made himself right at home. She let him help her out of her linen jacket and gestured to the hall closet, where he hung it up. "Can I offer you a drink?"

"Beer, if you have any."

"Yes, as a matter of fact I do. From a party I gave three or four months ago. I don't think beer gets old, does it? Come into the kitchen. I promised you an omelet."

"So you did."

With his beer in hand, Hunt prowled the spacious old-fashioned kitchen with its warm oak paneling, old cabinets and brick fireplace. "Nice," he said.

"Some of the furniture came with the apartment, some I kept when I sold the house and most of its contents. I was a great collector once, but frankly, I lost the bug. Unfortunately the fireplace in the kitchen doesn't work, although the one in the living room does."

"Maybe all it needs is a good cleaning. I'll check it out the next time I'm here."

"Next time?" Jemma opened the refrigerator and pulled out some eggs and butter. Then on a whim, she reached for an onion, a green pepper, and some ham. Might as well make it a Western omelet while she was at it.

"Next time. Haven't you heard? There's always a next time."

She smiled and put some bread into the toaster. Hunt remained at the fireplace, examining the photographs on the mantel: her parents, her sister and her sister's children, Seth as a baby.

"Where are your parents now?" he asked. He picked up a picture of her father in his army uniform, with his arm around her brown-haired, snub-nosed mother, just out of her teens when the photograph was taken.

Jemma came over and said, "My father died six years ago. My mother moved to California to be near my sister."

"Ah, you have a sister." He put her father's picture back in place and picked up the charming color snapshot of her sister holding a baby on her lap. "Blonde, blue-eyed, decades older."

Jemma took the picture out of his hands and put it back on the mantel. "Five years older, and we're not competitive. In fact, I wish she were here. My mother, too. Sometimes . . ."

"Sometimes what?" He reached out and briefly placed his hand around her wrist. "You have a habit of beginning a sentence and not finishing it, Jemma. You're all alone in Ramsey Falls, obviously fighting exhausting mental battles with your ex-husband while your family is three thousand miles away. Sometimes what?"

"I've a son and an ex-husband who's a lawyer. That adds up to my being locked into Ramsey Falls because the divorce decree I signed restricts where I live. Because of Seth, I mean. I want him to see his father on a regular basis, you understand. A son needs a strong man in his life."

Hunt's expression was one of admiration, not for Jemma but for Walt. "If I ever get in trouble and need a lawyer, your ex sounds like the kind of man I'd hire."

"Come on," she said, expelling a sigh. "I've had quite enough of the man for one night. Let's get on with that omelet."

"Need help?"

She carefully broke four eggs into a bowl. "Sure, I'm going to make it a Western omelet. You stir and I'll cut."

She was peeling the onion when the telephone rang, the sound harsh in the evening quiet. "Not the hospital." She dashed for it, picking the receiver up on the second ring.

"Oh, hi," she said at once to the fire chief, "I was going to call you." She assured him that Seth was all right and had barely hung up when the telephone rang once again. This time it was Victor Bosworth.

"Hi, Victor." She covertly turned and glanced at Hunt who had taken over the task of dicing the ingredients for the omelet.

"I called the hospital," Victor said. "That was Celie's idea, clever lady. We know Seth is okay. What I want to know is if there's anything I can do."

"Nothing, thank you. Incidentally, the first thing Seth talked about was the dog. He wants it tomorrow but frankly, Victor, I didn't say yes and I didn't say no. If he's supposed to stay quiet, I'd like to hold off for a couple of days."

"It's okay, Jemma, Niko isn't going anywhere. I've taken him into the house and he gets along with the pugs."

"Housebroken?" She laughed.

"Housebroken. I'll stop by tomorrow to say hello. Get some sleep now."

"'Bye."

When she came over to the kitchen counter, the peppers and onions were diced into neat little piles, and Hunt was at work on the ham. "Victor Bosworth," he said.

"He told me I should get some sleep now." That she hadn't mentioned Hunt's being with her had somehow unsettled the air.

"My friend Victor seems to spend a lot of time worrying about you," Hunt said.

"Celie put him up to it."

"Celie?" He gave her a keen, incredulous look. "You and I can't be talking about the same Celie." He pushed the diced ham toward her across the wooden counter.

"Or about the same Victor Bosworth. You'll find salt and pepper in the spice cabinet."

"Not too much salt," Hunt said. "The ham will do enough damage to our arteries as it is."

She put a dollop of butter into an omelet pan and turned the heat up. "If you're not careful, I may ask you to finish what I started." The scent of cooking butter began to fill the room. Jemma poured in the egg mixture.

"Tell me, Jemma," Hunt said, leaning back against the counter and watching her, "why this air of boundless independence, this incredible cool? You invited me up for an omelet, and we're damn well going to have that omelet. And incidentally, when Victor calls, you don't bother telling him you have a visitor, his old pal Hunt, and that you won't be going to sleep quite yet."

The remark took Jemma aback, but all she could do was stutter her answer. "He...he doesn't have to know my business. It's none of his business knowing my...business. And it's none of your business knowing my business, either." She turned the flame up and pushed angrily at the eggs with a wooden spatula.

He laughed and took the spatula out of her hand. "You're turning that omelet into scrambled eggs. Here, let me. You put on a pot of coffee and heat up the toast."

Jemma relinquished the spatula. "Why did I invite you up here, anyway?"

"Your son? Remember? You wanted to show me how grateful you are by feeding me."

"Next time I'll send you flowers." She began to set the table quickly and efficiently. It was only when her patterned china and old silver were in place on the round oak table and she was considering lighting some candles that she drew back. Candles. What in the world could she be thinking of? She looked over at Hunt, still occupied with the omelet. Her son in the hospital, and here she was with the peripatetic professor, planning on candles. She regarded him across the room, his back to her as he stood over the omelet.

She decided she liked the way his dark hair grew slightly long and unruly at the back and the way it brushed against his shirt collar. She liked his broad back, slender hips and easy stance. Cooking eggs, rescuing little boys, applying first aid in Thailand, lecturing in an obscure upstate college, apparently the man was at home everywhere. And she liked that about him, too. "Tell me something," she remarked, the question spontaneous and surprising even her, "why aren't you married?"

He turned and smiled. "Are you asking that because I make a mean omelet?"

"I haven't tasted your omelet yet. How about answering my question? Don't pull back when it's your turn on the hot seat."

"I'm not ready to make the kind of commitment I think you need for a marriage to work."

"Slippery, professor."

"I don't make promises I can't keep."

She set the toaster and then took the coffeepot over to the sink and carefully filled it. "Still slippery. What if your heart, that is if you have a heart, fell madly, passionately, incredibly in love, but your head told you it wasn't time for a commitment?"

"Oh, I fall once in a while," he said casually. "I just never let it take over."

She came to the stove and looked down at the omelet. "It's gone past omelet into rubbery, I bet." The toaster clicked shut just as Hunt cut the flame under the omelet pan. "You're telling me something very interesting," she pursued.

"Am I now?"

She turned to him without backing away, although they stood so close she could feel his expelled breath lightly upon her cheek. "It's all right if *you* stay cool and independent, but quite another thing if *I* do. Perhaps I also allow my head to rule my heart. Perhaps I'm not ready for commitment, either. You seem to be faulting me for my independence."

"Are you in love?" he asked. "Passionately? The whole enchilada?"

She stared at him for a moment, then understood. It was possible he was referring to Victor. The idea was both disconcerting and yet funny. Victor! "Not even the whole omelet. Come on, we're both talking utter nonsense," she said, impulsively taking his hand then releasing it as if his touch had scalded her, "the food's getting cold."

But when she tried to reach around him for the pan, he grabbed her arm. "Shove the omelet."

The unexpectedness of his movement seemed to jar her heart loose and in a flash his lips were hard on hers.

She found a cry of resistance welling up in her throat, but as he drew her into him, crushing her close, something happened that changed it, turned the sound into a moan of sheer, unexpected joy. It happened quickly, the key in the lock, a spark against dry leaves, a tap turned. His mouth on hers, his tongue forcing her lips apart unleashed an explosion of exquisite intensity that rocketed through her body. She leaned into him, opening her mouth willingly, letting it signal the opening of every part of her. She couldn't think. She lost all power of judgment but for one extraordinary insight. Her life had been empty of sensation until this moment, in this man's arms.

She was drugged, hypnotized, and it was only Hunt's angry, "Damn," that brought her to her senses. The telephone was ringing.

"I'll get it. Don't move." He released her, and she stood there gulping deep breaths while he strode over to the phone.

"Seth," she said in a weakened voice.

He picked up the receiver. "Yes?" His eyes never left her face. "Hunt Gardner," he said, "who the hell are you?" He raised his hand signaling Jemma not to worry. "She's here." He held the receiver out, but cupped his hand over the mouthpiece. "It's your ex. Helluva time to be calling."

"Damn." She ran her hand quickly through her hair and went over and took the receiver. Hunt bent over and kissed her neck. Long, exquisite striations raced through her body, but she struggled away, shaking her head.

"Walt?" Even that one word came out shaky. Hunt had gone over to the counter and was leaning against it, unashamedly listening in.

"Who's Hunt Gardner?"

"Why are you calling? It's late."

"Your son's in the hospital, and you're entertaining male guests at home. Clever."

"Walt, what do you want?"

"I see, okay, I understand."

"You don't understand anything."

"Priscilla and I talked it over," Walt said. "We're picking Seth up at the hospital. He can recuperate at our place. We have the room and we have the quiet."

"No you're not. I won't hear of it. I'm bringing him back here."

"Tell you what, Jemma. I'll see you at the hospital. We'll talk about it then."

"We have nothing to talk about, Walt, and I'd appreciate it if you didn't use your I'll-see-you-in-court voice with me. Goodbye." She slammed the receiver down and stood staring at it until Hunt's voice gently broke the quiet.

"Jemma, you're burning enough anger to set off your smoke alarm."

She looked across the room at him, but it seemed to Jemma that he was far away, that she was gazing at him through the wrong end of a telescope. She'd been so careful. All she wanted was her son and the structured life she'd made for herself. And in one rash move she had put everything in jeopardy. Pandora's box. Hadn't Hunt said something about it earlier that evening? She touched the golden locket around her neck.

"I think you'd better go," she said quietly.

He took in her gesture, the expression on his face devoid of judgment. Then he turned on his heels and was gone.

CHAPTER SEVEN

"Ah, Victor, I'll bet you're calling about Niko. I'm beginning to feel terribly guilty. I do stick to my promises, you know that." Jemma busily collated some advertising brochures for the mall as she talked, the phone cradled awkwardly between chin and shoulder.

"I know you do. The dog is the farthest thing from my mind. How's your son?"

"Fine, enjoying the fuss. No concussion, although the lump on his forehead is the size of a walnut. He's with his father until Wednesday, which makes sense as Mrs. Lawson wanted some days off because her grandson's here on a visit. Anyway, I promise we'll come for the beast as soon as Seth is home."

"Right now the beast is sprawled on my Persian rug watching me as if I were a very large, very rare steak. He has extremely expressive eyes, incidentally. Niko isn't why I called, Jemma. There are two reasons, actually. One, is to remind you about the cookout tonight."

"Oh, I'm afraid you'll have to count me out, Victor. I realize it's a charitable event and the tricentennial is a good cause, but..." She stopped and frowned. She had totally forgotten her conversation with Sarah Crewes. What tricentennial? Perhaps they could change it to a bicentennial plus ninety-nine.

"But," Victor was prompting. "Go on."

"Victor, the plain and simple fact is I can't afford the hundred-fifty-dollar donation right now."

"You're coming as my guest," he said in a manner that told her it was all settled. "You're the press, aren't you?"

"Not according to the publisher of the *Times Herald*."

"The publisher of the *Times Herald* ought to know that competition's a good thing. You're my guest tonight, Jemma. I won't have it any other way."

She glanced at her calendar knowing full well it was empty, as Monday night usually was. "You're a darling. What time?"

"Eight. Save your appetite. Oh, that other thing. Cousin Sarah just called. She had something interesting to tell me and wanted me to pass it on to you."

"Decided to come clean, did she?" Jemma relaxed. Sarah had told Victor about the misplaced year and the tricentennial after all. Well, that was one less worry.

"What's Sarah supposed to come clean about?" Victor went on. "Did I miss something here?"

"Are we talking about the tricentennial?" Jemma asked cautiously.

"There's a penny saver for sale in the town of Merriman. Sarah thought you might want to look into it. Owner is Ray Xeller, you know, Xeller Printing. He lives in Manhattan and he's retiring to Florida What's this about the tricentennial?"

"That's a nice little penny saver," she interposed quickly. "I occasionally send Xeller Printing work I can't handle, business cards, engraved stationery. Is the whole operation for sale?"

"So Sarah tells me. Along with the printing shop. The operation is similar to yours, but frankly larger. Sarah wanted me to pass the information on to you."

Jemma changed the receiver around and cupped it in her hand, her collating abandoned. "Sarah's an absolute fount of information," she said and frowned once more. She was still left with the decision to make about the tricentennial, and now something else was thrown into her lap.

"It might make sense to look into it, Jemma. There's a lot of duplication going on between your penny saver and the one in Merriman, don't you think?"

"The towns are thirty miles apart," Jemma said. "Anyway, the truth is, I don't believe I can afford to think about adding on new debt."

"There's every reason for you to consider the purchase."

"I've just been giving some thought to adding on a full-time assistant here," Jemma said. "I'm at the point where Whiting Printing can't stand still and it has only one place to go and that's forward, meaning infusions of cash. I need additional software programs and they cost the world. Thanks for thinking of me, Victor, and thank Sarah, but I'll have to pass on this one."

"According to Sarah, they've some pretty sophisticated presses there. You might be able to consolidate your work. It would pay in the long run."

"I'm not crazy about taking on more debt, Victor. Maybe in another year."

"What if I could see about financing?" Victor remarked.

"Look," she began, but he interrupted her.

"Sarah suggested it, and when my young cousin speaks, I obey. I'll look into financing, you look at the print shop. It's on Harbor Street near the town hall, the only one in the center of Merriman."

"Thanks, Victor. I know the place although I haven't been there since Ray Xeller took over. They have a pick-up service so we do most of our talking over the phone."

"Ray originally inherited the business from a brother, from what I understand. Anyway, if he wants to sell, you should hear him out."

"I promise I'll look at the place if I have a chance. But I'm warning you, I don't want to take on any more debt. See you tonight." She hung up, shook her head over how easy it was for people with money to offer advice to people without money, and went back to work. Another shopper's guide. Another print shop. She continued to collate furiously. A shopper's guide in Merriman. A print shop with a lot more capacity to turn out orders.

She'd have to borrow against her assets, but of course her accounts receivable would double, or triple. Just how ambitious was she?

The tiniest mote of interest took hold. No, she'd be a fool to think about it. It required a certain kind of mind to make a bargain with the future. You had to believe in yourself, first of all, believe you had the knowledge and energy to make it all work. She had done it once with the *Ramsey Falls Shopper's Guide*, put everything on the line, including her belief in herself. No, she couldn't add to her debt load, not now. Time. She needed time to think.

She glanced at the clock. It was nearly four. Outside the street was empty, even of occasional strollers. The

July heat dazzled, as if it had substance. Summer Mondays were often drowsy, but today especially so. Anyone with any sense was immersed in water: pool, lake, river, even Ramsey Falls.

Her son was away, it was a sleepy summer afternoon and Jemma was perfectly free to close up shop, post her Gone Fishin' sign in front and take a drive into Merriman. She would merely glance in the window of the printing shop, but it would be enough to either whet or dull her appetite. She could justify the visit by stopping off to see a few of her far-flung customers on the way back. She'd be through with everything before eight o'clock and Victor's charity cookout.

"Done." She finished collating and then toured the shop turning off switches and lights and setting her answering machine. She hadn't had a vacation in three years, and she'd have to make up for it one summer afternoon, and this was it. She pulled out her yellowed, precious Gone Fishin' sign and posted it on the front door.

She ran quickly up to her apartment, stripped off her clothes and stepped into the shower. As the cool needle spray washed over her, Jemma allowed herself to relax for the first time that day. She had given in to Walt on the matter of her son because Seth wanted it, and because he'd be safe, quiet and cared for, and she couldn't afford to spare the time.

Fine state of affairs. All activity, that was Jemma Whiting. Thirty-two years of energy spilling out, every minute taken up and accounted for. Her son, her business, her business, her son, no time for contemplation, no time for worrying about what was missing. No time for examining that hidden bit of herself waiting in the shadows that had been unexpectedly revealed under Hunt Gardner's touch. She pushed it back as though it were some terrible demon she would never be able to control.

Jemma turned off the shower, reached for the soap and began to scrub herself vigorously. Try as she might to rid herself of the memory, she couldn't. The fire hadn't gone out, the longing, the mystery, the magic of having someone's touch call up the fiercest, most overwhelming desire she had ever felt. She turned on the shower again, once again welcoming the needle spray. The soap washed down her body and away. She watched it sluice toward the drain. Her body was soft, pliant, shining. She turned the shower off and drew her hands along her arms. His touch. What was it? Was it because she had waited so long?

A fire in her loins banked all her life. What a miracle that such a splendid man had awakened something she hadn't even known was missing. She stepped out of the shower and dried herself with a thick, fluffy towel. She rummaged in her clothes closet, deciding on a white silk blouse and black linen pants. The day would cool off by the time she reached Victor's farm high above the river. Sandals for walking on grass. She dried her hair, dressed and put on eye makeup and lipstick, studying herself in the mirror. She looked no different. No one would ever suspect Jemma Whiting had found a secret core of herself and that she ached for Hunt Gardner and his touch with the most inconceivable longing.

Only Hunt knew, and she had sent him away, telling him with a gesture that he couldn't interfere in her life. She was tied up with her son and ultimately with her son's father. He knew, he understood, and he was staying away. For a moment she remained very still, wishing he had misunderstood her or pretended he had. The thought of not seeing him again filled her with the deepest sadness.

She reached for her mother's cameo brooch and pinned it to her collar. Then a pair of small pearl earrings and a cooling spray of cologne. Something else. What was it? The locket, of course. It lay on her dressing table, curled inside its chain. *Forever*. She put it on, touched it, then grabbed her bag and a shawl and went quickly down the stairs into the street.

It was still hot, the air thick and heavy. She scarcely glanced at the antique car at the curb as she locked her door. As she fumbled with her key, the word was carelessly thrown at her.

"Taxi?"

Hunt, she had no doubt of it. A feeling of satisfaction flowed through her, that she could easily define as simple happiness. No, not allowed. She didn't want, she didn't need, she mustn't even allow herself momentary happiness followed by long years of regret. It took her seconds to collect herself, then Jemma turned.

Hunt was standing in front of an old thirties roadster with the top down. "Thanks, but I have a car," she said unsteadily. She went over to him, her hand extended. "Out of Victor's collection, if I'm not mistaken."

He grasped her hand and held it. "He said to take any car, and I have. Come on, get in. I saw that Gone Fishin' sign and almost gave up on you."

"I *am* going fishing. Sorry, Hunt."

"Get in. Where's Seth? He's invited, too."

"He's with his father."

"How is he?"

"Thanks to you, splendid except for a lump on his forehead. Invited where?"

"For a drive, then on to Bosworth Stud for a charity cookout."

"I'm headed for Merriman. This old jalopy would never make it. Anyway, it isn't air-conditioned."

"Just the way I like it, not air-conditioned. Get in. In a hurry?"

"No, I suppose not."

"Then I'm taking you to Merriman in this jalopy at a whopping twenty-five miles an hour. Without air-conditioning."

She shook her head no. It had to stay hidden, that demon. Less than three weeks and he'd be gone, out of her life, taking his power with him.

"Let's go."

"You're a pretty persuasive fellow."

"When the stakes are worth having, I'm the best."

Jemma laughed and gave in. "Believe it or not, I could win prizes for my usual powers of resistance, but I always wanted to ride in an antique automobile."

When she was seated beside him, Hunt didn't start the car right away. Instead he put his hand on hers for the briefest time. "Jemma, about what happened on Saturday. It's all right," he said quietly. "Don't give it a thought. I won't. I haven't."

They regarded each other quietly. He was referring to their shared kiss, to her reaction. Then the thought struck Jemma suddenly, and she realized it was an idea she had skirted around but had scarcely dared face: was she his target for the month, his little amusement, his way of passing the time? Her tone when she answered him was measured. "No, I don't suppose you have given it a thought."

They continued to gaze at each other. "Jemma," Hunt began, then shook his head. "Let's go." He applied himself to the stick shift. "What I like about these roadsters is their roominess. Great for sparkin' in."

"You just mind the road." She relaxed. She wanted no dark thoughts, no imaginings, no taking herself or Hunt Gardner seriously. The parameters of what they could mean to each other were clearly set.

"Merriman. Shall we take the scenic route?"

"I'd like to get there before dark. We can follow the river on the way back. Better take the highway."

Jemma was grateful for the summer heat, for the open car and noise of the motor, which prevented sustained conversation. She kept herself close to the door on her side, with a wide space between them. The highway to Merriman was heavy with traffic at that time of day, and the car with its old rumble seat received its share of admiration as it made its leisurely way into Merriman. More than one occupant of an air-conditioned car smiled and waved in passing.

Her business did not take her into the county seat often. She usually enjoyed her trips to Merriman, although busy Harbor Street had not had the same prettily self-conscious Victorian make-over as Main Street in Ramsey Falls. Once in Merriman, she directed Hunt to Harbor Street, and when they found the print shop, asked him to pull up. "I'll only be a minute, if you don't mind."

The street was lined with cars. "I'll have to double-park," Hunt said.

"Just need a look-see into the printing shop."

"Checking the competition?"

"You might say."

She went quickly over to the shop, her eyes greedily taking in everything about the place, from the large slightly garish sign overhead to the dusty snake plant in the window.

Xeller Printing. The name sat in black letters on gold above the shop. Jemma automatically substituted the sign with her own Whiting Printing. The snake plant could stay, with a good washing down and a little love. She peered indoors. The interior was harshly lit from above with fluorescent lighting. There were cartons and piles of paper everywhere and several presses in operation. There were three people working at the presses and duplicating machine, as well as a fourth seated at the back using a computer.

She wondered whether they were part- or full-time employees. The idea of paying so many salaries was daunting. However, the traffic in and out of the shop was impressive. There were a couple of customers waiting at the counter, and two more came in while she watched. The woman at the computer answered the telephone, once, twice, yet a third time. There was a general air of activity even at that late hour and on that hot day.

If Xeller Printing had good cash flow and a healthy accounts receivable with no heavy debt, the owner would be asking a fortune for the place. Anything less, and she'd have to use a magnifying glass to search for worm holes. No, impossible. She was the corner candy store offering to buy Macy's. She went back to the car.

"What was that all about?" Hunt asked.

"Not worth going into."

"That's what I like, a snippy self-starter who needs no advice from any man. Or woman."

"You wanted to come along, Professor."

"So I did, fool that I am. Where now? Any more mysterious Merriman errands?"

"No, and anyway it's too hot to think. I was going to visit a couple of my customers, but it's okay, I'll take care of it another day."

"Can I buy you an ice-cream soda, lady?"

She brightened. "Come to think of it, a glass of iced coffee would go down very well. I know an air-conditioned café about two blocks down."

"You're on."

As she stepped into the car, Jemma said, "Afterward we can go back along the river. To show how grateful I can be, we'll take a detour to the genuine Ramsey Falls, the high point of any trip to these parts. It's on the way to Victor's farm."

"Ramsey Falls. That's where it all began," Hunt said, "three hundred years ago."

"Oh," Jemma groaned. "Three hundred years. I almost forgot." But her last words were lost in the motor's roar, and she tucked them away again. It didn't bear thinking about.

The café was agreeably dark, deliciously cool and smelled of chocolate. Jemma changed her mind about the coffee and ordered a chocolate sundae with all the works laid on. Hunt settled for an espresso, regarding her unexpected gluttony with an indulgent smile.

"Right now you look as if you've just met Santa Claus," he said when she dug in. "Chocolate in all the right, kissable spots, like dabbed in the corner of your lips."

"Don't even try. Have some, you coward. Chocolate is good for you." She picked up a spoonful, including the cherry and whipped cream and offered it to him. "Go ahead, don't be shy."

He laughed, and carefully licked the ice cream from the spoon. "Mentioning things that are good for me brings back memories of an uneaten Western omelet. Consume it all yourself?"

Jemma at once avoided his eyes, knowing she had asked for it, that the subject of their kiss was there between them and that she had, with a simple gesture, brought it out into the open. She dabbed at the ice cream with her spoon. "Uneaten. Still in the refrigerator. I'm a little uncertain about how to deal with a cold omelet."

"Not in the same way as with relationships."

She put the spoon down, her appetite suddenly gone. "My ex-husband was worried about Seth," she said quietly. "His call was—"

"Unfortunate?"

"Fortuitous, Hunt." She felt her heart beating strangely. "We should have stuck to eating the omelet."

He reached over and with his thumb rubbed away at the chocolate stain in the corner of her lips. "No, we should have stuck to what we were doing. There's no law that says you have to pick up the telephone on the first ring."

"My son," she began. "You knew I needed to be near the telephone."

"No," he said. "I don't know. Your son was okay, you understood that and so did I."

"But you were the one who raced for it."

"Just doing my duty."

"So you would," she remarked with a solemn expression. "That's why you're at Pack, isn't it? To educate the educators."

He ignored her remark and said, "I really don't know anything about you, Jemma, except that you have a son, an ex-husband given to calling at odd hours and a disconcertingly beautiful mouth. I want to know more but you have a way of stepping back, of covering up with a clever remark or an even cleverer change of subject." His eye went to the locket at her neck. He briefly touched it. "Old gold, smooth to the touch. Sleep with it on?"

"Only if I want to be choked to death."

"Come on," he said, pushing his chair back. "You're no more interested in that ice cream than I was in a Western omelet. Let's see those famous falls."

THEY WERE IN the Hudson Highlands where the air was faintly cooler and massive cliffs lapped at the river's edge.

"Nice bit of country you have here," Hunt said as the car made its way slowly along the tertiary road they had turned on to.

"Why don't you stay awhile and get further acquainted?" The question slipped out, and Jemma could have kicked herself.

"We talked about commitment, Jemma. I'm committed to a contract with the government of Thailand, and I'm due in Bangkok for meetings well before that in August.

"No way out."

He glanced at her with a fond smile. "No, I'm afraid no way out. I'm willing to live for the moment, however."

"I guess I asked for that remark. Come on, keep driving. I'm giving you the grand tour."

At the turnoff the tertiary road gave way to one lane, the forest dense on either side with oak, maple, tulip, quaking aspen, birch. Beneath were blueberry and blackberry bushes and the decaying stumps of fallen trees. The late sun sent brilliant shafts of light slicing through the foliage in crazy, flashing patterns. The road curved unevenly as it moved deeper and deeper into the green canopy.

"There's a bridge over Painted Creek," Jemma explained. "It's not used much anymore. Until around 1915, supplies were transported over it by horses to the other side of the falls, then the railroad built a spur about five miles upriver. Now Painted Creek and the Falls are just a paragraph or two in the guide books."

They rounded another curve and came upon the bridge, an old wooden structure that spanned a narrow gorge and a rushing stream far below. "Painted Creek is the word for it," Hunt remarked as he took in the gorge and its splay of gray, angular rocks, drape of ivy and twisted trees clinging to the sides. "Bridge looks a little shaky, though."

"It's pretty safe," Jemma said. "The town maintains the bridge and restricts it to pedestrian traffic."

"Impressive view. I can hear the falls."

"They do sing a rather pretty tune, don't they? It's the distance they fall that makes them so impressive."

Hunt pulled the car into a copse half-hidden by heavy underbrush. They stepped out to the sound of the falls and the heavy, mushroomy scent of decaying leaves. The air was still and hot; flies buzzed lazily and there was a steady purr of crickets.

"Over the bridge and through the trees to Ramsey Falls we go," Jemma cried gaily, running across the old wooden bridge ahead of Hunt, toward the sound of the falls.

Hunt came up to her. "Our friend, Mr. Ramsey, must have followed the stream below, not having a wooden bridge at his disposal at the time. That was three hundred years ago, if I'm right."

"Three hundred years, give or take a year. Incidentally, it's traditional to tell new visitors to the falls the legend of Painted Creek."

"I'm a collector of myths and legends, did you know that?"

She looked at him with surprise. "No. But then I don't know much about you, do I?"

They rounded the cliff, and through a bower of trees, caught the unchanged, primeval, roaring world of Ramsey Falls. "Come on," Jemma said, reaching for his hand and pulling him along. "Best view is from Outcrop Rock where there's an iron rail and it's deliciously misty, especially on a day like today."

The falls were a long, single thrust of water cut deep into the cliff and splashing a fine mist into the still summer air.

"The view has been painted by many an artist," Jemma said, when they came to the rock that cantilevered out over the stream far below. "It's a wonder there aren't any here today."

"A miracle," Hunt said, grabbing her by the waist and drawing her close.

"Hey, you're supposed to look and admire."

"I am."

"The falls, Hunt, the falls."

"Let 'em fall, I won't stop 'em."

"I promised you the legend." Jemma, feeling her breath catch in her throat, tried to pull away again.

This wasn't what she wanted, why she had come along with him. She was merely giving the visiting professor a tour of her corner of the land. Wasn't she?

"Of course," he said, brushing his lips against her ear. "Tell me about it."

"Not this way." She tore out of his arms and ran over to the railing. The delicate mist drew moisture along her skin, and she found herself quivering with the momentary cool.

"Jemma." He came up to her and drew an arm casually around her shoulder. "Tell me a story. The story of Painted Creek."

"You're such a phony," she said, unable to resist a smile. She put her hands out and gripped the railing, which was freshly painted and slightly damp. "Legend collector, I'll bet."

"Tell me. I'm a good listener." His words were delivered in a whisper almost lost under the crash of the falls. He drew her around once again, his eyes smiling. She pressed her hands against his chest, letting him know that he could hold her, but it stopped there, nothing else was allowed.

"An Indian maiden," she began, her mind scarcely on the story, but determined to stretch it out. Perhaps someone would come along, and she'd be rescued from Hunt Gardner and his power over her, like an Indian maid.

"Go on, you were telling me about an Indian maiden," he prompted, his face close to hers.

She could feel the warm, dulcet mood surround her and almost pull her in. He was a master, an absolute master. "An Indian maiden is discovered one starry night on Outcrop Rock," she began again in a determined voice, "discovered gazing at the falls by a young warrior called White Hawk."

Hunt drew his fingers slowly along her hair. "White Hawk. I like him already."

"Hunt, if you carry on, I'm not going to finish the story."

"But you have to, my collection of legends, remember?"

"Your collection, yes of course, we mustn't forget the collection. Where was I?"

"These two youngsters, falling in love on Outcrop Rock."

"The Indian maiden and White Hawk met every evening at the falls and gazed at them together. They were from differing tribes and her father, the chief of her tribe, wanted her to marry his bravest warrior. Oh damn, I'm not telling it right. It's supposed to be intoned, and no detail left out."

"Such as?"

"Such as how Outcrop Rock got to be this way."

"Force of nature, Jemma. What happened to the Indian maiden and her lover, White Hawk? I'm interested in romance at this moment, not geology."

"What happened was her fiancé found out she was spending her nights at Outcrop Rock with White Hawk. He spread evil rumors and claimed one night that White Hawk had stolen her away. White Hawk was captured—"

"And brought to camp and tied to a pole," Hunt continued for her. "The young maiden was handed a tomahawk and told to kill him. Instead, being a strong woman and one who'd take advice from no one, she slashed through the bonds with the tomahawk and freed White Hawk. They ran away in a hail of arrows to White Hawk's camp where his father, also a chief, and a man the United Nations could use, decided it was time to smoke a peace pipe. To say that the Indian maiden and White Hawk were married and lived happily ever after would not be putting too fine a point on the story. Case closed."

"You know the story, you knew it all along."

"Certainly. You can't be in Ramsey Falls for five minutes without having someone offer it up like the family jewels."

"Hunt," Jemma said from the circle of his arms, "Why am I here with you?"

He placed his lips gently against hers. "That's why."

A kiss, that's all it was, a soft pressing of flesh against flesh, and yet Jemma felt the rumble of the earth beneath her feet. Was it the falls or something so new it lacked a name? A shifting breeze sent a fresh spray of mist over them, the cooling bringing not reality but a dreamlike state.

She felt the softness, the tentativeness of his kiss. His arms had not tightened around her. It was a questing kiss, and yet her hands slackened against his chest. Almost involuntarily she raised them around his neck. "I believe in free will," she said against his mouth. She knew there was a pale charge waiting to be ignited but that he was wisely holding off. "I believe if I tell you this won't do, you'll back off."

He shifted against her. His arms tightened. "And I believe we're two grown-ups with a real-life situation and that I want you and that you," he paused, and gently bit her lower lip, then the tip of her ear and her neck. "And that you want me."

He kissed her lips harder to stay the response welling up in her throat, drawing her in as if the passion waiting for release could be captured between their bodies.

Jemma knew all at once that nothing mattered, there was no pretense, no make-believe. Life was not made up of long stretches of perfect time, but rather held rare moments of exquisite pleasure. Anticipation replaced caution and common sense. Every sensory receptor, every nerve ending flipped through her with wild abandon. Her body thrust forward in an action she couldn't have stopped, her mouth opening under the gentle prodding of his tongue. She curled into him, mindless, relaxing into pure sensation. Her hands tightened around his neck. She allowed her tongue to duel with his until a tremulous and unexpected sigh shook her body. The falls and the mist added to the sense of unreality. His hand tracked the length of her back, circling her waist to the delicate space under her breast.

He drew his lips from hers and gazed through dark and glittering eyes. There were tiny beads of moisture in his hair. "Come on, not here," he said. His voice was low, hoarse, almost lost in the tremendous crash of the falls.

She pulled back suddenly. "Hunt, please, don't." Her breath came in small quick spurts. She felt dazed as she had once before, afraid of a loss of control. "I'm confused. This is foolish. I should never have let it happen."

"Are you telling me you don't know what's going on between us?" His expression was dead serious, and she understood at once what he expected from the beginning. He was no amateur. He didn't play games. He expected beginnings to proceed in an orderly fashion to endings. He had chosen her, tasted her, and her own response was a foregone conclusion.

She pulled angrily away from him. "I know what's going on, Hunt, and I know what you're thinking. I'm an easy mark for you, aren't I, the divorcée who has a reputation in town for uncommon virtue. I might as well have hung out a shingle, but you manage to do your homework, don't you? You sail into town, take the lay of the land, so to speak, and decide Jemma Whiting will be only too happy to accommodate you until you sail away."

She was having a temper tantrum, trying to put the sole blame on him when she'd been equally culpable. She had let the magic of the moment carry her away. Still, she went doggedly on. Damn, she'd straighten it all out in her mind later. "It's the way you live your life, isn't it? And I suspect you've never had a failure. Until now."

Hunt shook his head slowly, letting her words wash right over him like the mist. He reached for her. "You have it all wrong."

She stepped back, clenching and unclenching her fists, cursing herself for the biggest fool alive. "Do I? But then why would you admit to the truth? I doubt if you could even recognize it as the truth. The trouble is I'm not so angry at you as myself. You're just doing what you've always done. I'm new at the game. No, don't," she said as he took another step toward her. "Let's go. I think it's time we left. Victor is expecting us."

CHAPTER EIGHT

THE LONG SILVER TWILIGHT shifted down to the mauve mist of a midsummer evening. The air was languid and fragrant with forest scents: loam, white Indian Pipes in their birth through layers of leaves, the decaying bark of fallen trees. In the distance the falls crashed, unmindful of day or night or shifts in human temperament.

There was something comical about the roadster parked under the canopy of trees. Hunt knew Jemma saw it, too. She stood several feet from the car, wavering. He had let her run ahead, let her cool off. She had it all wrong. And the heat was still in his loins. He could feel the pressure of her body against his, the desire for surrender that set the fire racing through him. He wondered for a brief, insane instant how she'd react if he took her in his arms again.

He came up behind her. At the sound of his footstep, Jemma turned. Her face held a mildly pleading expression that told Hunt they were past discussion. They were obliged to sit together in the comical car and to drive to Victor's, but that was all.

He was tempted to make a light joke of it, to tell her time flies when you're having fun, but her frown stopped him. Jemma went quickly to the car. "Victor's place is ten miles upriver."

"I know where it is." He went around to the driver's side, and when he was seated behind the wheel said, "I want to know what happened back there."

"We're late."

"Answer me, Jemma."

Her hands were clasped together, her knuckles white with the effort. "I thought I made myself perfectly clear. Now I'd like to go, please."

He didn't want to be emotionally tied up with her. If he had any sense, he'd turn the key in the ignition, press down on the starter pedal, head straight for Victor's and lose Jemma Whiting in the crowd. Contrary to all sense, Hunt made no effort to engage the engine. He wanted Jemma Whiting so badly he had to grip the wheel to keep himself from reaching for her. He knew with an absolute certainty that she wanted him, too. They were two fleshly creatures who, with a touch, turned each other on. Why in hell couldn't the lady leave it at that?

"Jemma, you're pretty smart," he said at last, "but when it comes to reading my motivations, you're all wrong. You'd fail Psychology I and a lot more with that theory. I didn't ride into town on a white horse looking for the most likely prospect to rescue from ennui—hers and mine—for the month of July. Incidentally, if your theory is correct, I'm a pretty bad planner. There are only two weeks left to the month."

She turned to him briefly, then twisted away and stared out the window.

"Two weeks," he pressed. "You're the best thing in Ramsey Falls, Jemma, but if I counted on you, I've been going mighty slow about it." He reached over and with a light touch drew his fingers across her neck. "Two weeks. Don't shut me out."

Her eyes met his, a smile playing around her lips. "We're going to present a few old-fashioned pageants in the town hall the last week in July. I believe they've been casting about for the part of snake-oil salesman. You wouldn't want to try out for it, would you? You'd be an absolute natural."

He laughed and took his hand away. At that moment he understood she was right. He had come into town with his usual swagger. He had lost his blonde for the month of July, but there were attractive, willing women everywhere. Jemma Whiting, he had decided, was easily the best thing in Ramsey Falls. He had wanted her from the first and dammit, he wanted her now. Physical wanting, finishing what they had begun. But the stakes had changed and he had to back away. She was no ordinary woman and the notion frightened the hell out of him.

"Let's go," he said and was surprised at her sudden exhalation of breath.

THE VAST BOSWORTH ESTATE came up on the right, its borders and interior paddocks defined by pure white wooden fencing. The colors of Bosworth Stud, navy and white, were visible on the barns and stables, white for the structure, navy for trim. Hunt turned off the secondary road to a two-lane expanse of macadam between acres of newly mowed emerald grass and massive oaks that led to the main house.

The parking area in front of the main stable was almost full. The stable was lit, both inside and out with wide bays open at either end. Some of Victor's guests wandered through, admiring his most valuable thoroughbreds. Hunt wedged the Ford between a stretch limousine and a silver Mercedes, but for once he could think of no clever remark to make.

"Victor wanted me to show up," he said as Jemma reached for the door handle, "although he knows I have little interest in the tricentennial goings-on." He stepped out of the car, but Jemma was already on her way to the back of the main house when he finished locking up. Hunt gazed after her. She made a slender graceful figure in the black pants and white blouse. Perfect poise, perfect self-possession. Dangerous stuff. He wasn't used to this new feeling of dead seriousness, of a loss of control. He started after her, then stopped. No, not a clever idea, not a clever idea at all.

"Hunt, I wondered whether you'd show up." The provost of Pack College came toward him, hand extended. "This will make the hundredth fund-raiser I've attended since we decided on the tricentennial bash. Enjoying yourself?"

"I like Ramsey Falls and everybody in it." Hunt saw past the provost's shoulder to a striped tent on the back lawn. Victor Bosworth was greeting Jemma with a bear hug and a kiss on her cheek. Then, arm in arm, they went smilingly into the tent.

"Well, we have good and bad like every place else," the provost was saying, "but in the main, it's as fine a place as there is."

The words were intoned affably in his ear but failed to make sense to Hunt, who mumbled that he needed a drink and left abruptly, to the man's evident surprise.

Celie Decatur found Hunt, however, before he could step into the tent, offering her cheek to be kissed and dragging him off. "You're a hard man to find," she said. "I was afraid you wouldn't show. I was talking to a friend of mine about you. He's a New York publisher and when I suggested it, he said he wouldn't mind seeing a draft. Said he's partial to travel books and particularly books about the Far East.''

"A draft?" Hunt looked at her stupidly. He still needed a drink, and drinks were being served in the tent. In the tent was where Jemma was, where Victor was, where it was danger to go, a jungle, as the deepest parts of Thailand never were.

"Darling, a *book*. About what you *do*. About the Far East. It's so necessary to your career.''

"Nothing's necessary to my career, Celie. I've published a book or two in my lifetime, enough to bore scores of college students now and forever. What I need at the moment is not to meet a publisher, but to order up a very strong drink or maybe two very strong drinks.'' He grabbed her hand and headed back toward the tent.

"Really, Hunt, you act as if you've had a couple too many already.''

He released her hand once they were inside the crowded, noisy tent, which was festooned with balloons and crepe paper ribbons. "What you see here, Celie, is a man who has a terrible thirst.'' A quick glance told him that Jemma was no longer there and for that he was thankful. He wanted to know where she was and what she was doing, and yet he had to stay away, far away. "Can I get you something?" he asked Celie politely.

"You're an angel. Vodka and cranberry juice.''

"Right.'' He came back in a moment with a Scotch neat for himself and the exotic concoction for Celie.

"Ah, there's my publishing friend,'' Celie said, raising her hand and waving.

With the comfort of the belt of Scotch warming his insides, Hunt followed along. Two weeks. In no time flat, it would all be history.

"JEMMA, I'VE ASKED YOU the same question three times, and all I get is a whimsical smile. Is that a yes or a no whimsical smile?" Victor and Jemma stood at the pool, drinks in hand. Guests who had thought to bring along bathing suits were disporting themselves in the water. Beyond the pool, near a carefully maintained rose garden, a band had been set up and old Cole Porter tunes, like a scent of flowers, drifted on the air.

It was that moment of dusk when the air becomes a wash of indigo, and the figures on the lawn, women in long gowns and men in summer suits, seemed to drift as if on light puffs of wind.

"Jemma, wake up." Victor prodded her gently.

"Oh, Victor, I'm sorry, what were you saying? I'm afraid I was lost a little in how pretty everything looks." She turned a bright, attentive smile on him. The Bosworth Estate was beautiful, and she realized with unexpected clarity that if she wanted it, Victor would hand it to her. Only she didn't. She wanted her life to go on as always, just Jemma Whiting and Seth and crowded days that stopped her from thinking about the future.

Victor took her hand between his. "Jemma," he said, "I don't think I've seen you look happier, nor more glowing."

"More glowing?" Her laugh was artificial. She gently took her hand away and touched her cheek. No, it couldn't be. She didn't want the kiss or the feel of Hunt's body imprinted on hers for all the world to see.

"Really, Victor, what are you drinking? Whatever it is, it's making you wax poetic."

"Nothing's in my drink," Victor said. "I only speak the truth."

"Thank you for your lovely compliment." She made a light bow, then hastily changed the subject. "Incidentally, I was very obedient. I took a run into Merriman for a quick look at Xeller Printing—from the outside, like a little girl staring through a toy shop window."

"Ah." Victor gave her a satisfied smile. "Were you impressed?"

"The snake plant is dusty."

"Come again?"

"Don't mind me, Victor." She was being silly, a little feverish and afraid the glow, the anger, the mixed emotions she felt, were visible one after the other like close-up pictures on a movie screen. She needed a moment alone, needed to pat her face with cold water, needed to calm down and take stock of what was happening to her.

Victor made a remark, which she missed. Someone jumped into the pool, screaming with delight. Someone else hooted with laughter. The band switched from Cole Porter to the Beatles.

Victor repeated his question patiently. "Niko's little nose must be up, smelling the barbecue." He waved his hand toward the striped tent. Off to the side spareribs were being turned on barbecue spits, smoke wafting into the air. "Isn't it about time you met your new pet?"

"Oh, of course, you're right, Niko. Where is he? You've been a darling to keep him all this time." She impulsively placed a light kiss on Victor's cheek. He put his arm briefly about her, his face flushed with pleasure.

"I'll send someone for him, Jemma. Have you eaten? Are you hungry? You sit down here," he told her, motioning to a lounge chair, "and I'll be right back."

She obeyed him, relaxing in the lounge chair, holding her drink in her hand, her eyes closed. The music was soothing and familiar, and she allowed her mind to wander back to the falls, to the feel of Hunt's body, to that exquisite moment when the whole world came alive for her.

"Come on, let's go." His words had been a terse command, his meaning absolutely clear. *Let's finish this thing in some comfortable place, girlie, just the way I want it.*

She had walked from Hunt just like that, letting him know she wasn't flattered being the best thing in Ramsey Falls. She was tired, exhausted, as if she had run a marathon or climbed the Himalayas.

"Hey, no time to fall asleep. I swear, Jemma, you're turning into a vegetable."

She opened her eyes. It was Sarah Crewes, carrying a plate of spareribs. "Have one, Jemma. They're great."

"No thanks."

"Give Celie credit for knowing how to turn on a great barbecue."

Jemma's eyes widened with surprise. "Celie? Responsible for all this?"

"Thank goodness. I was afraid Cousin Victor was going to rope me in. What he needs is a wife. Do you suppose Celie has set her cap for him?"

"I hope so," Jemma said.

Sarah plopped herself down on the lounge chair. "If you want my opinion, Ms Whiting, Victor's sweet on you."

"Victor's too set in his ways, Sarah. He has plenty of people to help him get through the day, and he's lived without a wife all these years. He's a bachelor born and bred. Don't go looking for trouble where there isn't any."

"And speaking of trouble," Sarah said, "what have you decided about the tri-you-know-what?"

"I've decided to throw the ball back in your lap and pretend you never said a word to me about papers of incorporation and the fact that our little town of Ramsey Falls is not three hundred years old but a young two hundred and ninety-nine."

"Whoops," said Sarah, nudging Jemma and shaking her head.

"I heard what Jemma said." It was Victor, bearing down on them carrying a squirming tricolored ball of fur with black droopy ears and a drooling mouth.

"Oh, he's darling," Jemma said reaching for the dog, which began at once to nip at her fingers and then to lick frantically at her with his tiny pink tongue, yelping all the while. "Hey, Niko, you're a real live wire," Jemma said. She snuggled her face into his warm, sweet fur.

"He's adorable," Sarah said. "What make and model number?" The puppy grabbed the sparerib out of her hand and she had a small tug of war to retrieve it. "Hey, that's mine."

"Australian shepherd," Victor said. "What papers of incorporation and what did you mean by Ramsey Falls being two hundred and ninety-nine years old?" He summoned one of his servants and asked him to take the puppy back into the house. "Better give him some water," he advised. "I hope he didn't chew any of the bone."

"No, it's intact," Sarah said. "But I think I'll go along with the pup and make sure."

"Stay here, Sarah," Victor commanded. "I don't like that guilty expression you're wearing."

"Guilty?" Sarah laughed but her cheeks had grown red. "I live in Manhattan, remember? What have I to do with the tricentennial?"

Jemma shook her head. "Sarah, you're digging yourself in deeper and deeper."

"Digging is right," Victor said. "Spill it, Sarah. What papers of incorporation? It's the first I've heard of any. I thought the originals were lost a long time ago."

"Tell him," Jemma said.

"The trouble with you, Cousin Victor, is that you think too quickly and too accurately. The best thing you can do is circulate among your guests and forget what you heard."

"Come along, young lady." Victor reached for her hand and pulled her to her feet. "You too, Jemma. I want a nice, private talk with you both." He led them to a gazebo at the back of the formal garden, a delicate, Edwardian affair with white iron furniture. The gazebo was at a remove from the center of the party, and in the lingering muted light the distant figures on the lawn seemed as posed as in a pointillist painting.

Victor, unmindful of the beauty of the view, faced Jemma and Sarah. "You two look as guilty as a couple of kids with their hands in the cookie jar."

"Stale cookies," Jemma threw in and forced down a sudden desire to laugh.

Sarah leaned back against the white railing and crossed her arms. "Then hold on to your cookie jar, cousin. I'm going to toss what I have at you, every last crumb, and then I'm heading for the bright lights of Broadway and you won't see me again until some time after Labor Day."

"I don't know," Victor said, eyeing her ruefully. "I always said you were too clever by half. What about the tricentennial?"

"Ramsey Falls is short a year, that's all."

Victor sat down on an iron bench. "Go ahead."

Jemma turned away, grasping the wooden railing with both hands, and gazing past the elegant garden to the crowd of guests in the distance. Would they laugh or cry or hide their heads in embarrassment when they learned about the mistake in time. At what moment in Ramsey Falls' history had the count gone wrong? She began to laugh again, silently, her shoulders shaking as Sarah recounted her discovery.

But Jemma ceased listening when she espied Hunt on the lawn with Celie, the laughter dying in her throat. His hand was wrapped around a glass. He seemed to be listening intently while Celie gestured and talked, their heads close together. Some guests came over to them, and for a while the group numbered half a dozen. Then Hunt broke away, walking rapidly around the side of the house. Jemma imagined he was leaving and had to repress a desire to run after him, to be with him no matter what the consequences.

"Sarah, you seem to think it funny." It was Victor. Jemma, brought back to reality, realized that Sarah, too, was trying to repress her laughter.

Celie left her friends abruptly, and as though she had known all along exactly where Victor was, began to thread her way through the rose garden toward the gazebo.

"You'd better think it's funny," Sarah said. "There's no other way to handle it. Anyway, the whole business is in your hands now," Sarah concluded, then added, "Victor, if you'll excuse me, I think I'll go get another plate of those ribs."

"Who else have you told besides Jemma and me?" Victor asked.

"Not a soul."

"Here's Celie," Jemma said with a warning in her voice as Celie came lightly up the steps into the gazebo.

"Powwow?" Celie asked. "May I join?"

Jemma exchanged a glance with Victor and Sarah. Victor, too, who had at last caught the mirth of the moment, smiled and said, "Celie, sit down, I think there's something you ought to know."

CELIE'S REASONED LITANY made sense. The walk-a-thon, the river-front festival, the art shows, the photography shows, the art exhibits, the personal appearances of local celebrities, the tableaux at the town hall, the mock battle staged by the Sons of the American Revolution, the tour of old houses, the tricentennial essay contest, the plays and poetry readings, the composition by the area's best known composer, the races, the parades and huge, concluding gala; the machinery for the tricentennial celebration had been in motion for more than a year. It was a juggernaut rolling downhill gathering speed.

"We'll cash in on the mistake," Celie said, "bring in the media and have a good laugh. When it's all over, we'll pat ourselves on the back for nearly three hundred years of continuity, and that will be that.''

The little party in the gazebo broke up, with Celie promising to talk to the mayor and suggesting a town meeting.

Celie tucked a friendly arm through Jemma's as though they were conspirators and directed her back toward the tent as Sarah and Victor followed behind. ''We're going to do a sensational little story on Sarah's discovery and follow it up with some detective work. Maybe we can pin the mistake on an actual moment in history.''

''Wonderful idea,'' Jemma said.

''And how do you intend to handle the story?'' Celie asked.

''I run a penny saver, not a newspaper, Celie.''

''Which, incidentally, brings up the subject of the Merriman penny saver. I heard it's for sale,'' Celie went on with an air of disapproval in her voice. ''The owner's retiring to Florida. I always felt he wasn't doing everything he could with it.''

As they neared the tent, Jemma turned to Celie. The last thing she wanted was to discuss the penny saver with her. ''I think I could do with a little water splashed on my face,'' she said. ''Could you excuse me?''

Victor heard her remark. ''Go through the garden room, and it's in the hallway off to your left.''

''Thanks, Victor.'' She ran up the steps to the flagstone terrace and through the sliding screen doors that led into the garden room. Off in the corner, half-hidden by the greenery, a young couple stood clasped in each other's arms. They kissed, unaware of Jemma.

Damn, love everywhere, Jemma thought. It seemed to drip from the luxurious ceiling plants. She stared at the couple for a long moment, then shook herself and hurried on through.

"I've never seen you look better. You're glowing." She examined herself in the mirror of the powder room, remembering Victor's compliment, and wondered where the glow was. Her makeup had worn away and her hair was ready for a good brushing. She turned on the cold-water tap and bent over the sink, scooping up water and rinsing her face. Then Jemma opened her bag and reached for her makeup case.

When she stepped back into the hall, hair combed and fresh makeup on, Jemma realized she didn't feel one whit better. Her nerve endings were raw, and she knew exactly where the problem lay and had no idea how to solve it.

Entering the garden room, her eye automatically slid to the corner where she had seen the young couple embracing. They were gone, and thinking she was alone, she remained rooted to the spot, reluctant to join the party and wondering how she might escape.

"Well, well, well, Jemma."

She turned sharply to find her ex-husband bearing down on her. "What are you doing here?" she managed, her heart sinking at the sight of him. "Where's Seth?"

"With his stepmother."

"Really? Outside?" She moved quickly past him to the sliding screens and gazed out. Night was folding in at last. The gardens were dramatically lit, and she was scanning the grounds for her son when Walt came up behind her. He held a half-consumed drink in his hand.

"He's home, with Priscilla. She chose to stay with him tonight rather than get a baby-sitter."

"Oh great, you left your son to come here," Jemma said. "You know Seth wanted to be with you this weekend. He expects you to make a fuss over him." She had an unpleasant vision of Priscilla with her son, holding him, putting him to bed, kissing him goodnight. What right did Walt have to leave the boy with her?

"My wife is extremely fond of Seth. She loves him." His tone was his familiar, irritating one. Jemma, with a cursory glance, took in his double-breasted suit, silk shirt and gold cuff links, and his carefully coiffed hair that looked as if it never ruffled in a breeze. How could she ever have imagined herself to be in love with him? And what right did Priscilla have to love her son?

"Priscilla also knows what constitutes good professional behavior," Walt went on, deliberately spacing his words. "Victor Bosworth is a very important man in the county. There wasn't any valid reason not to come. Seth isn't an infant. Priscilla loves the boy and he returns her affection."

Does he? Jemma thought. Funny, it was the first she'd heard of it. In the rare cases when Seth mentioned his stepmother, he referred to her as *she*. *She* said this or *she* did that. On one or two occasions Jemma had half-heartedly suggested to her son that he call Priscilla by her name, but then gave up when he stubbornly resisted the idea.

"Seth's fine and safe," Walt was telling her. "And besides, I thought it would be nice to see you out of context, so to speak."

"What?" She looked sharply at him. "You knew I'd be here? Now why in the world would my being here, out of context as you so cleverly put it, interest you?"

"Come on, Jemma," he said, "we're still connected through Seth. Everything you do is my business."

"You never stop, do you?" She should simply turn around and leave, but something, she wasn't even certain what, forced her to stay and face him down. There was a moment of silence while he regarded her. From outside a waltz started up. Some of Victor's guests had begun to dance on the terrace. The garden room was lit by glass-shaded lamps that cast the plants into a soft chiaroscuro.

Walt finished his drink in a gulp, then put the glass down. "Come on, Jemma, let's have a good old-fashioned talk." Walt motioned her to a chair, but when she shook her head in refusal, he shrugged. "Have it your way."

Still, she didn't do what common sense said she must, leave quickly without looking back.

Walt pulled up a white wicker chair and sat down in it, locking his hands behind his head and leaning back. He let his eyes run down her body. "In a hurry to get back to your friend, I suppose."

"That's right. I told Sarah I'd be right back."

"I was talking about Victor Bosworth." He smiled and Jemma wondered how she could remove the smile from his face without going near him.

"Get to the point, Walt."

"Hey Jemma, loosen up. We're not on opposite sides."

"We only share one thing, our son's welfare." She gasped at her stupid mistake. It was the wrong remark. He had only to bring up Seth's tumble from the fire engine, but he surprised her by not mentioning it at all.

"One hundred fifty dollars for the pleasure of roaming Bosworth Stud, three hundred considering I'd bought a ticket for Priscilla, too. All in a good cause, Jemma, only I wonder how Whiting Printing managed to ante it up for its president and general factotum."

"I'm Victor's guest," she shot back. She knew at once he had baited her, and she had taken it like a little fool.

His smile never reached above his lips. "Nice work. You're coming up in the world. Does Victor know about your midnight escapades with what's-his-name, that itinerant professor?"

The telephone call at midnight, Hunt answering it. She wouldn't even dignify his comment with an answer. She went over to the screen door and reached for the handle.

Walt came up behind her and put his hand out to stop her. "You're moving up in the world, Jemma, thanks to your friendship with Victor Bosworth. I'm impressed."

"Walt, get out of my way."

"He must be getting something in return."

"He is. My never-ending gratitude." She forced herself to remain calm.

"Never-ending gratitude. I'm doubly impressed."

Anger and heat boiled through her body. She had to wait until the sensation subsided before she could focus on him again. "You really believe you can control every facet of my life, don't you?"

"I'm interested in one thing only, our son," he began, but she didn't let him finish.

"Next time you have something to say to me, Walt, write me a letter. You're absolutely right there. I don't want contact with you about anything, except our son."

"Just one more thing, Jemma." He let his smile grow slowly. "You're a good-looking woman. You could do a little more with yourself, but still, not bad. I'm just surprised at your very active love life. I'm pretty impressed."

"You know nothing about me, about my life, about my hopes, my fears, my dreams, my anything. And now, if you'll excuse me." She reached past him for the door, but he stayed her with his hand.

"There isn't any reason for us to be enemies. Working together might actually prove beneficial." He lowered his voice, and his hand tightened on her arm. "We were always good together, Jemma. No reason why we can't be again. No one ever has to know."

"Walt," she said quietly. "Let go of me."

He released her, but bent over her, his voice low. She could smell the liquor on his breath. "You fool around and you'll be sorry. We have a little agreement written and signed that says you stay clean and pure."

"I know what it says, and don't threaten me."

He ignored her remark. "My son has to be brought up in a house with glass windows. Get out of line, and you'll discover a side of me you don't even know exists."

She pushed past him and opened the screen door. Then, turning to him, Jemma threw the words out. "Aren't we lucky, then, that Seth was so young and innocent and protected when you had your adulterous affair with the very loving Priscilla." She stepped onto the terrace, fighting an urge to run. She walked quickly down the length of the screened-in garden room toward the dancers on the terrace. Suddenly a hand was put around her arm, but when she turned furiously, she discovered not her ex-husband but Hunt Gardner.

He said in a quiet voice, "May I have this dance?"

CHAPTER NINE

JEMMA FELT HUNT fold her in his arms as if he was trying to take away the weariness that came over her in great waves. She let him lead her around the crowded dance floor, leaning into him, allowing everything to fall away, the anger, the unexpected fear, even the weariness.

"He's gone," Hunt said quietly. "Down the terrace steps and presumably to his car."

She looked at him, surprised. "How did you know?"

"I saw you heading for the garden room. I took up a seat outside, waiting for you to reappear, and I'm afraid I heard the entire confrontation with your ex-husband."

"Oh, Hunt, how could you? Why didn't you just walk away?"

"I hate to hear my name used in vain."

"Oh damn." She pulled away from him, expelling an exasperated sigh. She wasn't so angry as exposed. "You heard your name and then calmly kept right on listening. Was it because our conversation was so fascinating or because it merely confirmed what you've been saying all along?"

"Jemma, what have I been saying all along?"

She went quickly down the terrace steps to the garden below, throwing the words back at him as he came after her. "That both parties in a broken marriage are wrong. I assume I'll make chapter one in your case-book. Here you see Example A, the living, breathing debris of a once-happy union. Do I fit your theory? Should I have tried harder? Did I somehow overstep the bounds of good wifery? Should I have been more subservient? Prettier, smarter, sexier? I'm sure you've heard the local gossip. Walt walked out on me into the arms of a . . . more suitable woman."

Hunt came up to her, offering her a wry smile. "He's a horse's ass."

With that remark, some of the anger went out of her. "Believe it or not, he used to be a person. And he's a good father."

"You won't be insulted if I don't quite believe it."

"He'll be an important judge one day, or a politi-cian. There's no end to his ambition."

"Then the good citizens of this state ought to start watching its collective rear end."

"He was a rather nice, perfectly ordinary guy when I married him," she went on, slowly measuring her words. "He began to change once he landed a job with a prestigious Merriman law firm. I was busy with Seth, hearth and home. I certainly wasn't looking behind me to see who was catching up."

"Jemma, I'm not as narrow as you think. People grow, change, move, and if there was no chemistry to begin with, a marriage can break down with very little provocation." He looked deeply into her eyes. "Was there chemistry between you and Walt?"

Jemma returned his gaze thoughtfully. The discus-sion had nothing to do with her ex-husband. It only had to do with what had happened back at the falls, some unprecedented chemistry.

"Come on, not here." Those had been Hunt's words. They had cut through her, made her angry, furious, she never wanted to see him again. Chemistry. Hunt was waiting for an answer. She moved away from him, feeling her face grow disconcertingly warm. "It's not a subject for discussion."

"Pity." When a slight frown darkened her expression he added, "I'll take you home. Oh, and say goodbye to you in full view of Main Street."

She let a moment go by before answering, then shook her head, giving in. "I have every doubt about your intentions, but I think I can handle them. Let me say good-night to Victor and Sarah."

"I'll wait for you here."

She was a few steps away when he called her name. She turned. "Yes."

"One more thing, about Victor."

She waited curiously. "What about him?"

"I asked you this question once before. Is there anything between you?"

"You haven't heard a word I've said," she responded in a low, furious voice. "You listen in on a private conversation, then calmly use what you heard against me. Walt hints that there's something between Victor and me, and you take up on it."

She was about to turn away from him, when he caught her wrist. "Jemma, hold it. You spin on your heels so much it's a wonder you aren't dizzy with the effort."

"And as a commentator on the morés of common folk, you fail every reasonable test."

He laughed. "Perhaps I do. Right now I know only one thing. I want out of here, and I want you with me."

"No."

"No? I'm amazed at the passion you've put into one word."

"Oh, I'm tired, so tired," she said, suddenly going limp. The idea of seeing anyone else at that moment or of trying to cadge a ride home was irksome. She was especially reluctant to see Victor, who was so innocent and yet, it seemed, so much on everyone's mind. She'd apologize to him in the morning, claim a headache, anything. "Come on, cabbie," she said. "I'll take the hitch but only on sufferance." She led the way to the car, knowing that if she had any sense at all, she'd begin to consider Victor Bosworth a proper and suitable husband. Seth would be safe and her future gloriously assured.

As she stepped into the old Ford, she thought with a smile that even Victor's collection of antique automobiles would be hers. She cast a covert glance at Hunt as he backed the car out of its parking space. He had no right listening in on her conversation with Walt, and even less in believing what Walt had to say. There was only one thing she was certain Victor could never give her. She'd had a taste of it back there at the falls and it was a gift without price.

She looked away and out into the dark as the car lumbered onto the highway. As earlier that day, she was thankful for the combined noise of engine and wind. There was nothing she wanted to say to Hunt, either. He had come into her life; he had disturbed the very air about her, and she couldn't wait for him to be gone, for him to be a fading memory.

When the back tire blew halfway into Ramsey Falls, it was with a loud firecracker pop, and Jemma thought it was somehow inevitable.

"What the hell was that?" Hunt said. The car went slowly out of control, veering with a series of slapping tharrumps into the left lane. Hunt managed to bring it under control and onto the right shoulder.

"Back tire," Jemma said. The stretch of road in both directions appeared black with no vehicle approaching. "I hope there's a spare."

"There's a spare. Victor keeps these things in top shape, ready to roll."

"And tires ready to blow."

"Talk to him." Hunt reached past Jemma to the glove compartment. "Must be a flashlight in here somewhere."

"Two miles at least to the nearest house. This is all state parkland," Jemma pointed out.

"Try not to rub it in. I'll have the tire changed in a jiffy." He paused, then said, "No flashlight."

"Probably in the trunk."

"Jemma, the rumble seat is the trunk. I doubt Victor keeps a flashlight in a rumble seat."

"Try, Hunt."

"It's black out there. I'll need a flashlight to find the flashlight."

"Fortunately us primitive country folk carry such things around at all times." She rummaged in her bag and came up with a small, flat flashlight that produced a narrow, useful beam.

"Come on, pal," he said, getting out of the car, "I'll need your help."

When she joined him, the rumble seat was pulled up and Hunt was searching noisily in it for the flashlight. "You know how to change a tire on these old things," Jemma said.

"I've changed tires on Jeeps, trucks and assorted rusting vehicles in back countries everywhere."

"Oh, then this certainly qualifies. You're in the right place for it, too."

"Flashlight," he announced triumphantly. "Trust Victor. This one should be sixty years old if it's a day."

"Not with sixty-year-old batteries, I hope."

"Nope." He flashed it on. "Victor's no fool. Here's a wrench, ah, and a car jack. I hate a man who plans ahead. Do you suppose he fixed the tire so it would blow at say a hundred miles, just so we could use this paraphernalia?"

"Somehow I doubt he's that thoughtless."

Hunt handed her the wrench and the flashlight. "Make yourself useful. First we have to lift the spare from its metal housing. Then we apply the car jack, lift off the guilty tire, slip the spare in place, and we're back on the road."

"Sounds logical. You *are* an expert." She followed him around to the passenger side where the spare tire was set into the running board.

"Where the devil's the lock holding it together?" he asked, referring to the round metal jacket that encased the spare tire.

"Here." Jemma took the key out of his hand. The lock turned smoothly, and she removed the casing for him as well.

"Great," said Hunt. "Tire looks in perfect condition. Shine the flashlight for me, Jemma, and I'll have it off in a jiffy. Not there, *there*. Watch what I'm doing, buck private."

"Oh, aye, aye, sergeant. I'm watching all right," Jemma told him, "and a clumsier effort I've never seen. I really hate a man who panics under pressure."

"Mind your manners, young lady."

It was only when Hunt, grappling with the antique tire jack, at last managed to raise the rear left of the car, that Jemma took the matter in hand. "The wrench," she said. "You've lost a half hour trying to manipulate that jack. I'll complete the rest of the job, if you don't mind." She shone the flashlight into his face in order to have the pleasure of registering his reaction.

"Half hour, my foot," he said. "It took maybe ten minutes to figure it out."

"Twenty minutes to make it work. I finished a course in car maintenance last year when I realized I couldn't afford a new car, and I might have an emergency on some dark country lane sometime."

He handed her the key. "You don't have to convince me. You've got independence written all over your face."

"I've had to learn a lot, fast."

Ten minutes later the spare tire was in place, and Jemma secured the last of the nuts. "Done, except for the hubcap. Shine the light a little to the left, Hunt."

Instead, Hunt flashed it on her face. "You have half the axel grease on your nose and the other half on your chin. I'm not certain we'll be able to make our way into Ramsey Falls under those conditions."

"We'll manage. Shine the light on the hubcap, please."

He obliged, and when the hubcap had been tapped home, Jemma stood up and dusted her hands. "Let's go. Oh, wait, the old tire."

"I'll handle it, you just make yourself comfortable."

"Right." Jemma sat on the running board and reached for her bag, a tissue and her makeup case. She was using her flashlight and hand mirror to check for smudges, when she heard the thump and a long, low curse.

"Hunt?" She jumped up and ran around to the back. Hunt was nowhere in sight.

Then she heard a soft groan coming from below where the shoulder fell away in a grassy embankment. "Oh, no," she cried, focusing the beam of her flashlight in the direction of the sound. "Hunt?"

The silence was profound. The moon had not yet risen in a sky cast with the dim beauty of distant stars.

"Hunt? Where the devil are you?" The narrow beam of Jemma's flashlight couldn't penetrate the blackness. She peered down the embankment, gripped by a sense of dread. "Hunt?"

At last she heard it, a low groan that rose in pitch and then faded.

"Hunt?" She bent her head uncertainly. "Don't fool around. Where are you?"

"Jem?" His voice was weak and she imagined him lying broken and bleeding in the gulley below. She quickly slipped her sandals off and scrambled down the embankment. "I'm here, I'm coming, everything's going to be all right. Just keep talking, let me know where you are."

Another low groan came from her right. She went gingerly along the bottom of the embankment, calling words of encouragement until the tiny beam of her flashlight picked him out. He lay on his back, his eyes closed, his face pale. "Hunt, it's okay, I'm here. Don't move." She bent down and touched his face gently.

He opened one eye. "I think every bone in my body is broken. I need doctoring. I may bleed to death." He opened the other eye.

She reached over and tweaked his nose. He jumped and sat up.

"What'd you do that for?"

"Beast. It's my miraculous cure. Worked, didn't it?"

"I tell you I'm a broken man."

"Charlatan, imposter."

"Desperate, that's all." He grabbed her and pulled her down. "Look, you keep running from me," he said, holding her fast. "Can you blame me for resorting to a groan or two to get your attention?"

"I should've followed my first instincts and sped out of here and left you behind."

"Jemma, the tire got away from me. I started after it and went flying down the embankment. As for your instincts, pardon me if I don't believe a word you're saying. I heard your voice, and panic never sounded more beautiful."

She pushed her hands against his chest. "Let go of me," she told him evenly, "right now, or I *will* break every bone in your body."

"Not quite yet, Jemma. It took a little trickery to get you here—"

"For which I'll never forgive you."

"You don't know how hard it's been to keep my hands off you."

"Hunt, I swear—" She never finished the sentence. A moan of animal pleasure rumbled in his chest as his mouth came down on hers, hard and insistent. She didn't want to let it happen, but suddenly Jemma knew that she no longer possessed the will to stop him. He bent her back against the ground and pressed his body over hers. His tongue traced her bottom lip, bathing it with moisture and without meaning to, she reached up and wound her arms around his shoulders, dragging him closer in. When his tongue pressed home, embedding snugly in her mouth, she picked up the signal, playfully darting her tongue around his. All around her the night seemed to chime with joy. He had, with a touch, brought her to a private space that was no longer alien under that dark sky with its mysterious and watchful stars.

"Jemma." The word was a whisper, a groan, a pleading. He placed his mouth against hers and opened his lips slowly. For one long moment, they savored their heightened pulses, the realization of where they were headed. Then he whispered her name again before descending once more to her waiting mouth. He teased, explored and stroked until the possibility of surrender drifted out from somewhere deep within her, a moan that started low and told him there was no ending but one.

His hands inched up her sides until he found the soft underswelling of her breasts. His touch was sure and skillful and Jemma trembled, no longer aware of the unyielding ground below them. Her nipples grew hard and sensitive against the cool silk of her blouse. She had needed this for so long, she thought, so long.

"It would be so good, Jemma," he said softly against her mouth. "Here, now."

His words jolted her, giving her that little space she needed, even though her body was alive and it would be so easy.

"Jemma, just you and me, now."

A car came quickly down the road slowing up a bit as it passed the old Ford. She could all but hear the driver thinking. An antique car in the middle of nowhere. He might stop, come over to investigate. That slight diversion helped restore her sanity. "No, not now, not ever. I can't let this happen, Hunt."

He looked at her for a long moment. She could see him quite clearly. Then he pulled away, stood and drew her to her feet. "You're absolutely right, my lady. When it happens, it's going to be between two consenting adults, between white sheets and in a bed with good springs, and all the time in the world."

He bent and picked up the tire and flashlight.

Jemma exploded. He'd been playing her as if she were some musical instrument and he the maestro. She tore past him and began to climb the embankment toward the car. "Hunt, take me home. After that, I don't want to see you again. You're too much to handle. Trying to figure out all your angles is giving me a headache."

She heard his laugh and shook her head. He was pleased, damn him, and he didn't believe a word she had said.

He respected her silence, however, and her anger, all the way into Ramsey Falls. When they reached Main Street, he pulled into a parking spot.

"Don't bother," she said, when he opened his door. She stepped out and headed for her front door with a scant thanks and even scanter good-night. But he was there beside her, taking the key out of her hand and opening the door for her.

"Good night, Jemma," he said, handing the key back.

Their eyes held for an instant, then Jemma pocketed the key. "Goodbye, Hunt."

She had no idea how it happened, but in the shadowed hallway, he held her in his arms, his mouth to hers in a slow, engulfing kiss. The kiss lingered, deepened, and when Jemma felt the familiar flood of pure sensuality begin to ride through her, he released her. He said nothing, but continued to gaze at her, as though filling himself up with the sight of her, memorizing every part of her. They would never see each other again, she thought with surprise and anguish. Now, or two weeks from now when it was all over. He turned and without a word left, closing the door behind him with a final little slam.

JEMMA STARED at the clever front-page headline in the *Times Herald*: The Town That Couldn't Count Straight. Tri Turns into Bicentennial-Plus-99.

Sitting at her kitchen table and nursing a noon cup of coffee, Jemma was beginning to think she had Celie all wrong. Not only could the publisher of the *Times Herald* take bad news and turn it around, she did it with high good humor. Jemma eyed the telephone across the room and thought seriously of calling Celie up and congratulating her.

"Mommy." There was a plaintive quality to her son's voice. He lay flat on his stomach on the kitchen floor.

He had come back the evening before, delivered like so much baggage by Walt's chauffeur, who had carried the sleeping child up and thrust him at her. When Seth awoke in the morning, he was completely disoriented since he had no recollection of leaving his father's house.

She had taken Seth to the shop where he spent the morning underfoot, complaining and whining and coming over to lean against her, even sucking his thumb. Exasperated, she asked Adriana to watch the shop and brought her son upstairs to rest.

"Mom-my."

She looked fondly over at him. "What is it?"

He made a grinding noise, spread his hands and legs and began making believe he was swimming. "I hate brocurli."

"We're having tuna fish for lunch."

"*She* says I have to eat vegetables even if I don't like them."

"Who?" Jemma said, but she already knew.

"Pres-silly."

"Priscilla, silly. Vegetables are good for you."

"But *you* don't make me eat them."

"Sure I do. I just disguise them so you don't know you're eating them."

Seth picked up a miniature truck and began pushing it to and fro. "She made me get all dressed up in a yucky jacket and sit at the table with everybody and Daddy said I had to."

Jemma had to tread very carefully. Her son had never offered much before about his visits to the estate in Merriman and if she seemed too eager to learn of those weekends with Walt, he'd just pull back.

"Must have been something pretty special, that dinner," she said.

"*She* said that if I wanted to go to the right school I had to have manners." He looked up at his mother. "I don't want to go to a right school. I *like* my school."

Jemma felt a cold, sharp edge of anger creep along her skin. "Priscilla means when you grow up, darling, that's all." But she wasn't certain. Walt had mentioned more than once that the area held a couple of very good private schools. Jemma had scarcely let him finish each time, but it was obvious to her now that he was laying the groundwork.

"Daddy had a party when I was there, and he made me shake hands with everyone."

"Is that when you wore the jacket?"

Seth pushed his truck aside and scrambled to his feet. He came over and rested his head in his mother's lap and stuck his thumb in his mouth. "I don't like Priscilla. She smells funny."

Jemma stroked his head. Poor baby, she thought, he wasn't used to one-hundred-dollar-an-ounce perfume. "She wants you to feel at home when you're there."

"And she holds me too tight and Daddy makes me kiss her."

Jemma picked him up and cradled him in her arms. He was sweet and bright and still a baby. He was telling her something; she wasn't certain what, but it was clear that Priscilla was making moves that upset the boy. In fact, Jemma had always suspected Priscilla tolerated Seth because she had no choice in the matter. Leopards don't change their spots, so why her sudden concern over his eating and clothes habits, and why his reaction to it? Perhaps he felt disloyal to his mother, allowing this other woman to pet him. She gave a faint shake of her head. No, Seth had spent every other weekend for the past three years with Walt and Priscilla. It was something new, something unexpected, and she had no idea what it could be.

"Let's get some lunch, baby," she said, as she gently took his thumb from his mouth and set him on his feet. "Wonderful, lovely, exciting tuna fish with a side order of potato chips. How about that?"

"Yeah," he said with a bright smile that told her whatever had been bothering him was forgotten.

She had just placed some sandwich triangles on a plate when the telephone rang. "Start eating, honey," she said as she picked up the receiver.

It was Sarah Crewes. "Jemma, clue me in. Are you interested in Xeller Printing and the Merriman penny saver or not?"

"Interested, but not ready to buy."

"The owner is ready to sell. I have that on the most exacting authority. You have to act quickly."

Jemma glanced over at her son who was reaching for a sandwich. "I agree the shop has some first-rate equipment. They've always handled work for me, business cards, engraving stationery, that sort of thing. What I have in comparison looks as if it were left over from the Inquisition. Sarah, I don't know if I can risk going further into debt. It means borrowing against the shop. If I make a wrong move I could lose everything."

"Well, thought I'd tell you in my gossipy, friendly way that Celie Decatur's been making sudden, unexpected noises in that direction. If she took up the Merriman penny saver, she'd aim her guns at you, my dear."

"Oh." Jemma groaned. "I don't stand a chance against her. She could buy it with a bagful of money this afternoon. And to think I was going to call her and congratulate her for taking the tricentennial bull by the horns and running with it. And that's about the worst metaphor I ever mixed."

"Never mind the messy metaphors. You're in a better position, Jemma. Celie's bogged down with a passel of lawyers and accountants who'll compute and investigate into the next century. You have the advantage of being able to travel light and fast."

"I'll want to look at Xeller's profit-and-loss picture, too."

"Jemma, I'm related to somebody in this county who only has to raise the correct eyebrow to get answers."

"Victor."

"Spelled Victory."

"I can't ask him for special favors."

There was a short silence, then Sarah said, "There must be something in the water in your part of the county, Jemma. It makes all of you so dim-witted. In spite of everything, the penny saver is a good investment. Why am I nagging you? Because I love my Jemma as I always have, and I'd hate to see Celie any more powerful than she is already. I'm going to give Victor a ring and see what he can come up with, vis-à-vis how well Xeller Printing is really doing."

"Can I stop a train doing a hundred miles an hour?"

"Not the Sarah Crewes Special, you can't. Talk soon."

"Sarah, wait." But the line was dead. Jemma shook her head. *I love my Jemma.* She and Sarah saw little enough of each other but memories of good times in college held them fast. She turned to her son just as he pulled apart his sandwich and the contents dropped to the floor. "Good," she said, "that's right where I wanted it." He looked up and smiled and then got down on all fours and began to clean up with his napkin.

Tossed in a zillion directions, that was Jemma Whiting. She'd had her act together and then along came a hurricane and she was caught dead center. She loved Sarah, too, but didn't want anyone to make her decisions for her, not Sarah, not Victor, not Walt, not Hunt. Her mind was clouded. Try as she might, she had about as much concentration as a hen with pepper on its tail.

"That's fine, Seth," she said as her son dropped the sandwich into the garbage can.

"Can I go down and help Adriana?"

"You won't bother her? She has lots of work to do."

"I always help her," he said indignantly.

"Then, scoot. Tell her I'll be along in a few minutes."

"Mommy," he said from the door. "When can I see Tommy?" He was referring to Mrs. Lawson's grandson who was Seth's age.

"We agreed on tomorrow. She has to go somewhere with him today."

"What time?"

"First thing in the morning and all day. Won't that be nice?"

"Uh-huh." Without another word he ran down the stairs and into the print shop.

She was happy to have a few minutes to herself. Every once in a while she had to fight a sudden, hemmed-in feeling. It wasn't easy bringing Seth up alone, and although she had long ago given up the raw anger she felt toward Walt, his behavior on Monday at Victor's party aroused fresh resentment. She went over to the sink with her cup, rinsed it and poured herself another cup of coffee. She glanced out the window to the street below.

Tricentennial banners in red, white and blue were strung across Main, and every shop window including her own had been decorated with themes dating back to the seventeenth century. The window of Whiting Printing was filled with artfully arranged quill pens, scrolls, leather books and old ink bottles. The street was crowded with summer tourists. There was a festive air, although the actual parade date was a week away.

She smiled, wondering how Hunt had explained to Victor the tire blowout and its subsequent repair. The smile lingered although he hadn't called after their parting Monday night. The last kiss had been a necessary seal to what had happened at the falls and to the reckless abandon with which they had held each other later. A proper goodbye without words, without apologies, without a promise. He had come along at a time when she was fresh out of dreams and took away the blackness that had filled the nights.

Jemma could no longer fool herself. She'd been hiding behind her repressive divorce decree, using it as a shield whenever someone made a move in her direction. It allowed her to keep her emotions in cold storage, to put the blame on Walt every time a relationship threatened to turn into something else.

Oh, she and Hunt were a pair, all right; the feckless divorcée who had gone three years without letting a man close and the professor who picked out his woman where and when he wanted her.

She had let him kiss her, let an undiscovered part of herself come awake with the promise of fulfillment, but then turned him away. What was the matter with her? She should move on breaking Walt's decree. The trouble was facing him on his own turf. If only she could resurrect Clarence Darrow.

The sound of the telephone broke into her thoughts, and she reached gratefully for the receiver. Victor's warm friendly voice was on the other end.

"Cousin Sarah's been giving orders again," he said at once. "It took a discreet call to the Merriman Savings and Loan to discover in simple terms that Xeller Printing is solvent, makes its payments on time and isn't in over its ears. The Merriman penny saver was always a little underfinanced, which is why yours has the greater distribution. Together they'd cover the most populated part of the county."

"I was hoping for bad news," Jemma said, "so I could say no and that was that."

"You're not the only one interested."

"I heard about Celie."

"One or two others, from what I hear. I hadn't heard about Celie," he said with a note of surprise in his voice.

"I'll have to move fast, won't I?"

"I'm afraid so."

"I could never get all my papers together, Victor, to apply for a loan. They'll want to know things about Whiting Printing, too. I still think I ought to pass."

Victor said, "I'll ask you one question, Jemma. Give me a yes or no answer. If you could conclude the deal, would you like to go for Xeller Printing?"

She thought a moment. It took her longer to consider buying a pair of shoes or a blouse. "Yes."

"Call Ray Xeller in New York." He gave her the man's telephone number. "Go down to see him, and when you're ready for financing, call me."

She hesitated. He couldn't be offering to finance the business deal without expecting something in return.

"Jemma, I'm being selfish," he said. "I enjoy doing things for you. Let me know what's happening."

"Victor, wait." But she heard the sound of his receiver hanging up. She wondered, staring down at Xeller's telephone number, just how much trouble she was buying herself.

CHAPTER TEN

THERE WASN'T a damn thing Hunt wrote that made sense to him. He crumpled the sheet of paper and tossed it with an overhead shot into the waste basket where it joined a dozen others equally crumpled. His office was hot and clammy. The air-conditioning had conked out in the morning, and he had forgotten to report it. An old, hastily requisitioned floor fan whirled noisily in the corner recirculating the hot air. The last of his students had come and gone in the early afternoon. It was nearing four, and Hunt Gardner was hungry, bored and generally out of sorts.

He remembered a crushed candy bar he had dropped in his desk drawer. When he unwrapped the paper, the chocolate melted onto his fingers. *It's okay,* he thought, *the day has to end sometime, and if I just don't go out and play in traffic, I'm safe.* He consumed the candy greedily, licking his fingers afterward. Then he leaned back in his chair, hands locked behind his head, and gazed up at the white painted ceiling. He gave in to what he had been fighting all that week, Jemma Whiting.

Ordinarily Hunt Gardner was no daydreamer. He was a man who dealt with reality every moment of his life. He occupied a world of positives and negatives. You do this, you get this result. You do that, you get that result.

You find yourself attracted to a woman, you signal her that you're attracted. Chances are it works both ways. You kiss. You let it move on from there slow or fast, according to the circumstances; everybody's happy.

Why this strange magic concerning Jemma Whiting in this unexpectedly hot, misty corner of the civilized world? Why had their making love turned into a challenge? Even with the better part of the week gone by, he could still feel her heat, and the very remembrance sent his loins swelling.

It was her essence he wanted, her body, her legs wrapped around him, her breasts under his touch. He closed his eyes and let her float about him. Go with the fantasy, he told himself, just let it happen.

She was almost real. If he put his hand out he could touch her, this Jemma Whiting of his fantasy, this shapely creature floating in space. She was wearing something unexpectedly clinging, silken and red that outlined her breasts and their peaked tips. Her hair spun delicately about her face; with a sly dip of her head, she flicked her tongue beckoningly over her lips. She was moving slowly to unheard music, her hips swaying with the melody.

He felt his throat go dry and shifted in his chair as the familiar ache surged through his body. He knew what he would dream next if he let the fantasy go on. Yet he couldn't have stopped it, even if he wanted to.

She came closer, a slim strap slipping from her shoulder and revealing a glistening rise of flesh, pink-tipped and ripe for the taking.

He reached for her; his chair creaked, the unheard melody turned into the groan of the floor fan. He opened his eyes to reality, knowing his feelings about Jemma Whiting were moving beyond his control.

He hadn't counted on meeting a woman like her, and he didn't want one whit of it. He wanted no fantasies, no Circe drawing him on and he following like a besotted idiot.

Hell, he'd be a besotted idiot if he walked straight into her arms, her problems, her reality, a divorcée whose husband hung over her like a black cloud. A son, a business, a tight place in a small community.

No, he wanted breathing space, he always had. But the trouble was Jemma wasn't the kind of woman to love for a time and then leave with a quick kiss and a squeeze. No, and no again. His leave-taking was a little more than a week away, and he probably wouldn't even remember her name come December. All he knew for an absolute fact was that he was going to stay away from Jemma Whiting for the rest of the time he was in Ramsey Falls.

Six and a half minutes later he picked up the phone and dialed her number.

Jemma answered on the third ring. He had only to say her name when she broke in. "Hello, Hunt."

He gripped the phone, a man about to drown in his own stupidity. "I . . . I want to see you."

She hesitated for a moment, then said softly, "Do you think it's a good idea?"

"No, it's the lousiest idea I've had in a long time, but I don't seem to be operating on all my pistons. What do you say?"

Again the hesitation. He supposed she had as many options to weigh as he. Dammit, all he wanted was a date, a good old-fashioned American down-home apple-pie date with the girl of his dreams, not a meeting between two heads of state.

"It'll have to be some time next week," she said at last, her voice neutral. "I'm going to New York City for the weekend."

"The Big Apple. Pretty hot down there this time of the year." He wanted to ask more but didn't for fear of learning something he'd be sorry about.

"I heard New York in July is the place to be," she put in. "All the locals are out of town and it's given over to tourists. I'm going there on business, but I figured on a little sight-seeing while I'm about it."

"Taking Seth?"

"No, he'll be spending the weekend with Mrs. Lawson. She has a grandson visiting her who's Seth's age, and they get along famously. Perfect all around. Adriana will take care of the shop until noon, then close up. I'm free as a bird and feeling wonderful about it."

Seth with his baby-sitter, perfect all around. It took no time at all for the idea to form. "Want some company?"

"Talk about lousy ideas," Jemma said, but there was an oddly light note in her voice that didn't quite cut him off.

"Hey, what's one more?"

"One more too many. No, Hunt. I don't think so. I'm considering buying a print shop in Merriman, and I've an appointment with the owner on Saturday, noon to be exact." She gave a small laugh. "I have to keep my wits about me."

"I'll pick you up at eight."

"I'm taking the train down, Hunt. I figured it all out. It's the most efficient way."

"Jemma, eight on the button."

"I don't think—"

"That's right, don't think. Let's pretend there's a yellow brick road leading right to the land of Oz. What about hotel reservations?"

She was a long time answering him. "As a matter of fact, I already have a room booked at the Plaza."

"Nice work."

"If you must know," she stated quietly, "it's being lent to me by Victor Bosworth."

He didn't miss a beat. He was past believing Victor was the problem. The problem lay in the lady herself, and Hunt had spent his whole life seeing around problems. "I'll call in a second reservation. See you tomorrow morning." He disconnected on her very audible sucked-in breath, dialed information and asked for the number of the Plaza Hotel in Manhattan. What was needed was action, plenty of action and no thought at all of traveling a one-way road on the side of a very steep cliff scattered with signs reading No Turnaround.

"MANAGE A HOTEL ROOM?" Jemma asked first thing upon settling into Hunt's air-conditioned rented car the next morning.

"At the Plaza, dangerously near the Bosworth suite."

She leaned back, tightening the safety belt and taking in a glimpse of a tantalizingly blue sky. "On a day like today, I'm not even going to fault that remark, Hunt."

"Rules of the trip, Jemma. No fancy remarks that lead to disagreement. If we do get tangled up, though, we flip a coin to decide who wins."

"You supplying the coin, of course."

"Of course, pure Confederate. Incidentally," he added, throwing her an admiring glance, "unarguable is the way you look this morning."

"Well, thank you." She grinned, pleased, needing someone to tell her she looked good. She had been careful about getting ready for her business interview. And for Hunt, too, though she scarcely admitted it at the time. She wore a white linen dress with a small lace collar. She had tamed her thick brown hair by pulling it back and fastening it with an antique silver comb. She stretched her foot out and looked at her high-heeled shoes that pinched a bit in the toes. She hoped she'd be able to walk in them on New York's tough pavements.

"You're being very quiet," Hunt remarked when they were ten miles into their trip downstate. "Deep thoughts? Worried thoughts? Fiscal thoughts? Want to talk to old Professor Hunt about it? Results guaranteed."

Jemma shook her head. "No thoughts. I'm just winding down."

"The print shop in Merriman," he said. "The one I took you to last Monday, that the one you're considering?"

"Yes." She turned to him, twisting her fingers together in her lap. "I have to make up my mind pretty fast. There are a couple of people after it, plus Celie Decatur."

"Celie. That should put a fine imprimatur on it."

"She can also get her hands on some cash a lot easier than I. Except of course, she has a dozen advisers who could gum up the works, and I've only got me."

"To gum up the works."

"To say yes or no."

"And that's how you like it, Jemma. Getting up in the morning and asking yourself what's new and supplying the answer. Same routine repeated at night, of course, as you undress and head for your pristine, narrow little bed."

Jemma started and turned angrily to him but checked herself when he went good-naturedly on. "No woman is an island, etcetera, etcetera. Do you really want to buy the print shop or is something goading you into it?"

"I have to think of my future and my son's future. I have to take advantage of opportunities as they come along, and if I want your advice, Professor, I'll ask for it."

"Jemma," he said in a softened tone, "ask for it."

She sat silently for a while, remembering the profound joy that had come over her when she found him standing on her doorstep at precisely eight that morning. She recalled the faint warm kiss on her cheek that anyone abroad at that time would see, the starched and awkward silence that followed.

She had scarcely slept through the night for worrying about the coming meeting with Ray Xeller. The difficult decision about the shop would have been enough to keep her awake, the thought of being with Hunt exacerbated it. She was willingly breaking the cardinal rule of being with a man who can't be pinned down: be careful and stay out of his way. She gave Hunt a sidelong glance. He knew it without even turning, and a smile started that made her heart quicken.

She found herself considering things about him that she had never noticed in a man before: the way his hair curled softly at his neck, the square cut of his jaw, his hands braced on the wheel, fingers lithe and strong.

There was an easy animal grace to the way he moved. And if he touched her, if he held her in his arms a moment too long, everything would change forever.

"Jemma?"

She caught his glance and his smile and everything melted away. "Help," she offered him in a quiet, mirthful little cry.

"You don't like going it alone."

"Sometimes I hate being my own best friend. Victor's been pressuring me about purchasing Xeller Printing and so has Sarah. Neither really knows the meaning of 'Help, where's the rent money coming from?'"

He slowed the car to a crawl, took the up ramp that led to the parkway going south and eased into the right-hand lane. "What are your options?" he asked crisply.

"Sticking with what I know and hoping that the new owners of the Merriman penny saver won't expand into my territory. Putting all my eggs into my own shop against using the state-of-the-art presses and typography that Xeller Printing has. Going big-time or staying small-time."

"Important to become big-time?"

"If it means I can prove my mettle, yes."

"Can you kick in the dough?"

She shrugged. "I'm seeing Ray Xeller this morning. I'll find out what his asking price is."

"He's solvent, is he?"

"According to Victor, he is."

Victor. The word came out like an admonition and that, too, was on her mind. Victor had dropped by the evening before and had helped her prepare for the meeting with Xeller. He had made vague hints about accompanying her, but when Jemma didn't respond, he dropped the subject. She didn't tell him about Hunt and dreaded his finding out. She could offer no excuses for her behavior. One thing she *did* know: her silence had everything to do with having to live with her decision long after Hunt was gone.

She was headed willingly down dangerous pathways that led to tangled undergrowth, with no machete, no map, no way back. "Victor will make getting funding a lot easier for me," Jemma told Hunt at last.

"Well, what the hell, he certainly came through for me. The man's a saint."

"He is, and a pretty unselfish saint, too."

"I believe that's the function of sainthood, Jemma. I'd never qualify."

"Being selfish is your thing, then."

He cast her a quick glance. "I'm a long time about wanting something. I don't like excess baggage, mental or physical."

"You'd never have a problem over whether to buy or sell, would you, Hunt?"

He laughed. "On the contrary, your problem right now is my problem. If all systems are go, you'd be a fool to hesitate."

"I've been a fool once or twice in my life."

"And," he said, applying his foot to the gas and exceeding the speed limit, as if to emphasize his words, "I looked in a shop window in Ramsey Falls and discovered something I wanted."

"Not for sale, Hunt."

He laughed. "I asked for that one." He put his foot on the brake pedal and eased the car to the speed limit.

"Listen," he said, "there's a small inn about two miles off the main road. They have the best coffee and cranberry muffins in these parts. How about it? Have you had breakfast?''

"I haven't and I know the inn. How do you know it, though?"

"You'd be surprised at the kind of reading you do when you're new in town and want to discover the lay of the land, to coin a phrase."

"Lay of the land. You're good, Hunt."

He pulled onto the service road and in a couple of minutes drew into the parking lot of a white clapboard inn. "Fortunately not called Dew Droppe," he told her as they were seated in one of the small rooms off the parlor. The inn was surprisingly crowded for that time of the day.

"Bring us half a dozen muffins with an emphasis on cranberry," he told the pretty young waitress who came up to them almost immediately. "A pot of coffee and some jam, too. Anything else?" he asked Jemma.

She shook her head, and with her elbow crooked on the table, rested her chin on her hand. She experienced a kind of mindless happiness over the simple act of sitting opposite Hunt in the quiet little inn with its rose-spattered wallpaper, riot of green plants and scent of baking and fresh coffee. Funny, she thought, *forever* was no grand crescendo. It was soft, unexpected moments strung together that formed the stuff of memory.

"Small quirky smile on your face," he remarked. "Contemplating success?"

"I suppose you'd call it that."

"We'll spend the weekend celebrating."

"Wonderful. Any specific plans?"

"Every minute, except for that irksome time when you'll be out of my grasp, so to speak. I figure your meeting will take a couple of hours, which should bring you back to the hotel around two. We'll make the rounds of the city's more impressive watering holes—''

"About which, I gather, you've extensive experience. I mean for someone who's spent the better part of his life living in grass huts."

"You'd be surprised what a thirst a man raises in those grass huts. When I return to Western civilization, it's with a vengeance."

"And after Manhattan's watering holes? What do we do then?"

"Back to the hotel, change, shower, put on our fancy duds—''

"You counted on my bringing fancy duds."

He reached for her hand and grasped it between his. He put his lips gently to her palm. "I counted on everything."

The waitress appeared with a tray, and Jemma drew her hand away. "It sounds like an expensive day, Hunt, the one you've cooked up. Expensive and with a hitch."

He carefully buttered a cranberry muffin for her. "Look, Jemma, I keep stumbling over myself with you. There aren't any hitches, catches or tricks. Come on, take a bite, and I have nothing fancy up my sleeve to go along with it. What you see is what you get."

She laughed. "Well, I won't fight it. So far I truly like what I see." She bit into the muffin, and he took the uneaten half and downed it.

"I invited myself along for the weekend because there's nothing I'd rather do," he remarked. "As for it being expensive, there's no place in Ramsey Falls to spend my money in. I have a couple of checks from

Pack College I haven't even cashed yet. Get your interview out of the way, and after that I want you to relax and pretend it's your birthday. I'm the fellow they've sent to grant your every wish."

She looked at him solemnly, then carefully buttered a piece of muffin, coated it with jam and offered it to him. "It *is* my birthday."

Hunt seemed inordinately pleased and took her hand in his, the muffin still between her fingers. "Then you're the giver of gifts. I like the idea of spending your birthday with you." He took the muffin and put it on his plate. He opened her palm and placed his mouth once more upon it in another soft kiss. "Happy Birthday."

"I lied a little. The actual event won't be until Monday."

"Not your tricentennial, I hope."

She laughed and slipped her hand away, flushing and glancing around, wondering whether her utter happiness was evident to everyone in the room. But no, they sipped their coffee and buttered their muffins and took no notice at all. She felt a momentary annoyance, as though what was happening to her was a cataclysmic event, not to be ignored.

Hunt glanced at his watch. "Damn, I think we'd better make tracks."

"Do you know, for one long, wild moment I forgot about Xeller Printing, New York, the works. I forgot about everything."

"But us."

They exchanged a long gaze, then Jemma said, "but us."

THE BUILDING where Ray Xeller had his office was modern, gray and nondescript. "This is it, Jemma," Hunt told her when they pulled up a scant two hours later. "Got you here with ten minutes to spare. Anything you want to go over with me?"

"No. I feel pretty secure." Jemma took up her leather briefcase and checked through it once more to make certain she had all the papers she needed. Then she offered Hunt a nervous smile. "All here and ready to go."

"Want me to come along?"

"No, I can handle it."

He reached over, placed his finger under her chin and tilted her face up. When he pressed his lips to hers, Jemma took in his kiss thirstily. It lasted no more than a second or two, but left her flushed and breathless.

She reached hastily into her bag and pulled out a small mirror and glanced at her image. She needed a touch of lipstick, but there was no mistaking the glitter in her eyes. She quickly applied a soft pink shade, then turned to Hunt who sat watching her. "Thanks for coming with me," she said.

He gave her a reckless flashing grin. "I'll see you back at the hotel."

"Back at the hotel, then."

Within minutes of making her way through the doors of the large, anonymous building, however, Jemma managed to push Hunt Gardner to the back of her mind. Her future lay straight ahead. Hunt was only a delicious yet dangerous stop along the road.

IT WAS A LITTLE PAST TWO when Jemma stepped out of the cool cab and ran up the steps into the Plaza Hotel. The day was already the scorcher the announcer had promised on the cab radio. The lobby was pale and cool, and Jemma felt a rush of excitement that came as easily from the dramatic change in temperature as from the highly charged world in which she found herself. Whenever she came down to the city, she was astonished by the air of movement and purpose she sensed in everyone about her.

When she asked the desk clerk for her room key, she was given two call messages, one from Victor and one from Hunt.

The Bosworth suite was on the fourth floor, a large, airy, bright room with a small dressing room attached. There was a bouquet of flowers in a vase with a note from Victor. She'd have to call him at once and tell him that she'd been impressed with Xeller's figures. There was no doubt about competition, however. Xeller had also scheduled interviews with the other interested parties, including she supposed, Celie's battery of lawyers and accountants.

She placed a telephone call to Mrs. Lawson who confirmed that Seth was settled in and playing happily with her grandson. Jemma hung up satisfied. She was about to phone Victor when she discovered the bud vase with one white rose in it. No ferns, no baby's breath, and no note, just the white rose sitting in a small crystal vase on the table next to her bed.

Jemma picked up the vase; it was slender, narrow with sharp-edged facets. The rose was pristine and she buried her face in the scent, ignoring the larger bouquet from Victor.

She reached for the phone and asked for Hunt's room but was disappointed when there was no answer. From where she stood, she could see directly through the windows to Central Park. Horse-drawn carriages lined the curb opposite and one, carrying a family of four, began to move slowly into traffic. Jemma sat down on the side of the bed and dialed Victor's number, but he wasn't in, either. Suddenly the whole world was someplace else and she was perfectly alone. But then wasn't that how she had ordered her life these past three years? Why now did the sense of her independence come upon her with such a frighteningly slow ache? She dialed Hunt's number again and settled for leaving him a message at the front desk.

JEMMA DECIDED upon a lavender-scented bubble bath from the selection of toiletries provided by the hotel. She slipped into the warm, fragrant bath, and a sensation of pure luxury came over her. This simple pleasure was a rare indulgence.

Thinking about herself as a physical human being had been low on her list of priorities for a long time. She was a mother, a mass of tender warmth for her son. She was the level-headed proprietor of a printing establishment, carrying facts and figures and knowledge around with her like so many leather briefcases. A quick shower, a quick brush through her hair in the morning, a quick application of makeup and she was raring to go. Rest wasn't time for contemplation, merely nature's way of catching up so that she could begin again. Who was she? What did she look like? Her thirty-second birthday was on the horizon, and where had everything gone?

She raised her arms out of the water and traced her fingers along her wet skin, feeling its silky texture. Was she still desirable? Was her body still young? How had she looked before her son was born? She couldn't remember. Were her breasts as firm? Would Hunt find her attractive? She didn't know; she had locked herself away, seeing only men who were safe because they didn't interest her. Good-nights at the door. *Keep your distance, please, I'm cold, cold as ice.*

No, not as cold as ice. Deep down was something that was almost frightening, something sultry, vibrating, a part of herself waiting to spring. It was Hunt alone who held the key. Hunt! What would she do about Hunt Gardner?

She could keep up the pretense that he had no motive for coming along but one of pure unselfishness. She could also pretend that Mars was a large round apple waiting to be squeezed into cider.

He hadn't picked her out because she was the *only* thing in Ramsey Falls, merely, according to him, the *best* thing. The best thing. Was she? Would she fail him? She knew that if he wanted her, she would come to him, no questions asked, no answers required. The future didn't exist, only the present, only the learning.

She lay in the bath for a long time with her eyes closed, forgetting everything except the certain knowledge that she was on a honeymoon from that other world. She would have to return to it soon enough.

The quick tap at her door roused Jemma from her torpor a half hour later. "Hunt." She stepped out of the tub and wrapped herself in a thick, thirsty towel and ran barefoot to the door. "Hunt? Just a second, I'm soaking wet. Oh, what's the difference." Still, it took her a minute to collect herself. She gave a small, anticipatory shiver. She'd get dressed, they'd go out on the town, and when they returned, she'd be in absolute possession of herself. A handshake at the door, and it would all be over. "Come on," she said brightly, pulling the door open and feeling perfectly collected, "no use your standing out there."

For a moment they remained on opposite sides of the door, Jemma wrapped in the huge towel, the tips of her hair wet, Hunt grinning at her from a forest of colorfully wrapped packages. He looked her over, his eyes raking in the towel, her bare shoulders and bare feet.

"What's all this?" Jemma said, referring to the packages. She stood aside to let him in.

"Celebration time." He went over to the chair and spilled the packages over it. "How'd everything go with Xeller?"

"Nothing to celebrate yet."

"What happened?"

"We got along famously, but Xeller wants to see a couple of other prospects. I'm adopting a 'whatever happens happens' attitude."

"Whatever happens happens." He gave her a smile of approval. "A philosophy I could live with."

She glanced down at the packages. "You've been enjoying yourself."

"For your birthday and something for Seth."

"No, Hunt, impossible. Really, I shouldn't have mentioned my birthday. And that crystal vase with the rose in it."

He turned and glanced at the larger bouquet. He seemed to know instinctively that it was from Victor. "The competition is obviously a dozen up on me."

"Competition has nothing to do with anything," Jemma said a little sharply. "Look," she added, knowing she was too much on edge, "it'll take me fifteen minutes to get dressed, that's all. I'm starved." She began to collect her clothes when she felt Hunt's touch on her arm.

"Jemma."

She turned to face him, clutching her bra and panties in one hand, a blouse in the other. She was intensely aware of the moment, of the faint sounds outside the window: the rumble of cars, a horn blowing, the shriek of a whistle summoning a cab. The air was cool on her bare skin. She could feel the softness of the cotton blouse between her fingers. She dared to gaze at his eyes, which held the same deep secret as always. She thought she would never understand him, that when he was gone, she'd be left with a will o' the wisp and nothing more.

"We're not going anywhere," he said.

She wasn't even aware of the clothes slipping out of her grasp to the floor. "No, I suppose we're not," she said.

There was an inevitability to the way his lips came down on hers. His kiss was violent, desperate, an explosive release of longing matching hers that had been held in check too long. Daggers of desire sliced through her. She pulled away and they gazed wordlessly at each other. There was no hiding from it; she wanted him with a passion that had no beginning and no end. With a little whimper, Jemma flung herself against him with reckless abandon, lifting her mouth to his and accepting his kiss with a raw sexuality that overwhelmed her. It was why she had run from him twice before. She had been shocked at the unfamiliarity of her own body, at what his touch could unleash.

He crushed her close, burying his face in her hair, running his hands down her body, whispering her name over and over. She took his face between her hands and kissed his eyes, his nose, his lips. She wound her arms around his neck and placed her lips on his in a feverish kiss that lost her in his taste and feel. His mouth was hard, demanding, sweet.

Her lips parted, allowing the swift probing of his tongue. A flame ignited deep inside her; she curled against it, twisting her body closer into his. She had been waiting all her life for this deep, exquisite mystery, this fire imagined but never known. She hadn't even been aware it was missing with Walt.

Again Hunt pulled away and gazed at her, and this time his dark, penetrating gaze held a question she could read quite clearly. Commitment for this moment alone, now, or it would all be ended. "Jemma," he began.

She put her finger against his lips. "Ssshh." She loosened the towel and let it fall to her feet. She heard his sharp intake of breath. She stood before him, feeling his eyes travel over her naked body as though with a smooth, silken, natural touch.

"You're beautiful," he said. "Just as I imagined."

"Am I?" She asked the question artlessly. "I was afraid I might not please you." Then she added almost inaudibly. "It's been so long—"

"If you pleased me more, I'd splinter into a thousand pieces. I'd need a team of surgeons to put me back together again." He gave a low growl as he reached for her. In one easy movement he had lifted her and with a long stride was at the bed, nestling her in the center. Her mouth went dry. She met his eyes bravely as he bent over her, then with shaking fingers she began to open his shirt, pulling it free. His skin was golden, bronzed by the sun. The sight of his half-naked body mesmerized her.

"Oh, Hunt," she said, "you've traveled halfway around the world and found me, no, discovered me, set something loose and I'll never be the same again." She drew him close, letting him nuzzle his mouth against her breast, feeling the sensitive tips beneath his heated breath. He ran his fingers down the length of her body. She shivered under his touch as he traced her breasts, her thighs, the high arch of her foot, then softly, quickly, a whispered, tantalizing touch between her legs.

She gave a little cry and strained, trying to turn toward him but he placed a hand on her stomach and held her down. Then he was over her, his mouth on her nipple; he sucked strongly and the thrilling sensation drew yet another cry from her. She trembled wildly as he straightened up and swiftly removed his clothes, flinging them to the floor. Jemma watched him, every nerve alive with desire. He stood before her, broad-shouldered with a lean, taut frame, strong muscular thighs and his manhood, aroused and ready.

He smiled down at her, silently mouthing her name. Then he was on her again, sweeping his hand along her thighs, demanding that she open herself to him. He tested her lips, her throat, the curve of her shoulder with gentle bites. When he found her breasts again, waves of roiling pleasure swept through her, her skin burning with a new and fragile sensitivity. She clenched her legs together, trying to control the ache churning through her. She wanted to hold off, memorize, savor every sensation, but he lifted his head and gazed down at her. He was holding back equally and the strain was visible in his heated eyes and ragged breath.

For a moment time lay suspended between them, hushed yet fierce.

"Now," he said. His mouth hovered over hers. He tipped her chin up, touching his lips to hers and licked them delicately, soothingly.

Slowly she relaxed and he spread her legs gently. His fingers moved smoothly along her flesh, exploring, driving her along with him. As she began to tremble wildly and chant his name in a shaking, helpless plea, he drew himself over her, stroking her hair, whispering words of desire. His eyes glistened with a need that was soaring and molten. Slowly he sank his flesh into hers.

Something broke in Jemma and shock waves battered her body. She clenched the sheets and then surged upward, taking all of him in, reaching her arms up to pull him closer.

"You okay?" He breathed the words into her mouth.

"Yes, oh yes."

She stroked her hands along his back, luxuriating in the heat he threw off, in his silken, rippling muscles. And then he surged and began a primal rhythm. She dug her nails into his back; he was claiming her, devouring her with searing tenderness. He was slow at first, setting the tempo, sealing her mouth with his. When his mouth moved to her throat and found the pulse spot, he exerted just enough pressure to send a roaring through her ears. She clenched her muscles as the roar subsided to something unknown and wonderful, deep within her.

He pulled back and gazed at her. "Jemma." Her name was wrenched out of him as he clasped her close. He drove into her deep and hard, pounding with relentless power. When he exploded within her, Jemma understood that she had never been truly alive before.

JEMMA HAD NO IDEA how much time had passed, and yet she knew she hadn't slept. She felt suspended, floating in a time warp that had no beginning, no middle and an end she couldn't bear thinking about.

She looked across at Hunt and ran her fingers delicately against his flesh. He stirred, moved against her and opened his eyes. "Hi," she said. She couldn't say more for the lump in her throat.

"Hi."

"Had a nice sleep?"

"I wasn't sleeping."

"I like your deep, even breathing when you don't sleep."

He reached for her. "I was busy contemplating my next move."

"Which is?"

He reached for her and claimed her lips with a sweet, lazy touch. "We have to celebrate, you know that."

"My birthday? I told you, it's not until Monday."

He moved over her, pinning her down with his body. "You silly little fool," he breathed into her mouth. "That's not what we're celebrating."

"Hunt..." But she stopped, feeling the quick unfolding of desire again. She drew her arms around him, pressing her body to his and responding willingly to his kiss.

CHAPTER ELEVEN

JEMMA CAUGHT A GLIMPSE of herself in the mirror as she sauntered with Hunt through the lobby of the Plaza Hotel. Damn, it stood out a mile. Everyone would know. Her cheeks were flushed, her eyes glittered, and in spite of the freshness of her taupe linen pants and paler taupe cotton blouse, she knew she carried a certain air of dishevelment about her. She wore, quite simply, the look of a woman in love, a woman who had discovered her sensual nature, and once having discovered it, could hide it no more than she could the errant curl in her hair or the green of her eyes.

"I picked this up at the reception desk," Hunt said, dragging a folder out of his jacket pocket. "*This Week in New York*." Neither wanted to eat at one of New York's stuffy, prestigious restaurants. They decided to wander around until something unostentatious and romantic presented itself.

Jemma peered around his shoulder at the brochure. "Pretty impressive. Ramsey Falls' activities leading up to and including the tricentennial don't cover a tenth of what's listed there."

Hunt ran his finger down the page covering weekend activities. "Central Park. List of events for a Saturday night. Concerts, jazz, dance and Shakespeare. Your choice, madam."

"Not Shakespeare. There's no way I could concentrate."

He smiled at her. "Nor I, come to think of it. Let's find a place to eat, then head over to the park."

"I've a better idea," Jemma said as they stepped out into the soft early-evening air. "I think there are a couple of stores open on Second Avenue. We need some bread, cheese and a bottle of wine. Then we'll amble over to Central Park and pick out a large, friendly crowd and follow where they lead us."

"Smart kid. Remind me to recommend you to Mr. Xeller of Xeller Printing."

They arrived at Central Park a half hour later, carrying a shopping bag holding a long French bread, wine and cheese. They found the place well lit and crowded with evening strollers.

"Why don't we head for the Bethesda Fountain?" Hunt said. "I recall that from my student days. It should be a circus at this time of night."

"Your student days?" She looked at him in surprise.

"I took my Ph.D. at Columbia."

"Did you? You never told me."

"Among the things I've wanted to tell you, Jemma, where and how I got my Ph.D. never seemed to matter much."

She considered his remark as they strolled along a busy path that led to the Bethesda Fountain. They had traded barbs and kisses, but had done very little in the way of learning about each other. Now she wanted to know everything; she wanted to see photographs of him as a boy on that farm in Minnesota, wanted to know what his father and mother were like and whom he resembled most, why he had decided on education for his life's work and what his hobbies were. Yet the questions died on her lips. She couldn't afford to know. She and Hunt existed in the here and now; she had bought it when she thrust herself into his arms, and there were no other payments due.

"I smell smoke," he said, putting his arm protectively around her. "The kind that comes when you rub two thoughts together."

"Hunt." Jemma stopped in the middle of the path, turning toward him and letting people part and walk around them. "There's no thinking, just pure sensation, I promise you."

He gazed thoughtfully at her. "Tigers think, they can't afford not to." He put his arm through hers and resumed strolling. "Want to share some of it?"

"No."

"Let me tell you, then."

"Don't, Hunt. Look," she said to distract him, pointing at a couple of kids on skateboards. "They'll break their necks."

"And everybody else's, too. Why aren't they home in bed where they belong? Why aren't we home in bed where we belong?"

"Because we're famished."

"For food?" Hunt said. "That's not what I'm famished for."

"Glutton."

"Tiger."

"I suppose you've had a great deal of experience with tigers," Jemma remarked.

"An occasional pussycat, never a tiger."

She laughed. "You're being silly. When are we going to eat?"

"When we get to the fountain. Now why do you suppose she's shaved her head, and he's dyed his hair and is wearing it in spikes," Hunt remarked about a young couple scurrying ahead of them.

"Goes with the leather and high button boots, I suppose." Both were dressed in similar fashion, although the young man carried a large portable radio which blared out heavy rock music. "Are they from outer space or are we?"

"You'd better ask them."

"In what language? I feel a million years old."

Hunt smiled appreciatively at her. "I go for older women."

The young couple and their music had disappeared when Jemma and Hunt arrived on the balustrade that overlooked the fountain and surrounding terrace. The area was well lit and crowded with strollers, guitarists, skaters, joggers, children, dogs and couples arm in arm.

"Apropos of crowds," Jemma said, "I suppose you've heard about our missing tricentennial year."

"Had a good laugh over it," he told her. "Celie said the committee had been looking for something out of the ordinary to entice tourists, and a tricentennial that isn't should do the trick."

"I'd have preferred something a little less accidental than that."

Hunt turned away from the scene below and leaned against the balustrade. The moon had risen in a sky too lighted from below to reveal many stars. "Your own roots," he asked, "do they go way back in Ramsey Falls?" he asked. "To the founding father, Mr. Ramsey himself?"

"They go back far enough," Jemma said. "Late eighteenth century. My ancestors started out as dairy farmers."

"Related to everyone in Ramsey Falls?"

"An awful lot of us have roots that join, way back when."

"And where's the old homestead?"

"None." She shook her head. "It's a housing tract, now. My grandfather sold pieces off until there was nothing left. My father was an engineer. We lived in a twenties cottage outside of Ramsey Falls. He died after I married. My mother sold the house and moved to California. The trouble with my roots is I can tell just about everything in a paragraph and a short one at that."

"And you've had no desire to move on?" he asked.

She shook her head once again. "No choice in the matter, Hunt. I can't think about it. I don't even dare question the alternatives. 'I should have' is not exactly my favorite phrase. I'm exceedingly pragmatic."

He pulled her over so that their bodies touched at every warm point. "We're from two different places, you and I. Physical, mental." He tipped her chin up. "You're rooted, I'm footloose. You have responsibilities, I've none except for the need to pass my knowledge on." He placed his lips on hers in a simple, chaste kiss.

Jemma felt the long, slow welling up of desire stretch through her body. "I haven't asked you to explain yourself or me," she said at last.

"What the hell are we doing here when there's a nice, warm bed awaiting us?"

He kissed her. She could feel him stir against her. There was a faint clip-clopping of a horse's hooves as a carriage passed them along the road that wound through the park. Someone laughed as their kiss held, a laugh of sheer pleasure. And from the band shell in the distance, on the ghostliest of winds, she could hear the strains of a soprano singing Mozart.

Hunt drew his mouth away from hers. "Let's go."

She took his hand and raised it to her lips. She laid a soft kiss on his open palm. "Yes, let's."

They did not speak again even when they reached the hotel lobby. Hunt had long before spontaneously handed their picnic to an indigent sitting on a bench outside the park. In the elevator Jemma stood awkwardly to one side, her eyes averted, afraid the other passengers would see the need she knew burned in their depths. They were the only passengers to step off on the fourth floor and for that Jemma was grateful. As the elevator door closed and it continued silently up, Hunt took her in his arms again. They stood in a tight embrace as though to contain the power of what was between them.

Say it, she thought. *Tell me you love me and that this will go on forever. No.* She caught her breath into a little sigh. *Don't. This is just a ferocious little moment in time that I want every bit as much as you do.*

"Jemma." His voice was husky but she silenced him with a shake of her head.

Still holding each other close, they hurried down the corridor to her door. He kissed her once more as he fumbled with the lock. Once inside, as the door closed with a final little click, a kind of savage fury overtook them. Her mouth was against his. Blood pounded through her veins as his fingers, hot and quick, worked at her clothes. When she strained her nude body against him, the roughness of his shirt and his heated breath sent long driving currents of desire through her.

She had no idea when he removed his own clothes, but suddenly they were at the bed and he pulled her onto him. She shuddered, clamping her thighs around his. She was all instinct, all feeling, the tigress released and fighting toward a newer ecstasy. He urged her on, arching higher and higher until she collapsed against him, drained and exhausted.

HIS BODY WAS HEAVY, and Jemma could feel his heart still knocking unevenly against her chest. She took in a deep breath and released it slowly.

"I thought you were asleep," he said.

"No need to sleep. It's all a dream." She looked into his face and his soft, caressing smile. She still felt the need to move against him, to feel his flesh joined with hers. As though he sensed this fresh need, he eased off her without lifting his body from hers. He rolled sideways and pulled her with him. She lay against him, feeling his arms tight around her and his chin on her hair. They breathed in unison and after a while Hunt murmured, "Did it surprise you as much as it did me? First times aren't supposed to be that good."

"Hunt, nothing about you has surprised me."

"And everything about you has."

"From the moment we met?"

"Mmm," Hunt said. "Especially your line about 'Stop the presses.' And your racing after me down the street to show me the plug for my lecture in your column. *And* your review of said lecture. That took the wind out of my sails."

"My earthshaking column."

"It certainly shakes the earth beneath Celie's feet."

She raised her head and grinned at him. "You small-town gossip, you. I think you've fallen in love with Ramsey Falls and all the nonsense that passes for daily living there."

He regarded her for some time, his expression thoughtful. "I left all that behind me when I drove away from the family farm in Minnesota. If it was going to be small-town gossip, I wanted it exotic and in some other language."

Jemma knew then that the parameters hadn't changed, and she had no right to expect them to. She put her head on his chest, her hand flat against his flesh. She listened for a while to his even breathing and then closed her eyes.

When next she opened them, it was to a gray dawn making tentative forays into the room through slatted blinds and gauzy curtains. Hunt lay against her, his head on her breast, one arm flung possessively about her. She slipped carefully out from under him and reached for her robe. She went silently across the floor and parted the curtains. There was a fine mist falling on deserted streets. The road was shiny, and although it was early morning, the street lamps were still lit. Jemma had the unreal feeling that the world belonged to her to do with as she pleased. She stretched luxuriously and then turned toward the bed. The covers had been thrown back, and Hunt lay in a soft light that picked out his warm, burnished skin and pale dusting of hair across his chest.

He slept silently with only the occasional sound of a breath being drawn in. Jemma moved to the foot of the bed and gazed down at him, admiring his smooth expanse of tanned flesh and the tumbled mass of dark hair that fell across his forehead. He didn't seem real to her. He was like something she dreamed up, something she was only allowed a glimpse of before being awakened.

She had wanted that dream, made it happen, and now knew that his leaving her would be devastating. No matter what else she had in her life, no matter what the future held, there would always be a part of her that would belong to Hunt alone.

She felt a sudden chill although she wasn't really cold. She hugged her arms and rocked forward. A ribbon of sensation spiraled through her at the thought of what had passed between them. She opened her robe and dropped it to the floor. *Let tomorrow take care of itself.* She went quickly over to Hunt and slid in beside him.

He opened his eyes. "I dreamed you went away," he said, putting his arms around her. "It was turning into a nightmare."

Oh God, she thought, he had it all wrong. It was he who was going away, going far away forever. And still she wanted him, felt she couldn't get enough of him. He touched her breast gently and a wildfire of longing swept through her. When his mouth claimed hers, she responded with hot hungry kisses. She ground against him, rotating her hips. Stunned by her aggression and ever-mounting desire, she drew out a long groan of ecstasy. And then he was in her, kissing her again and again as the full, hard, warm pressure of his body filled her completely. And yet at the moment of fulfillment, tears started to her eyes. She felt more alive than ever before, yet she knew in her heart this was all an illusion, nothing more.

RAMSEY FALLS looked exactly the same. The streets
ran north to south, the kids played in the deepening,
incandescent dusk, dogs barked and the tricentennial
banner at the entrance to the town of Ramsey Falls
billowed in a fresh breeze coming off the river.

It was amazing. Everything had changed for Jemma
and Ramsey Falls was still the same. She was intensely
aware of her body, her skin, her hair, the blood cours-
ing through her veins, and more than that, of the man
sitting beside her in the car. She stole a glance at him.
His hands were steady, his fingers drumming in time to
a tune on the radio. He sensed her scrutiny and gave
her a quick smile. "When are you picking up Seth?"

"I wasn't certain what time I'd be back. He's staying with Mrs. Lawson until tomorrow morning."

They neared Main Street, and Hunt slowed the car
to a crawl while he searched for a parking spot. "What
about dinner?"

"I thought we decided we weren't hungry," Jemma
said.

"We weren't. Not that way. I'm not certain I am
now, but that doesn't do away with the fact that we
ought to have dinner together." He found a spot,
pulled in and then turned to her, his hand still resting
on the wheel.

Jemma glanced briefly at Whiting Printing several
stores down. It was there, safe and waiting in a street
of shops with windows softly lit, their charming dis-
plays like so many good dishes at a banquet. The streets
were filled with Sunday strollers, and there was an in-
definable air of the celebration to come. The world was
at that pivotal point of a hushed, breathless waiting.
Let the celebration begin she thought with a wistful

smile. And she wondered if everyone in town knew they were away, and knew they were back.

"Let me pick up some makings for dinner. Somehow I want to show off my culinary powers," Hunt said. "You'd be surprised what I can do with rice, onions, a lot of garlic and some very hot peppers."

"Hunt." She reached out and placed her hand on his. "I don't think it's a very good idea."

"Why not? We can have a candlelight dinner. A quiet, romantic evening at home." He turned a boyish smile on her. "We won't have to stop celebrating until tomorrow morning."

"No," she said in a tone whose sharpness surprised even her.

"No? What do you mean, 'no'." His voice was tight with a rising impatience.

"I live in this town," she said quietly, "and I raise my son here." She didn't want to be the subject of gossip; when Walt had left her, she instinctively understood it was on everyone's lips.

He muttered something under his breath and turned away, but not before she caught the arrogant tilt to his jaw. "I can't have you staying in my apartment overnight," she added. "I thought you understood that."

"I'm beginning to think I understand nothing about you."

She was silent for a moment, then said, "Look, it's a small town. I've lived here my whole life. What I do, what anyone does, what somebody's pet cockatoo does, is fed into the gossip mill. Stepping into this car and driving out of town and heading for New York with you could have set a lot of tongues wagging. Jemma Whiting, Seth's mommy," she said in a mimicking tone, "the very correct lady who owns the

Ramsey Falls Shopper's Guide, that Jemma Whiting, taking up with the handsome professor, you know, the one who's leaving at the end of the month and never coming back? Now why do you suppose she's done that?''

Hunt shook his head all the while she spoke. "It's not local gossip that's bothering you, Jemma. I think it's Walt and whatever hold he still has over you." He made the remark sympathetically, but Jemma flinched nonetheless. "You're a grown woman," he continued. "No one has the right to force you to live like a nun." He reached over and took both her hands in his. "I thought maybe you learned something this weekend about breaking out?"

"Really?" She drew her hands away. "Is that what it was all about?"

"No, dammit, you know that."

"If you think small-town attitudes have changed along with the divorce statistics, let me tell you, they haven't. It hasn't a thing to do with Walt, but with people's perceptions of my behavior. If they saw me leave with you, if they know we're back—"

"And exactly what meaning do you suppose they'll attach to all those ifs, Jemma?"

"Oh, Hunt." She raised her hand to touch him, but drew back. "This weekend was...*special*. Surely you know that. I don't want it to be the subject of idle speculation. I'll never forget the love we made."

"Then why are you sending me away?"

"Because nothing is simple." She twisted her fingers together, staring down at them. "I'm going to sound like a hypocrite and fool if I tell you that it could happen in New York and it can't here, but it's true."

She gazed at him entreatingly. "Don't make this more difficult than it already is. Let me be."

"I already tried that, Jemma. It didn't work."

She reached for the door handle. "I think I've said all I can on the subject."

Hunt was out of the car first, taking her luggage and the wrapped boxes of presents that she had pointedly left wrapped. He came up to her as she opened the door to her shop. Somehow it seemed important to Jemma that she step inside, get her bearings. Hunt followed her in, saying, "I suppose it's totally out of the question for me to come upstairs even for a moment. To help with the packages, of course. What would the neighbors think if I let you cart all this upstairs by yourself?"

She went into her office and put her briefcase down on her desk. Everything was in shape. She came back outside and glanced quickly at the order pad and automatically took in the number and nature of sales Adriana had made.

"Jemma." Hunt stood looking at her.

Her smile was involuntary. It was difficult to leave him, to say goodbye. It seemed so natural to want him in spite of the consequences.

"You promise you'll leave when I say so."

"Scout's honor," he said, raising three fingers.

"Liar." She went over and unlocked the door leading to her apartment above. He gathered her packages and followed her upstairs.

It was all wordless. Once inside her apartment, the packages tumbled to the floor. Jemma didn't even reach for the light. Hunt folded her in his arms. In a moment they were at her bed, the covers pulled roughly back, their clothes hurriedly discarded.

His hands traveled her flesh along a now familiar route. When Jemma arched her back and gave a tiny whimper, Hunt raised up, poised over her body, studying her face. He seemed about to say something, but then, with an almost imperceptible shake of his head, appeared to dismiss whatever it was. Even in the dim light, through half-closed eyes, Jemma could see the fine line of perspiration above his mouth. She stifled a sob. He bent to kiss her as he entered her body. He didn't pause or hesitate, just pressed deeply and slowly. Then, as she rocked with him, he whispered in her ear, "Go ahead, I dare you, tell me to go away."

WHEN JEMMA AWOKE, the morning silence had a certain empty ring to it. She reached across the bed to touch him, but even without opening her eyes, knew Hunt was no longer there. Some time during the early morning he had slipped away, leaving her to face the daylight by herself. She sat up in bed and pulled the sheet around her, feeling the emptiness of the room as equally as the emptiness of a future without Hunt Gardner. Her life, she thought with a weary little sigh, was coming unraveled. During the past three years she had become used to being without a man; used to waking up in a room by herself; used to a single-cup coffee maker; used to putting one slice of bread in the toaster. She no longer slept on the right side of her large double bed, but instead roamed the mattress at night.

She reached for her robe and climbed out of bed. She went over to the window and saw that it had rained overnight. The sky was still overcast, and there was a fresh, cool scent in the air. She yawned deeply. The dream was over and with any luck it might fade away along with memories that were too good, that could spill over into the rest of her life if she didn't take care.

She found Hunt's note in the kitchen on top of his boxes of presents. She remembered now his dropping the packages hastily to the floor and a long slow rise of red drew along her cheeks. She hadn't opened them at the Plaza Hotel and hesitated even now. He had torn a piece of paper from her memo pad near her telephone. It read:

Jemma, it wasn't a dream. I'll call around eleven. Bogged down with students from eight on.

Love,
Hunt

P.S. Happy Birthday

Happy Birthday. She sat shakily down at the table and stared at the words. Love. It seemed to carry all the weight of the Magna Carta. She could place any interpretation on it: "You're a lovely roll in the hay. Love, Hunt." "For a small-town babe, you're great where it counts. Love, Hunt." "Someday when I pass this way again, I'll call. Love, Hunt." Or did it mean, "I love you, I'll stay"? She threw the note down and contemplated the boxes piled on the table. There were half a dozen of varying sizes and in varying colors. She had delayed opening them at the hotel because the love they made was too new, too frightening, something she couldn't cope with. It held a wealth of meaning she wasn't ready to explore. Back in her own world she felt more able to face whatever went on between them.

"Oh Hunt, you're crazy," she said aloud to the empty room. Then, in a sudden gleeful fit, Jemma pounced upon the three largest, all from F. A. O. Schwartz, and all for Seth. She gave each a good shaking but could deduce nothing of the contents. She had no idea how she'd explain them to her son but Hunt's generosity didn't fill her with rancor as Walt's always did. She even wondered what feelings Hunt had when he purchased them; how he explained Seth to the sales clerk.

There were two presents for Jemma, one from Bergdorf Goodman, which Jemma unwrapped quickly with trembling fingers. The box contained a silk scarf printed with a jungle motif, its center a tiger. A tiger! She burst out laughing. He had expected everything, foretold everything, the beast.

The smallest box of all was of a soft blue, a box with the Tiffany imprint upon it. She hesitated before undoing the white satin ribbon, examining the small note that had been tucked in beneath the ribbon. *For Jemma from Hunt. Happy Birthday.* No *love.* Certainly not thanks or anticipation of thanks. If anything, the *loves*, the *thanks* were for later, for goodbyes. She opened the package carefully, preserving the ribbon as one might a lock of hair. Against blue velvet lay a pair of diamond earrings, tiny, wistful, exquisite. She did not dare touch them. In a way his generosity puzzled her, but before she could work it out, the phone rang, awakening Jemma from her reverie.

"I know it's early," Victor said at once.

She glanced at the clock. It was just past nine-thirty, and the shop was not yet opened. What could she have been thinking of? And she hadn't even called Mrs. Lawson about picking up Seth.

"Hi, Victor, I was going to call you as soon as I opened the shop." With a stab of conscience, she thought of his next logical question, about how she found her room at the Plaza. Victor, however, surprised her.

"I set the wheels in motion for your loan, you know that, Jemma."

"Victor, nothing was concluded. Ray Xeller had to see some other people, and I was extremely happy for the respite."

"Did you like what the man had to say?"

"Yes, I liked him from the first, and what I liked best is that he'd stick around for a couple of weeks to help me through the rough parts."

"He apparently has been on to your bank checking into your assets, Jemma."

"So soon? And is that good, bad or indifferent?"

"Apparently he called your Ramsey Falls bank on Saturday morning, even before you were scheduled to meet with him. At any rate, I gather that your competition, with the exception of Celie, fell through for lack of proper financing."

"Victor, your gnomes have certainly been busy on my behalf."

"Celie's, actually. She told all this to me when we had breakfast together this morning. Her gnomes are a lot cleverer than my gnomes."

"Do her gnomes tell her to buy Xeller Printing?"

"As far as Celie is concerned, her advisors tell her to stick to what she knows, advice I've also given her. Incidentally, Ray Xeller is back at his shop, and he'll stay around for the tricentennial bash, anyway."

"Let me think," Jemma said. "I can't think."

"You'll be buying a thoroughbred with known winners in its background."

"I'll call him," Jemma decided. "See him in Merriman and go over every piece of equipment."

"I want you to use my lawyer when you're ready to draw up papers," Victor said.

"Just a phone call to Merriman, Victor. I can't be rushed on the first day of the rest of my life."

"Understand. Incidentally, how was your trip?"

She didn't hesitate with her answer, because she didn't dare. "Fine. And thanks for the flowers, they were gorgeous." She had left them behind, remembering only to scoop up the crystal vase with its lone white rose. "Victor, I'll call you back as soon as I talk to Mr. Xeller." She replaced the receiver quickly, and without allowing herself time to think, raced into the shower. It was only later, fully awake and gulping her first cup of coffee in her office downstairs that she picked up the telephone receiver and dialed Mrs. Lawson.

"Tommy and Seth are outside," Mrs. Lawson told her, "and acting up. They had a couple of temper tantrums apiece this morning because I'm delivering my grandson down to his parents in New York, and both kids are upset about it. Can you beat that?"

"Oh, Mrs. Lawson," Jemma said, "poor Seth. I know he loves Tommy."

"The feeling is mutual, believe me. I'll bring Seth back around quarter to twelve on my way to the bus."

"I can't thank you enough," Jemma told her.

"Thank *you*. Having Seth here made my life a little easier. See you later."

Jemma next called Ray Xeller at his shop in Merriman. He wanted to see her and set a date for the afternoon, which meant she would have to take Seth along with her. She could just imagine sitting in Xeller's office trying to tough out negotiations with a small boy tugging at her blouse, asking to go to the bathroom every ten minutes, but she had no choice. Adriana was due in at one. Jemma couldn't expect the teenager to handle the shop and a noisy youngster at the same time.

She tried a couple of the baby-sitters she used in a pinch, but the tricentennial had everyone booked solid for one event or another. Then the shop became too busy for her to think about finding someone. Nearing eleven, she made herself a fresh cup of coffee and offered one to a customer who sat waiting for the duplicating machine to run off a hundred pages of a manuscript. The phone rang several times, interrupting a delicate paste-up job she was doing, and there were several other orders to be put through the press. There wasn't any doubt about it. She needed full-time help at Whiting Printing unless she could consolidate her work with the shop in Merriman. Which meant, of course, that buying Xeller Printing was beginning to look better and better.

The sun came out. Whenever the door opened and the cowbell jangled, warm air gusted into the shop. Outside the street was filled with people bustling to and fro. There was an air of jovial purpose to the way they walked. Ramsey Falls had made a silly, wonderful mistake about its age, and tourists wanted to be in on the celebration. It was a great story, all right. They were smack in the middle of a long hot summer with an abiding quality that made one forget the other seasons.

At precisely eleven o'clock the telephone rang. As she reached for it with a crazy racing of her heart, she knew she was in trouble. *Hunt,* she wanted to say, *why did you have to happen?*

His voice was a caress. "I miss you."

She looked distractedly through her office window that connected with the shop. Her lone customer was still leafing through a magazine. "Hunt, don't do that, please," she said. "It isn't fair."

"Hell, if I waited for things to be fair, I'd still be counting ears of corn in Minnesota. You move, Jemma, you stir the air up, you make things happen." He paused, then added in a sombre tone, "I wouldn't have missed you for the world."

"That's great, Hunt. It's nice to know I'll be a footnote when you write your autobiography, but meanwhile I have to get on with my life."

"Don't turn me off," he said, a touch defensively.

It was time to pull apart, let go. She thought of Seth and Tommy fighting, getting in each other's way to ease the hurt of saying goodbye. Was she being childish like her son, allowing instinct to make her decisions for her? "Sorry," she said at last. "I have a lot on my mind this morning. I have to run into Merriman to meet with Ray Xeller at one. At noon my son will be delivered to me, and I haven't found a babysitter for him, which means I'm going to have a rambunctious child on my hands while I'm trying to learn something about the Xeller operation. And to top it off, I seem to have my teenage assistant running my business for me."

"I'll watch Seth."

"What?"

"Leave Seth with me while you take care of your business in Merriman. I know my way around kids. I've a few things to finish off here in my office, and he can keep me company. I'll treat him to lunch and then show him how to play baseball. All in a day's work. How about it?"

"You're asking for a passel of trouble."

"Some passels I like. I'll pick him up at noon."

"Hunt, no." She wanted to count on nothing about Hunt Gardner. She wanted to shout at him to leave, just leave, without goodbyes, without unexpected kindnesses.

"Remind him that I'm the nice man who took him to the hospital."

The one he called Daddy, she thought. "Yes," she said, and with the word, relief drained through her. "I'll tell him that you're Mommy's friend, that nice man who took him to the hospital."

"That's right, Mommy's friend," Hunt said softly, just before he hung up.

CHAPTER TWELVE

"REALLY, HUNT, a baseball uniform and hat." Jemma shook her head in admonition when Hunt arrived to pick up Seth.

"And a mitt and baseball bat and ball," Seth chimed in.

"Glad you like them," Hunt said, pretending a certain amount of innocence in the matter of spoiling six-year-olds.

"Did you thank Mr. Gardner properly?" Jemma asked her son.

Seth held out his hand and muttered a thank you.

"How about dinner tonight," Hunt asked Jemma when the boy was safely seated in the car.

"I'm sorry, I promised to spend this evening with Seth. I feel as if I've been away from him for a year."

Hunt suspected that it was just an excuse to put distance between them, and the trouble was he understood. He swung into the car and told Jemma that he'd have Seth back in Ramsey Falls at six.

Later that morning the boy sat on the floor in Hunt's office, with sheets of paper strewn around him. He wore the Yankee baseball uniform Hunt had bought him, with the cap, which was a size too large, low on his ears.

Hunt had provided the boy with colored marking pens and paper. Seth willingly threw himself into the

drawing of dinosaurs, intoning a litany of names while
Hunt worked at his desk. Triceratops, stegosaurus, al-
losaurus, brontosaurus. The words floated up to Hunt,
as though the boy had become adept at a foreign language. Smart mother, smart son, he thought more than
once.

Hunt lined up the manila folders that held his students' work, vague, imprecise and wordy attempts at
understanding his lectures. Hunt had a sudden feeling
that he had tried too much in too short a time. To whip
these students into shape he'd need a year, two years.
No, leave that to others. The lectures were a public relations effort to enlist their interest in setting up education programs in third-world countries, and that was
all. When he moved the folders aside, he gave in to a
nagging feeling that was beginning to drive a stake
through his heart: moving fast and alighting infre-
quently wasn't all it was cracked up to be.

He pushed back his chair, stretched his legs out and
studied the child who was sitting happily at his feet. It
wasn't supposed to be this way, had never been before. Someone had broken the rules. All he had to do
was exercise his old logic, think the whole thing
through and come to the only conclusion he could. He
didn't belong in Ramsey Falls, a claustrophobic, tight
little beehive of a community that couldn't even count
straight, and where a man could spend his life trying to
find breathing space. Hadn't he left Minnesota for the
same reason?

It was that first intriguing sight of Jemma that did
him in, those frowning, green eyes accusing him of
stealing her press time. Not love at first sight, just
coming-back-for-more sight. Dead-serious Jemma,
seriously intent Jemma. Jemma who was funny, chal-

lenging, beautiful. Damn. She was everything that would keep his life exciting, even in this quiet little burg.

When Jemma first saw him, he knew something had stirred in her, too. Just how had she seen him, the man who was busy stealing her press time? Hunt didn't want to believe all the moves had been his alone, that he had wanted to zero in on someone whose life he could mess up. He had always been so careful about that.

Hello, goodbye. No one hurt, no one left in the lurch. Was he capable of precisely that behavior he railed against in his public lectures at Bosworth Hall?

Leave tomatoes at home.

Maybe he could have used a few square in his face. What the hell was happening to him?

"This," Seth said, breaking the intense silence, "is the biggest, *biggest*, biggest biggest. Brach-io-saurus. Seventy-five tons."

Hunt glanced at the respectable drawing the boy had made. "Brachiosaurus, seventy-five tons," he said. "Pretty mean-looking character. I'd hate to bump into him coming around a corner."

Seth threw the paper aside and picked up another sheet. "No, he doesn't look like that. I'll do another one."

Hunt turned back to his desk and reached for the letter that had been waiting for him when he arrived in his office that morning. It was from Victor Bosworth. Hunt scanned the contents once more, skipping the compliments and settling on the last paragraph. "If you decide to settle down after this next trip, I would like you to consider a post at Pack College. I'm certain we can always arrange a tenured position with the appropriate compensation."

Good Lord, Pack College. He had turned down Harvard and Stanford, why in hell would he settle for Pack? Packed away Pack College in the middle of nowhere, no way. He shoved the letter into his top drawer and slammed it shut.

Seth glanced up at the noise and gave Hunt a shy, tentative smile. "Want to see this?"

"Sure," Hunt said and immediately joined the boy on the floor. Coming back to Ramsey Falls would turn his life upside down. He'd be tied to Jemma, her child, and in the odd way of the American divorce system, even to Walt Whiting. He'd end up knee-deep in printer's ink resenting everything about the place.

Seth solemnly handed him a blue marking pen and a piece of paper. "Here, you draw one."

"Okay, how about a giraffosaurus?"

Seth giggled. "There's no such thing."

"A rhinosaurus."

Seth giggled once more.

Hunt bent low over the paper and began a rudimentary sketch of a dinosaur. Seth squatted on his knees and leaned slightly against him, watching every stroke that Hunt made.

Hunt found himself taking shallow little breaths, as though the moment were so fragile, any wrong move would shatter it. The pen made swishing noises on the paper.

"What kind of skin does a dinosaur have?" he asked Seth.

Seth shrugged.

"Like a lizard maybe." The last thing Hunt wanted to do was to think about why he was thirty-five years old and not even contemplating marriage and a family. It was a mistake all around, becoming involved with Jemma Whiting and now her son.

"His head's too big," Seth said.

"Come on, young man," Hunt told him, rising to his feet and feeling suddenly more tired than he had in a long while, "time for lunch."

"Just one more."

Hunt smiled, looking down at the boy. Seth held the pen awkwardly in his right hand and began to cover the paper with quick strokes. Yeah, it was close with Jemma, real close, but he wasn't quite ready, in spite of her storybook son, in spite of her warm, luminous skin and the wanton way she reveled in the sex they had together.

Who could Walt have found to replace her, and why in hell would he want to?

He shook himself and said, "Come on, Seth, how about it? It's a nice day out there, and we've got a lot of baseball to play."

No, in a short while, he'd be half a world away. She'd fade. Jemma was right when she accused him of picking her out of the crowd, the gay divorcée looking for a little love. That's just what happened; it was his modus operandi. It wasn't a bad choice for one hot summer. Maybe with any luck he'd forget her in time. He took in a deep breath. In a pig's eye.

"Can I take them with me?"

"The drawings? Of course, and the pens, too, while you're at it. First lunch. We'll buy you a greasy hamburger, french fries and a Coke. How's that for a special treat?"

"My mom doesn't let me eat that stuff," Seth said, watching him out of solemn eyes.

"Then I guess you and I are going to have to keep a secret."

Seth started a slow smile and Hunt reached out and tugged at the baseball cap. The smile turned into a wide grin, all solemnity gone. Hunt found himself gazing at Jemma's beautiful eyes. He bent, scooped the youngster into his arms and headed for the door before he had time to investigate the possessive, melting need that took hold of his heart when Jemma's son looked at him.

IT WAS FOUR O'CLOCK when Jemma returned to Ramsey Falls from her meeting with Ray Xeller. She was unexpectedly taken aback by the contrast between her small place and the larger one in Merriman that she now suddenly, daringly had agreed to buy. She had been impressed with Xeller's operation, knew it would meld perfectly with Whiting Printing and ultimately be far more efficiently for both. But as she stepped into her comfortable little shop, she couldn't quell an unreasoning panic over having bitten off more than she could chew.

Adriana was waiting on a customer, talking on the telephone and running the printer all at the same time. She waved Jemma over to the phone. "The doctor asking where his new stationery is," she whispered with her hand over the receiver.

"Not ready," Jemma whispered back. "Not even begun. We're waiting for a shipment of paper." She took the receiver and dealt with the doctor in as charming a manner as she could. She had the odd feeling that everything was getting away from her, flying off into space like so many remnants of a huge explosion.

When she put the receiver down, Adriana was running a comb through her hair. "I'm sorry, Mrs. Whiting, but I have to go. Here are all the telephone messages, the mail and the order pad. Oh, and the order on the press is rush rush. Mr. Fields is coming back at five for it. And the rest is packed or—" she shrugged apologetically "—unpacked. I'm sorry, I couldn't get to everything. Oh, and your mother called. Nothing to worry about. She read about the tri—whoops—bi, you know what I mean, in the *Los Angeles Times* and wanted to talk to you. She said it's your birthday. Happy birthday, Mrs. Whiting. She asked you to call when you have a chance. Also Mrs. Lawson called and said she'll be around tomorrow if you need her."

"You're an outright angel, Adriana," Jemma said, spontaneously hugging the girl.

"And we're selling picture postcards like crazy," Adriana said.

"Well," Jemma said, pleased, "I guess I had a good idea, for a change."

Early in the year Jemma had printed a line of souvenir postcards illustrated with appropriate old photographs of Ramsey Falls. She had also designed and ordered from a silk screen house several hundred posters depicting Main Street and the date of the Ramsey Falls tricentennial. In spite of its being off a year, or perhaps because of it, postcards and posters were selling briskly.

"I have to run now," Adriana told her.

"See you tomorrow."

The girl stepped out the door, the cowbell ringing, and the local travel agent stepped in at the same time. She brought in her current business card and asked Jemma for a box of a thousand, to be printed on gray stock. "You couldn't get them to me by Thursday?" she asked hopefully.

"I have to send them into Merriman to be printed," Jemma told her with a dubious note in her voice. "Oh, wait a minute, of course." She smiled. Xeller Printing was hers now. "I'll get them to you for sure. A thousand cards on gray stock, and the information remains the same, right?"

"Right. I figure with all the tourists in town I might be able to pick up some business. Thanks to all the media coverage, we might experience a mini real-estate boom."

"The town that couldn't add straight," Jemma said. "I'm not certain of the value of that kind of publicity."

"Ramsey Falls has always been beautiful, Jemma. A charming backwater. Now everyone knows about it."

"Oh, they do. They do, indeed." She handed the woman her invoice. "I'll call you and let you know the exact delivery date."

The travel agent, however, didn't leave at once. She seemed inclined to gossip and joined Jemma for a cup of coffee. "So we're losing our handsome professor," she said, stirring in the sugar and cream. "He asked me to book a flight for him first to Minneapolis, then to Los Angeles, then on to Thailand. He's leaving Sunday, and it isn't a round trip."

Jemma waited on a delicately inhaled sigh.

"Leaving Sunday and taking half the hearts of Ramsey Falls with him. If I weren't married, ah me. What about you, Jemma? You seem to know him pretty well."

Jemma was saved the trouble of having to make an appropriate remark because the phone rang and the street door opened at the same time. When the dust cleared, she was alone. She grabbed the order pad and telephone messages and retreated to her office. There was a finality to knowing Hunt had booked a flight and was about to do what he planned all along. She felt oddly hurt that he hadn't said a word about it, even though she understood he was leaving when she allowed him to make love to her. No, not allowed. She had never *allowed*. She had merely thrown herself into his arms.

He was leaving, and she was numbed by the thought. Being with her hadn't made one damn bit of difference to his plans.

Numb, frozen, without feeling. It was easy enough to concentrate on business when her heart had been emptied of all hope. She bent to her task, grateful for the interruptions that kept her busy until late afternoon.

As she made her way upstairs to her apartment, she realized the queasy feeling hadn't subsided that had first come over her in Merriman when she left Ray Xeller. With a handshake, she had agreed to purchase Xeller Printing and was about to put up all her assets as collateral. Panic over a decision she had made on her own almost seemed a natural event. Halfway back to Ramsey Falls she had wanted to stop at a phone booth to call Hunt, to hear him tell her she had done the right thing.

She didn't even try. He was off with her son playing baseball, and she couldn't discuss her life or her plans or her feelings with Hunt, anyway. The distance between them had widened perceptibly. She had seen to that, as well as he. He needn't take a plane to make it any wider, and there was no sense pretending he was going to be around for her.

As she began preparations in her kitchen for a birthday dinner with her son, Jemma decided that the purchase of Xeller's shop had come along at the right time. She was going to need something to fill in the empty space that Hunt's leaving would cause. It could take a lifetime.

The downstairs buzzer rang sharply. Her heart leaped. Hunt had promised to bring Seth back at six. A glance at the clock told her he was early. She pressed the button to release the door and then raced for the hallway.

"Jemma." It was Walt, coming slowly up the stairs.

She closed her eyes for an instant, but he wasn't an apparition. When she next spoke, she tried to keep her voice steady. She never trusted Walt's surprises. "What are you doing here?"

"I remembered it was your birthday."

"Really? You're not even a charming liar." She tried to block his way into the apartment, but he brushed past her as though he had every right to be there.

"Where's my son?" He stalked over to Seth's room and peered in.

"He's with the baby-sitter. I don't want you here, Walt. Our agreement doesn't call for you to drop by to see him anytime you like."

"Baby-sitter. Mrs. Lawson, right." He looked at Jemma with the most curiously chilling expression she had ever seen.

She didn't even try to correct him. "If you have a message for Seth, perhaps I can pass it on to him."

"I can always stop at Mrs. Lawson's on my way home, although why he's with his baby-sitter and you're here, I won't even venture to guess."

"If you'll excuse me, I'm in the midst of making dinner. Don't slam the door when you leave." She moved past him on her way to the kitchen.

"We have a few things to talk about," Walt said, unhesitatingly following her, "and it works out fine that my son isn't around at the moment."

"I'll give you five minutes." Jemma grabbed an onion and began to peel it furiously with a paring knife. Walt sat down at the table, his hands folded. Jemma knew that he never did anything accidentally. If he had settled on a chair, it was because he didn't want to appear threatening, which meant she had to keep her wits as sharpened as her knife.

"Had a successful day today?" he asked.

"Walt, what does that mean?"

"I take it you sealed your deal with Xeller." He looked as if he were about to lick some cream from his lips.

She tried to hide her surprise, cutting away at the onion, feeling her eyes smart.

"I came to congratulate you on your expanding empire." When Jemma didn't answer, he continued. "Just want you to know I'm impressed. I never thought—" He stopped, letting Jemma finish the sentence in her mind.

No, Jemma thought, he never believed she had any character at all, his little wife who would do anything for him, including suppressing the best parts of herself.

"Just shows," he went on expansively, "how a person can grow with the times. Like your newfound ability to make men dance to your tune."

An icy warning slid along her spine. "I'm not interested in your five-and-dime philosophy, Walt. I'm still waiting for you to leave, gracefully or otherwise."

"How was your weekend at the Plaza?"

The knife slipped and she cut her finger. "Damn."

"Cut yourself," Walt commented.

She dropped the knife into the sink and quickly turned on the tap water and began to rinse her finger. Walt knew nothing about her weekend in New York, nothing.

"Need a bandage?"

"No, I don't need a bandage." She examined the cut and saw it was superficial.

"Yeah, must have been some weekend in Victor Bosworth's suite with a man who didn't resemble Bosworth, not a whit. Tall, impressive fellow, the kind who looks like he's wearing tweeds even when he isn't wearing tweeds. You know, the intellectual type," he added, drawing out the word.

"You bastard." She turned on him. It seemed to Jemma that something had happened to the air in the room. Suddenly it was difficult to breathe.

"Professor Hunt Gardner, over at the college, on his way to Thailand end of the week." Walt regarded her out of narrowed eyes. "I don't think you two even came up for air." He tilted his head as if he was waiting for confirmation. "Now, some things can be assumed, Jemma. For instance, Victor didn't know the interesting purposes to which you put his expensive little suite at the Plaza. And since Victor seems to be behind this purchase of yours, I'd say he's being cuckolded by the very man he brought to Ramsey Falls in the first place.''

"I want you to leave, Walt, now." Jemma pulled the door open, marched into the hall and waited for him to appear.

It took Walt several minutes to come out. "Jemma, I have a little proposition that might interest you now that your life seems to be moving into another lane."

"I'm not interested in anything you have to say. Good night."

He wagged his head. "Not 'good night' quite yet. You have a choice, though. You can either listen or expect your private life with Hunt Gardner to be aired around Ramsey Falls."

Jemma felt the heat rise to her face, and it was only with great effort that she could regard her ex-husband without flinching. Her knees were weak and she realized she was clutching the doorknob so tightly her knuckles had turned white with the effort. That the spontaneous burst of happiness she'd had with Hunt might be made common knowledge hurt her so deeply, she relented with a sigh. "Get to the point, Walt. You always had a flair for the dramatic. I just want to warn you that juries may be impressed with your tactics, but I'm not."

"The chap we used is the soul of discretion," he began. "The kind of private investigator that fits very nicely into the woodwork of such places as the Plaza Hotel. Two grown-ups acting like a couple of silly teenagers wouldn't notice him at all, not even the faintest click of his camera."

Jemma kept her face impassive. Private investigator. Click of a camera. What the devil for? What in the world had her weekend away with Hunt to do with anything? She thought with sudden anguish of her divorce decree and how she had never made a move to change its repressive contents. She could see past Walt to the kitchen clock. If Hunt was on time, he'd be there with Seth in another quarter hour. She had to get rid of her ex-husband quickly.

"Stupid, Jemma," Walt was saying. He gave her a sly grin. "What in hell possessed you to bring the man back here for the night with our son in the house?"

Her intake of breath was audible, and Walt smiled when he caught it. Jemma stopped herself from screaming words of denial at him, simply because she remembered the advice Walt had given her while he was still in law school. *"Never offer any information. Just answer the question at hand, and that's all."* It was time to take his advice seriously. Seth wasn't in the house when Hunt was with her. What she did when her son wasn't around was her own business. As a lawyer, Walt might be faster on his feet than she was, but it struck her that she had a weapon best kept hidden for the time being.

"Priscilla can't have any children." The words were blurted out, and Jemma saw a look of extraordinary pain come over Walt's face, replaced almost at once by an air of bravado. "It's the last thing we expected," he went on, "but fortunately we have Seth."

Jemma concentrated on his eyes, on the brightness of the irises. She tried not to blink. She felt as if she were waiting for a sledgehammer to drop and crush her.

"You're at a turning point, Jemma." Walt's tone was his most reasonable. He leaned back against the wall in an effort to seem casual. "Things could really move for you if you had time at your disposal. He's my

only child, Seth. Frankly, I'd like to avoid a court fight
for his custody. It wouldn't be good for you. It
wouldn't be good for him. I want to be reasonable, and
I've thought it through carefully. You've been a good
mother to Seth, but your life is on a different track
now. He'll be the first one to suffer. Priscilla and I are
set up to give him everything he needs."

"All right, I've heard you," she burst in. "The answer is an unequivocal no."

"I'm not pushing you out," he went doggedly on in
an infuriatingly calm voice. "You can have the same
visiting rights as I have. I'll even sweeten the pot by
giving you some cash for your new enterprise. You'll
be on your way free and clear, and Seth will have the
kind of home he needs. Priscilla can cut down her
hours on the Family Court bench to be with him."

Family Court, it would all end up in Family Court.
Jemma felt as if the marrow had been drained from her
bones. She'd have to fight Walt and Priscilla on turf
they both knew exceedingly well.

"Good, you're being smart," Walt put in. "You're
thinking about it. Victor doesn't have to know a thing
about your professor. Not a bad catch, the head of the
Bosworth Foundation. I have to give you credit there."

"You're not in a position to give out chits of credit,
Walt. I'm truly sorry about Priscilla, but I'm not about
to hand her my son."

"The court will do the handing," he retorted.

"Good night," she said calmly, her hand still firmly
on the door.

He went past her without saying another word. She
closed the door behind him very quietly. She had
wanted to do something about her divorce decree, and

if Walt meant to fight her for their son, she'd counter-sue, if it took every penny she had.

Every penny. That very afternoon she and Ray Xeller had shaken hands, and now he had virtually everything she owned.

Her son's voice reached up through the dark thoughts and cloudy emotions that swirled through her brain. A squeal, a giggle and the slam of a car door. She raced to the bathroom, patted cold water on her face, then dotted on some lipstick. She was combing her hair when she heard Seth's chattering and laughter in the hall. She raced to open the front door and found him perched on Hunt's shoulders, the baseball cap plunked sideways on his head. She could see spills of everything he had eaten that day on his shirtfront. His laces were untied, and it even seemed as if his sneakers were on the wrong feet.

She managed a smile. "I see you guys had a good time." Hunt looked as disheveled as her son. His hair was mussed and his jeans had streaks of dirt on them. There was a rip in his shirtsleeve.

"I'm as good as Ron Darling," Seth announced. "Hunt said so. Hey, where's my bat and my glove?"

"Forgot," Hunt said. He swung Seth to the floor. "In the trunk of the car."

"Let's go get 'em," Seth said.

"A kiss first, young man," Jemma said.

Hunt grinned and spontaneously gave her a light kiss on the lips.

"Not you, I was talking to Seth."

Seth giggled and allowed Jemma to hug him.

"How do you keep up with him? I need a week in a rest home." Hunt reached over and pulled Seth's cap off and messed the boy's hair.

"Hey," Seth said and grabbed the hat and flopped it back on his head.

"Hungry?" Jemma asked.

"I don't think so." Hunt winked at Seth. "We had a bite before we hit the road, eh, kid?"

Seth looked sheepishly at his mother and then ran to Hunt and buried his face against Hunt's leg.

Jemma felt her heart flutter with all the possibilities of love that could never be. "Okay, out with it," she said hastily and with a rueful smile. "Did you fill yourselves up with junk food?"

"Of course not." Hunt feigned hurt. "We ate vegetables. Broccoli is one of Seth's favorites, right, kid?"

At that Seth fell to the floor laughing. "We had hot dogs and dinosaur hamburgers and pickles and French fries and pizza and soda and—"

"I thought we had a pact," Hunt broke in. "Remember, we swore on a stack of brachiosaurus."

"One thing I forgot to tell you about my son," Jemma said. "He can't keep a secret."

"Now the lady tells me." He reached for her and tried to pull her close.

"Hunt." She said it more sharply than she intended. "Seth, go get ready for your bath." She had not let her gaze stray from Hunt's.

"Can I get my bat?"

"Your bath."

The boy headed slowly for his room.

It was a moment before either of them spoke.

"He's a great kid," Hunt remarked. "Smart, easy to be with, and he made me think about what I was missing."

"I'm sure when you're ready, you'll have it all." The remark sounded false, even to her ears.

There was an instant of awkward silence before Hunt said, "How'd it go today, with Xeller, I mean."

"Oh." She had almost forgotten. "I agreed to purchase his place on a handshake and every asset I own."

"Happy?"

She turned from him and went quickly into the kitchen. "Of course I'm happy," she said, hoping he wouldn't hear the catch in her voice. "What more could I want?"

He came up behind her. "I know your life is here in Ramsey Falls and that you've just managed to tie it up in a neat little package with a sailor's knot that would be tough to undo. My life happens to be halfway across the world."

She turned to face him and without realizing it, laid her hand on his arm. "Don't, Hunt." She could feel his uncertainty. If she were to say anything, now was the time. She'd have to tell him about Walt and what lay ahead for her. She couldn't do that, couldn't burden him with it. The silence surrounded them, heavy with expectation and sudden heat.

He took her in his arms and kissed her.

"Mom?" Her son's voice issued from his room.

She broke away. "Be with you in a second, love."

"I'll get his bat and glove," Hunt said.

"Just leave them on the stairs," Jemma said. "I'll pick them up later."

"Mo-om."

"Coming, sweetheart." She hurried toward her son's room.

"Jemma."

She turned. Hunt was at the front door. She shook her head slowly.

"I'll be here until Sunday. It's inevitable that we'll meet, if not one way then another," he said.

She turned away, not daring to speak.

CHAPTER THIRTEEN

TUESDAY. Jemma thought of the impending week as a countdown, not to the celebration that would culminate in fireworks on Saturday night, but to the day after, to Sunday when Hunt would leave Ramsey Falls. When she returned to the shop on Tuesday after a buffet luncheon with members of the tricentennial committee, she found Adriana alone in the shop, operating the offset press. It clanked noisily, and she thought of how obsolete it was compared to the presses at Xeller Printing. She'd have to make decisions about what to keep, what to discard.

It took Jemma a couple of seconds to get Adriana's attention.

"Your mother called again," Adriana told her at once, "and said if you don't get back to her, she's going to report you as a missing person. And Professor Gardner called twice." The latter news was announced with a dimpled smile. "He said he'd call back."

Jemma rubbed a sudden itch on her arm. The week until his leaving was going to be a trying one, and she had no doubt Hunt would keep calling and she'd keep avoiding him. "Did Mrs. Lawson say when she'd have Seth back?"

"He's at his karate class. Then she's taking him over to the school. They're having a tryout for the Little League."

"He's too young for Little League," Jemma said.

"Well, he was carrying a baseball and a bat and wearing a baseball suit when he left, so I guess no one told him he's too young."

Jemma groaned. She hated to think of her son's disappointment and instinctively blamed Hunt Gardner for buying the uniform in the first place.

"Here are the rest of your messages," Adriana said, handing her half a dozen slips of paper, "and the order pad. Also, the shipment of twenty-pound stock came in and I stashed it under the counter. Oh, and your costume came from Sarah Crewes for the fair on Friday. It's *gorgeous*. She said you're going to be a gypsy fortune-teller."

"Complete with crystal ball. Sarah didn't send that along did she?"

Adriana shook her head. "She said she's still scouting one up. Oh, Mrs. Whiting, my mother made me the most incredible dress. Pale blue. I'm selling raffle tickets on the Ford, which isn't nearly as neat as telling fortunes."

I can't even predict my life five minutes from now, Jemma thought, feeling tired and impatient. Aloud she said, "You have to be a wise old lady like me to tell fortunes."

"Oh, Mrs. Whiting, old lady, gosh you're funny."

"Funny or not, I could use a tall glass of iced tea," Jemma said, "and a cold shower, but I think those are luxuries I may never have again." She went quickly into her office, opened her briefcase and withdrew an updated list of activities given to her by the tricentennial committee. "Adriana, how soon can I have the small press?" she called out. "I need two hundred copies of the new tri-bi schedule."

"Tri-bi," Adriana said, coming over to the window that separated the office from the shop. "That's what everybody's calling it. Do you realize Ramsey Falls is the laughing stock of the entire country?"

"I think we should be given a medal of honor for making the country laugh," Jemma said. "How about the press?"

"I just have one thing running, then it's all yours. Mrs. Whiting," Adriana said in a suddenly serious tone, "is it true you're buying Xeller Printing in Merriman?"

Jemma drew her brows together. "Is the news all over town?"

"I'm sorry, Mrs. Whiting."

"I wanted you to know, Adriana, but until everything is signed, sealed and delivered—"

"Keeping this place?"

"Yes, and you. It'll all work out, I promise you."

Adriana gave her a wide smile, but the ringing of the phone interrupted them.

"Do me a favor, Adriana, keep taking calls for me," Jemma said. "I've got to get the shopper's guide started or it'll never see the light of day."

Although the call was from a customer, Jemma realized that she might never again be able to hear the phone ring without hoping it was Hunt.

Hunt did phone Jemma later that afternoon, just before Adriana was about to leave for the day. Adriana shouted the message from the shop. "Mr. Gardner."

"I can't take it," Jemma said, although she had to stop herself from reaching for the receiver. She wanted to feel the stirring, the flurry of excitement when she heard his voice. But what was the point? It would be far easier to accept his leaving if she resigned herself at once. She bent low over her work in a fit of concentration. Not seeing him, not talking to him gave her the small measure of control she desperately needed.

"Mrs. Whiting, he said he just wanted to have a word with you."

"I'm sorry, honey, but it's impossible."

"Okay, I told him. He said to call him back."

"Adriana, put on the answering machine before you leave, and slip the latch on the front door. I'm so far behind, I may never come up for air."

Adriana came to the door and peered in at her. "Mrs. Whiting, he's leaving for Thailand on Sunday. That's the other end of the world. I'd give up winning the lottery before I'd refuse a call from Professor Gardner."

Jemma forced a laugh. "But you see, with Xeller Printing, I believe I've just won the lottery."

"Oh, Mrs. Whiting, you're so cool."

"HAD DINNER?" Ray Xeller was at the door of his shop beckoning Jemma in when she arrived in Merriman early Tuesday evening.

"A quick sandwich with my son," Jemma told him.

"A quick sandwich with your son." He shook his head disapprovingly. "I'd have guessed as much." Xeller was a small, garrulous man whom Jemma had liked from the first. "Eating is part of living," he went on, wagging a finger at her, "maybe the best part. I want you to remember that, Jemma."

She laughed. "My body remembers, but I'm afraid my time schedule doesn't."

"I've a good mind to send out for something. You'll be here, two, three hours at best. Come along, come along."

He left the door open and Jemma almost immediately understood why. The place was sweltering in the evening heat.

"It's that cockamamy air conditioner," Xeller said with a dismissive wave of his hand. "Don't let it worry you. I'll have everything shipshape when you take over. How about coffee?"

"Fine, I'd love some."

Xeller beamed and went rushing over to the coffee machine. Jemma caught the eye of a tall, burly man working a noisy press. She was surprised to find someone still there so late, but presumed he was Frank Quincy, who ran the shop for Xeller. He winked at Jemma, as if to tell her that Xeller was vaguely manic but nice, nonetheless. She smiled, feeling suddenly awkward and holding on to her shoulder bag and briefcase as though they were a life-support system. Looking around the printing shop, she wasn't certain which emotion was taking precedence, awe or simple panic. She had decided on a combination of both when Xeller came back with a ceramic mug filled to the brim.

"I sent the others home," Xeller explained to Jemma. "Too hot, and I figured they could wait a day to meet you. The idea this evening is to get generally acquainted with the paperwork. Tomorrow night you can learn who does what and how. The staff promised to stay a little late for you."

"It's the week of our tricentennial," Jemma said, "the worst time in the world for concentrating on anything but having a good time."

Xeller burst out laughing. "Right. Ramsey Falls, the town that couldn't count straight."

"Ray, I'm afraid that line is engraved on my heart."

"Well, don't let it get you down. Ramsey Falls is a pretty little town and don't let anyone tell you different. Frank," he bellowed, "come here and meet Jemma Whiting. And make a good impression. She's your new boss."

Frank Quincy came over, wiping his hands on a dirt-blackened rag. "We've talked on the phone," he said in a surprisingly soft voice.

"Yes, of course, the business cards and everything else we haven't been able to handle in Ramsey Falls. From what Mr. Xeller tells me, this place couldn't exist without you."

He gave her a broad grin. "I appreciate your keeping us all on."

"I'd be a fool to do anything less."

"Frank, soon as the press run is over, clean up and hightail it out of here. Your wife is going to have my head if I keep you a minute longer." Xeller took Jemma's arm and led her to a small office at the back. "The one thing I've always stressed is being on good relations with my employees and paying them well. It works to everyone's advantage. *Your* desk now," he said grandly, pulling out his worn leather swivel chair for her.

"My desk." She mentally added exhilaration to the awe and panic she was feeling. She had acquired full-time employees who were as dependent upon her as she was on them. She could never be casual again about the way she ran her business. Overwhelming as it was, Jemma didn't even try to repress a smile of joy and anticipation.

When Jemma stepped into her car three hours later, her mind was filled with new words: employee benefits, pension plans, sick days, vacation time, overtime. She was inheriting Xeller's personal attachment to the people on his staff. She agreed with him that it was the best way to keep a business running efficiently, especially when its owner wouldn't be on hand full-time.

She had everything riding on her acquisition of Xeller Printing. Although she might want to curl up in bed, pull the covers over her head and brood about Hunt, she would fill every hour of her time so that she'd be too busy to dig into her feelings. Her nights would be sleepless anyway.

WEDNESDAY AFTERNOON. The feeling of helplessness, of the wrong kind of anticipation, colored every move she made. Wednesday marked the opening ceremonies for the tri-bi, and yet for Jemma the excitement that had been gathering all summer was at a further remove than ever.

When Seth came running over to her, his smile revealed the fact that he had lost a front tooth before breakfast. "The parade! Yay, the parade!"

In the distance the sound of a marching band burst through the air, shaking the shop windows—drums pounding, tubas blaring, trombones and trumpets blasting. Hearing the music, Jemma felt a welcome quickening of her pulse. Like her son, she loved a parade.

"Mo-om, come on, we'll mith everything."

"Everything? The parade will go on for a couple of hours."

Shopkeepers on Main Street had agreed to shut down after the opening ceremonies at the town hall for the parade that followed.

"Mom, come *on*." Seth pulled at Jemma's shirt-sleeve.

"Just a second young man, hold your horses. I have to close up shop."

"I'll help you, then."

"No you won't. Just put your nose to the door and watch."

"I can't *thee*."

Jemma came over and peered through the glass. Curbside was already crowded, and a small child would have no chance of seeing the parade except from the front row or on someone's shoulders. "Seth, we can probably watch it better if we go upstairs and look out the front window."

"No, I want to thee it cloth up," he pleaded.

"Okay, you old nag." She gave a desultory look around and left without her usual checks and precautions. She'd have to come back and work late anyway. "Let's go. Just remember," she added, pushing her son gently out the front door, "stay close by. I don't want to lose you."

Seth nodded enthusiastically and promptly ran toward the crowd and burrowed through to the curb. All Jemma caught were the flags and banners as the high school band marched past. Off to the right was a minivan with a television crew setting up equipment. She went over, hoping to position herself close to the curb.

"You aren't from around here, are you?" she asked a young man in well-worn jeans.

"Nope. From the network. They think it's cute that you people got your dates all wrong."

"It's easy to lose a year when you're counting from zero to three hundred," she said.

"Hey, smart," he said, giving her an admiring grin. "Stick around, we'll put you on television."

"Try Sarah Crewes. It's all her fault for digging up the mistake." She escaped quickly, stepping past the van and out into the street. The high school band was marching briskly past in its bright yellow and and gold outfits. The noise was deafening. She checked along the crowded curb to where Seth should be sitting and discovered he wasn't there.

"Looking for Seth?" The owner of the local drug-store touched her arm.

"I guess I couldn't expect him to stay put," Jemma said. "He was at the curb a couple of minutes ago."

"You're looking down when you should be looking up. He's sitting on somebody's shoulders. There he is. Lost a tooth, I see."

"First one." Her son, indeed, was high above the crowd, grinning and holding a candy apple in one hand and a bright blue balloon in the other. She made her way back past the minivan to her son and found him on Hunt's shoulders. Hunt. Her reaction was one of un-restrained joy. Tears started to her eyes. Perhaps it was the parade. She always cried at parades.

"Hi, Mommy. Look where I am."

"Hi, honey. I couldn't miss you if I tried. Hello, Hunt."

"We wondered where you were, old Toothless and I. I figured a kid needs a balloon and a candy apple to get through a long day of parade watching, not to mention a pair of shoulders." Hunt offered her his own candy apple. "Have a bite. The look on your face suggests a long, serious deprivation of candy apples, isn't that so, Seth?"

"Yeah."

"I think you've just made my son the happiest kid in the world," Jemma said taking the candy apple from Hunt. It was obviously hand-dipped and sat crookedly on the stick, resembling all the homemade candy apples of her childhood. Hunt had already bitten into it. Jemma hesitated, then moved her tongue over the bite mark, her eyes holding his. "Delicious," she said, handing it back to him. "Brings back the best parts of my childhood."

"You'll have to tell me about them."

"It would take an age."

"Look," Seth cried, "old carth. Can I get down? I want to thee them from the curb."

"Sure thing," Hunt said, swinging the boy to his feet.

"Hold thith for me," Seth said, thrusting the sticky candy apple and balloon at his mother before squirming through the crowd again.

There was an awkward moment before Jemma spoke. "Antique cars. I suppose the one with the rumble seat is amongst them."

Hunt's answer had nothing to do with a parade of antique automobiles. "Why didn't you answer my calls?"

"Let's not go into it now."

"Jemma, I want to talk to you."

She shook her head and turned away, moving hurriedly toward her apartment door.

"Jemma." He came up behind her as she reached into her pocket for the key. "Why didn't you answer my calls?"

"Because I didn't want to."

"Why don't I believe that?"

"You want to take the last ounce of blood out of me," she said hotly. "It's over. There isn't any more."

"We had something wonderful together," he said, "I don't want it to end on a note of anger."

She tried with trembling fingers to turn the key in the lock. She could hear the rumble of the old cars, and to the south, trumpets blaring as another band came marching up Main. She didn't want to think about Hunt, to discuss phone calls or travel reservations made or the relentless passage of time, marching like so many high school bands. The only thing she knew was that she had to get away from him. "It's not anger," she said. "It's finality. The play is over. The curtain has come down. The theater is empty." She heard the faint click that released the door latch, and before pushing the door open added, "I don't understand what you want from me, Hunt."

He placed his hands on her arms and drew her around. His eyes searched her face. "I want the impossible."

Jemma shook her head slowly before turning away. "You won't find it in Ramsey Falls. I'm sorry." She slipped into the hallway and closed the door behind her. The corridor was cool and smelled pleasantly of wax. She brushed her hand along her forehead. It was over, *over*. Jemma turned and ran lightly up the stairs. She would watch the parade and keep an eye on Seth from the living room window. She loved parades. She always cried at parades.

THURSDAY. Countdown to Sunday, not to the moment on Saturday when Ramsey Falls would declare it was three hundred years old, minus a year.

The town never looked prettier, an amalgam of flags, flowers and banners. Mrs. Lawson exclaimed that it was as if Ramsey Falls had been tied up with a bright red taffeta ribbon. The excitement, unabated, drifted around Jemma, who went about her business in a daze. She had promised Ray Xeller that she would come to Merriman to learn how to operate the press that printed business cards and cut them all in a simple operation. Some time around noon Jemma realized she'd be running late. She picked up the telephone and dialed Ray Xeller. "I don't think I can make it to Merriman until after the celebration," she told him.

"You call me when you're ready, Jemma."

"How about Sunday?" she asked. "I'll be free all day."

"If you think you can concentrate, I'll be there," he said. "If not, do us both a favor and take it easy, treat yourself to a day of rest."

"I've got a couple of business card orders, Ray. I want to learn that press operation. I'll see you early."

When she replaced the receiver, she turned her attention to a customer. No use contemplating her deliberate tying up of her Sunday, all day. Business cards. The first one would be Whiting Printing with two addresses on it and two telephone numbers.

Hunt did not call on Thursday, but she had no luck tucking him to the back of her mind. At least four people, including Adriana, found reasons for mentioning him. The last to do so was Celie, who wanted her to come to a small dinner she was giving for Hunt.

"Spontaneous, Jemma. It just sneaked up on us, his going away on Sunday. I hate it when everything comes to a culmination, and then pouf, it's all gone and you're left contemplating your navel."

"I'm afraid you'll have to count me out, Celie. I'm keeping the store open late tonight."

"But Hunt! I'd have thought you of all people."

Jemma cut her off at once. "Business before pleasure, Celie. You're talking to a workaholic, the genuine article."

"So I see. Incidentally, allow me to congratulate you on grabbing Xeller Printing. I wanted it but my accountant warned me off." She paused, then gave an embarrassed laugh. "Well, you know what I mean."

"I know what you mean, Celie."

"You're a good sport, Jemma, you always were. We really ought to have lunch one day."

"You're on, as soon as we're out from under." Celie had softened in the most curious way, Jemma thought and couldn't quite put her finger on why. Celie might always say what was on her mind, but the old harshness was gone.

Jemma kept the shop open until nine, the dinner party on her mind all that time. Hunt with Celie. Hunt with Victor. Hunt being toasted and telling stories of what he had done or what he expected to do in Thailand.

Business at the shop was brisk until the moment of her closing for the night. The posters of Ramsey Falls sold well in spite of the price tag. As the official printer for the tricentennial, Jemma went in for her share of ribbing. She was interviewed by newspaper and television reporters who seemed to think that she was stuck with unsold souvenirs. Precisely the opposite had happened. When she turned the key in the street door lock, Whiting Printing was completely sold out of souvenirs, and Jemma decided to carry the postcards in her regular inventory.

FRIDAY. The ache in Jemma's heart was replaced by a dull sense of something gone awry. What amazed her was how well she was able to function under the circumstances. On a couple of occasions, her son asked for Hunt and sulked when he learned that Hunt Gardner wouldn't be around anymore. That Seth didn't ask for his father puzzled Jemma, until she reasoned that the celebration was being held on the weekend he was to visit his father. Merriman was, in Seth's mind, a long way from Ramsey Falls, a long way from fireworks and more parades and parties.

Jemma knew she'd have to swallow her pride and talk to Walt about it. After dinner, she stood with Seth in front of the shop, waiting for his father to come for him. Seth was unnaturally quiet and Jemma's heart went out to him. When the car pulled up she saw that the chauffeur had come alone. She was informed that Walt was out for the evening.

"Can I come back tomorrow?" Seth asked her entreatingly.

She exchanged a glance with the chauffeur who gave the boy a sympathetic smile but said nothing.

Jemma ruffled her son's hair. "I'll talk to your father, okay? I'm sure he'll do everything in his power to make sure you don't miss the celebration." She could see a sob bubbling up and hastily gave him a kiss. Long after the car disappeared down Main Street, she remained at the curbside. He looked so small and vulnerable sitting in the front seat with only the top of his towhead visible. She had a feeling that Walt, by not picking up Seth himself on a weekend he knew was important to the boy, was making a statement. Seth was now a pawn in a battle his father had every intention of winning.

THE FIRST THING one noticed about the seventeenth-century fair on the grounds of Pack College were the banners and flags draped from tall ribbon-entwined poles, then the blue-and-white-striped tents and then the baroque music played by groups of roving minstrels, dressed in seventeenth-century costume. A scent of barbecue smoke and fresh popcorn hung over the grounds. Candy apples were in great supply. At the fringes of the fair, a small amusement park had been rigged up, complete with a Ferris wheel and games of chance.

Jemma arrived at dusk wearing her gypsy costume, which was composed of several layers of multicolored skirts, a red silk blouse that rode low over her shoulders, and a black cummerbund twisted around her waist. She wore a sequined turban, with large gold hoops dangling from her ears. She had carefully applied glistening makeup and a dark beauty spot at the corner of her mouth.

The grounds were already crowded. Excited children ran everywhere. Seth should be with her, she thought, but attempts to reach Walt had been fruitless and her patience was worn thin. She left a strongly worded message with his housekeeper and hoped Walt would forget his rancor enough to bring Seth to Ramsey Falls on Saturday for the fireworks.

Good sense hadn't been written into her divorce decree, either. Even if Walt had dropped the idea of fighting her for custody of Seth, she had made up her mind about one thing. She was going to court to have the decree changed to a more equitable one. It was a fight she was certain she'd win.

The tent given over to fortune-telling was small, situated near a white-elephant table manned by Sarah Crewes.

Sarah was dressed in pale pink with a white lace collar, her hair a mass of ringlets. "Jemma? That you?" She smiled and tilted her head prettily. "I've never seen you so gussied up. You certainly are one exotic gypsy."

"Well, thanks for the costume. You look very beautiful and very seventeenth-century. How are things going?"

"You'd be surprised at the junk people own and what people will buy." She waved her hand over the table of oddments. "Incidentally, your Professor Gardner stopped by and donated a bunch of paperbacks on philosophy, unread."

Jemma blanched. "My Professor Gardner." Knowing the fair was being held on the grounds of Pack College was bad enough; there was every probability that she'd run into Hunt. Their affair, which seemed to be on everyone's lips, was another thing entirely. *Did* everyone know, or was she just imagining it?

"You know what I mean," Sarah said and Jemma thought that no, she didn't. "Crystal ball's in the tent," Sarah added hastily. "It's old and a little scratched but venerable and absolutely guaranteed to reveal the future. I'll be in for a personal reading later on."

"Happy selling," Jemma said, deciding there was nothing to Sarah's remark, after all, merely a guess that unfortunately hit the bull's-eye.

There was a sign outside the tent that read Madame Jemma Lazanga, Gypsy Fortune-Teller. $5.00.

The interior of her tent had been prettily bedecked with an old-fashioned lamp on the table providing a soft, mysterious glow. Facing the table were two folding chairs with Turkish pillows on the seats. The chair she was to use was recognizably from Victor's garden room and had obviously been appropriated by Sarah. It was white wicker with a soft cushion seat. The table was covered with a Persian carpet that smelled vaguely of mothballs. A wooden cash box sat off to one side. The crystal ball had been polished to a high shine, although the top was laced with tiny scratches as though hands thick with rings had caressed it over the years.

Jemma had never examined the heart of a crystal ball before. She gazed down at it, holding the carved rosewood base between her hands. How dense it seemed, how thick with molten glass that refused to reveal its depths.

Neither crystal balls, nor dreams, nor expectations, nor hopes could envision what Jemma's future held. Once Sunday came and went, absolute reality would be the rule; Walt and his threats to take his son would fill her life, and all this tri-bi nonsense and the kisses of Hunt Gardner would be so much history.

"Five dollars? I expect my future to be told until the twenty-first century with that kind of money." It was Celie, a five-dollar bill in her hand, her favorite rose-scented perfume filling the tent. "You look like a proper gypsy, Jemma." She sat down and gestured toward the crystal ball. "Go ahead, tell me the good news."

Jemma took the money and with great ceremony placed it in the wooden box. Then with an attempt at seriousness, she bent over the crystal ball and slowly passed her hand over it. "I zee great sings in your future," she said. "I zee a figure of a man."

"Lovely. You're on the right track, Madame Lazanga."

"Ah, I zee more. I zee a lufly houze, and a great lawn. What what's zis? A fashionable party. A wedding? Could it be a wedding?"

"Never mind the wedding," Celie said. "I'd like a little more information on the fine figure of a man."

"Glasses. I zee glasses."

"In his hand or on his face?"

"Oh, on his faze." She was surprised to hear Celie's expelled breath of satisfaction and looked up quickly. Victor. The notion hit Jemma with extraordinary force. A lucky guess, or had it been in the air all along? She repressed a smile and turned back to the crystal ball. "Oh, ze picture she is fading," she said with a shrug. "Going down ze years into ze twenty-first century. Yes, my dear, wiz glasses."

Celie stood up and smoothed her dress. She reached across the table and offered Jemma her hand. "Madame Lazanga, as a reader of crystal balls, I'm going to recommend you to all my friends."

Jemma had little time after that to contemplate the development she had stumbled across. The cash box filled up, the crystal ball was much consulted and when at last her eyes threatened to close from overuse, a tall figure entered the tent.

"Madame Lazanga?"

"Ze same."

"I came for a reading."

"Five dollars, please." She didn't even try to still the fluttering of her heart.

Hunt Gardner stood at the entrance for a moment, his eyes never leaving her face. She felt the warmth ride slowly to her cheeks under his scrutiny and felt an unexpected ache chase through her at the sight of him and the seriousness with which he contemplated her.

"Come in," she said, at last finding her voice.

He bent his head in acknowledgement and handed her a ten-dollar bill before sitting down.

"We don't tell the future twice," she told him.

He waved away the change. "Once will suffice."

She bent over the crystal ball, wondering if at last something would materialize out of its mysterious depths.

"Looks as if you're trying to pick your way through the jungle on a South Seas island," Hunt remarked.

"It is a forest of sorts," Jemma said, "but whether here in Ramsey Falls or at the other end of the world, I can't tell." She looked up at him and caught an expression in his eyes that mirrored her own confused emotions. "But I see a future scarcely different from the present," she went on, gazing quickly down at the crystal ball. "I see a man alone. I see him waving goodbye to someone. I suspect it's a gesture he has made more than once in his life. I see a man who has discovered a dozen different ways to say the same thing—goodbye. He attempts to disguise from himself that he's a man with no hold on the present, no commitment, no roots. Perhaps he doesn't even realize how little his life changes, how his future resembles the present and no doubt the past. It's the way he likes to live, saying hello and then saying goodbye." Jemma hesitated, then added, "He must be a happy man." She looked up, surprised to find Hunt frowning. "Happy, Professor?"

But his answer was thwarted by a call from outside the tent. "Madame Lazanga, there's a line a mile long here waiting for a reading."

Hunt rose quickly to his feet. "I'd say that's ten dollars worth," he told her. He turned and left the tent and as her next customer pushed his way in, Jemma realized that Hunt hadn't even said goodbye.

SATURDAY MORNING brought a terse call from Walt. He informed Jemma that he had intended all along to take Seth to Ramsey Falls for the celebration. Before hanging up, Jemma had given him a simple thank you, but Walt's few words told her everything. The old overbearing superiority of tone was gone, replaced by an icy formality. She knew it was only a matter of time before he'd make his move to gain custody of their son.

And, as usual, Jemma kept everything to herself, consulting no one, although it would have helped to shout her anxiety to the whole world.

The whole world, it seemed, crowded into Ramsey Falls and its environs on Saturday. Main Street was beflowered, ballooned and bannered from one end to the other. At noon a biplane appeared overhead trailing a congratulatory message. At one o'clock, a crop-duster did some acrobatic tricks against a clear blue sky, spelling out Ramsey Falls on its tricentennial, and as usual, the wrong date of incorporation.

In the afternoon there was a bike-a-thon, which came down Main Street, while over in the high school auditorium the new junior class performed an enactment of the famous "Legend of Painted Creek." This was followed by a musical put on by the Ramsey Falls Theatrical Society of the original Ramsey arriving with his bride at the falls.

There were tours of the district's historic houses and an impressive art exhibition in the town hall by the painters of the Hudson River School. All four of the area's churches held book fairs and offered inexpensive lunches.

As a member of the tricentennial committee, Jemma, in spite of all her peregrinations through Ramsey Falls that day, didn't bump into her son or Hunt. About not seeing Hunt, she felt grateful; if running into Seth meant a confrontation with Walt, she felt it best they didn't meet. When she at last returned to her apartment at six and kicked off her shoes, she was exhausted and oddly exhilarated. She was proud of the party her town had put on, and with her natural high spirits, decided to give her worries a holiday, at least until after closing ceremonies, which would culminate in a fireworks display.

Jemma heard the telephone ringing just as she stepped out of the shower. She grabbed a towel and raced for it. There was something about Hunt still being in Ramsey Falls that made the telephone an instrument of hope.

It was Victor, and she had to swallow a combination of disappointment and relief that it wasn't Hunt. "All ready for the big ball tonight?"

"I expect I'll be there about nine, nine-thirty," Jemma said. "I've skipped all invitations to dinner."

"Let me send the car for you."

"I'll see you there, Victor," she said gaily. "And don't forget, I'm picking up the dog on my way back from Merriman on Sunday. Surprise for Seth when he returns from his weekend with Walt."

"Sure you still want the dog?"

"Sure I'm sure. See you soon."

When she stepped into her car three hours later, Jemma wore a black cotton halter-top dress, cut artfully low in front, that left her back bare to her waist. She wore high-heeled, slim-strapped sandals. She had hesitated over her jewelry, however. The tiny diamond earrings that Hunt had given her beckoned—and the gold locket. "B.W. Forever. M.S." Who were they, she wondered, fingering the old, satiny gold. Had it been forever? Then with a sigh and without further thought, she put both the earrings and the locket on. She'd leave B.W. and M.S. to Sarah Crewes.

The tricentennial ball was held outdoors on the sloping grounds of an old and venerable vineyard above the river. Jemma arrived in time to hear a number of self-congratulatory speeches that threatened to continue on until the display of fireworks. But at somewhere close to ten, a hush fell over the huge crowd attending the party, and everyone began to move naturally down the lawn to the cliff that scalloped the river. Jemma, wanting to be alone, drifted away from Celie and Victor and Sarah Crewes. She took her shoes off and wandered along a winding path that led through an herb garden, then past a display of small fruit trees, to come up at last to an outcropping of rocks above the river.

The fireworks barge sat stolidly in the middle of the river, with a small fire tug standing by. Off to her left, at the opposite end of the grove of fruit trees, she could see the gathering of people all along the cliff. She sat down close to the cliff edge on a flat-topped stone, clasping her hands around her legs. She cried at parades and felt a lump in her throat at fireworks. She wanted to be surrounded by the magic, to have it explode around her as though to illustrate her breaking heart.

She heard a rustling behind her and hugged her legs tighter. Damn! She wasn't fated to have the place to herself, after all. When the sound stopped several feet away, however, and there was a few seconds' silence, Jemma instinctively knew that somehow in that secret and remote place Hunt had found her.

"No," he said quietly, coming up behind her, "I didn't follow a silken thread laid down by Ariadne. I saw you come over here and willed you to be alone."

There was a sudden sizzle in the sky as the fireworks began, an opening starburst, an explosion of pale yellow that reached out toward them with a thousand fingers and then withdrew and disappeared. There was a rise of rockets, then another and another, the sky resounding with a hollow, thunderous sound, sizes and shapes and colors of fire in an outpouring, a rivalry, an impermanence that came and went so quickly, it could not even burn into memory. Hunt came over and sat down beside her, placing his hands on her cool skin and clasping her close.

The display stopped for a moment, and the watchers continued to stare at the sky, wanting more. Jemma felt his grip tighten, felt the strong beating of his heart against her bare skin and at last the touch of his lips to her shoulder, her neck, and then his cheek on hers. They sat quietly, gripped by the stillness, knowing there was nothing more to be said.

Then came a fresh overture, the pop of more fireworks, short sequined bursts one after the other as though trying to crowd the sky. It was ephemeral, wanton, reaching a grand crescendo in ever-widening circles of red, white and blue and then blackness with only the lights of the shore opposite and the stars providing a reminder of reality.

"It's all over," Jemma said, turning in his arms. He wore a tuxedo, his shirt collar open at the neck and his tie undone. Knowing it could be a memory that would haunt her for the rest of her life, she hungrily took in the sharpened shadows of his face, the heightened lights of his brow, his strong nose and well-chiseled chin. And she was aware of the way he watched her with an equal hunger.

"Gone with a bang and nary a whimper," he said at last. "Will you celebrate next year? You have all those tricentennial banners. It would be a mistake to let them go to waste."

She shook her head no. "It's all over, Hunt. Everything. There is no more. It was fun while it lasted. Perhaps more than will ever happen again."

He raised her chin with his hand and kissed her, a kiss that was simple, as though it, too, sealed a memory. "Forever," he said quietly when he released her. He touched the locket and then the earrings and seemed about to say something when she shook her head.

"Some forevers are meant to be locked away, Hunt, in a box full of shiny beads and fireworks. It's dangerous to release them." She drew out of his arms and stood, then in another moment, clasped her arms around his neck and kissed him slowly, once more savoring the taste of his mouth as though it were the most exotic of spices. "All over," she said, then turned quickly and walked away, knowing he would not, could not follow her.

CHAPTER FOURTEEN

THE UNIVERSITY reserved a room for Hunt at the Oriental Hotel in Bangkok. There was a planned week of high-level meetings with government officials before he'd be able to get away into the countryside. What he hated most was the time-consuming formality of the bureaucracy when all he wanted to do was set his program in motion where it was most needed. All the rest was flowery embroidery meant to impress foreign journalists, local reporters and government officials who had to approve matching funds.

And worst of all, the one man whom he had particularly wished to see, General Suthee Tantemsapya, had taken himself off to a monastery for a six-months period of meditation. Just like him, Hunt thought, hiding his disappointment. It was the general who had successfully guided Hunt's request for matching funds through labyrinthine government channels. Together they had worked out a successful approach to the problem of adult illiteracy in Thailand, and now the man was sitting in a monastery somewhere trying to get in touch with his soul.

With or without Tantemsapya, scheduled meetings and lunches and dinners dragged on, and Hunt counted the days until the weekend when Max Tam would arrive, and they'd head for the countryside.

Hunt had been to Thailand more than once; he was always charmed by the warmth of its people and the beauty of its women. This time, however, he was restless, impatient for things to begin, *and* to be over with. Part of him still resided in the States, in Ramsey Falls with Jemma.

Hunt hadn't been able to shake the memory of that last moment with Jemma and what struck him as its utter finality. This, in spite of the dramatic change of scenery from the calm green mountains and the cool ribbon of the Hudson River, to the brightly plumed bird that was Bangkok.

He had stopped as planned in Minnesota on his route west, arriving at the Gardner farm around dusk. He had to touch base, to see his family and be among familiar surroundings, to face the muddled thoughts that somehow wouldn't come into focus. His family gathered around Hunt, leaving him little time for solitude, for which he was thankful. It was his mother who at last drew him shrewdly aside just before his flight out.

"Hunt, have you anything to tell me?" she asked. She was a tall, slender woman, silver-haired and with eyes as deeply dark as her son's. If she and Hunt's father disapproved of their son's restlessness, neither ever showed it.

He grabbed his mother and soundly kissed her. "You could always read my mind," he said. "I can't tell you how hard I tried to avoid you when I first discovered girls."

"I can still read your mind," she said playfully, ruffling his hair and then with a quick, absent-minded gesture, straightening his collar.

"Everything?"

"I can tell when you're not happy. What's wrong?"

He thought that, like Jemma, he kept his own advice, and it wasn't always a good idea. "It's a woman," he said after a moment, and at once felt a long pent-up release.

"Now why is that a problem?"

"Trust me to find someone very down-home like you, but with enough problems to stuff a Thanksgiving turkey. She has a small business, which she's determined to make a success of, an ex-husband who forced a repressive divorce decree on her and a young son she'd never consider dragging all over the world."

His mother gazed at him for a while. "She must be something special."

"She is. Although why she has to be the one woman in the world with her feet nailed to the ground..." With a shrug he left the sentence unfinished.

"Maybe both of you want it that way."

"Maybe. Maybe she's afraid of a new commitment."

"And maybe you are, too."

"My commitment is to my work," he said, kissing his mother on the forehead. "And that's the end of that."

The talk with his mother hadn't settled anything except to confirm that he wore his dilemma on his sleeve for everyone to see. In Bangkok Hunt spent restless evenings wandering the bubbling, energetic city of skyscrapers and golden temples. He tried to lose himself amongst narrow lanes alive with shops selling exotic, scented fruits and colored silks, with wandering the grid of *klongs*, canals throughout the city where the native Thais live and upon which their entire lives are carried out.

He was a man trapped by a memory, however. In some ways he was a tourist, a sightseer looking in at the windows of his own life—a glimpse, and then on to some other foreign place. There had been women before Jemma, women more suited to his life-style, and he had let them go. He told himself that when he was in the field and busy, when he was away from the sheer beauty and the clamor of this spectacular, golden city, he'd come to his senses. No, indeed, he wasn't going to be snared into something that could put an end to his career, tie him to one tiny corner of the world and probably curl his hair with boredom.

THEY WERE IN THE MIDST of the monsoon season. A daily downpour of rain, mercifully short and usually in the afternoon, kept the countryside cool and verdant. Four weeks into the trip his small educational entourage arrived in a hamlet in Tahi, not far from the monastery where General Tantemsapya had gone to meditate. Somewhere along the line, Hunt planned to see the general, to let him know that his inspired approach to the problem of adult illiteracy was proving successful. And the truth was, he wanted to talk with him, perhaps even to take up where his conversation with his mother had left off.

There was nothing about this small community, sitting amidst sodden rice paddies under cloud-dappled skies, to make it any different from the others. The interest of community elders had to be piqued, local problems isolated in a series of informal meetings, and a method of teaching remedial reading to adults accomplished, all in record time. Hunt, Max Tam and the government official accompanying them on their tour would often leave a village in the midst of a conflict over local problems brought to light by Hunt's team, and no peace in sight. The real result of their work was far more subtle. What was left behind were adults raised out of lethargy and on the road to helping themselves.

Adult literacy classes in this quiet little place were held in a small, but remarkably beautiful, Buddhist temple where tables and chairs were set up and there was a scent of incense in the air. An earlier meeting with the town elders had established that the particular problem was the usual one in Tahi. Animals were kept under houses for protection and warmth—an unsanitary habit but one the natives were loathe to change.

Max Tam was well suited to the work. A natural charmer, he was at ease in the countryside and quickly won the respect of village elders. Tam, working with young local teachers, showed them cards upon which key words were printed. "*House* and *animals*," he explained. "These are the words around which discussions will be held. We're going to divide the class in half—those who are for keeping animals under houses, and those against. The cards are to be taken home and shown to other adults, so that everyone in the village is involved in this problem of house, animals and unsanitary conditions."

"The beauty of this," Hunt had long before pointed out to the Thai official accompanying them, "is the easy way adults tackle their own illiteracy along with local problems."

"Tackle is right," the official had said. "You'll leave behind you a lot of broken heads."

Days, as usual for Hunt, were busy enough to keep him from thinking about Jemma. Nights were tougher.

While he was used to primitive accommodations, Hunt often wondered whether his anxious, sleep-tossed, dream-heated restlessness was noticed by Max Tam or his hosts. It was Tam, in that small hamlet in the Thai countryside, who took Hunt aside one day.

"Want to tell me what your problem is?" he asked. "You've been off track since you left Ramsey Falls."

"Ramsey Falls," Hunt murmured. "Was that place real?"

"Thailand's the dream," Tam said, "and the trouble is, I think it's turning into a nightmare for you."

THE MONASTERY SAT in the flat countryside like a mirage, a huge temple with a golden roof glistening in the morning sun.

Hunt waited in the courtyard while monks in saffron robes, their heads shaved, went about their business, unmindful of the stranger in their midst. The place was alive, chattering and buzzing with their voices. Fragrant flowers mingled with incense to fill the air with a kind of peace and enchantment Hunt had never known.

When General Tantemsapya found him, Hunt made no effort to hide his surprise. The last time they had met, the General was resplendent in a perfectly tailored army uniform, his silken black hair full and luxurious, a trim mustache curved above a strong, resourceful mouth. Now he was clean-shaven and his robe hid the muscular angles of his body.

"I was surprised to learn you had given up your former life," Hunt said.

"It was time. I am a Buddhist. No matter how good the work is that one has done, no matter how perfect one's life seems to be, it's in our religion to enter a monastery for a period of time, to search for new answers to the meaning of life.''

"Your education program," Hunt began.

"It will do quite well without me. At any rate, I'll be back in uniform in another three months. Maybe I'll have a clearer idea of what I am meant to do."

"And will you take on the trappings of your former life? The luxury, the power?"

The general laughed. "Perhaps. It has its place, I suppose, but one must examine the nature of existence. If we don't take the time to ask ourselves what is important, then how can we be sure of anything?" He stopped, and his brilliant eyes seemed to reach deep into Hunt's soul. "You're in trouble, aren't you?"

Hunt nodded.

It was a few moments before Tantemsapya spoke, and when he did, his words were measured. "There's something humbling about taking a bowl and begging for food, about being dependent upon others for kindness and even your survival. Sometimes it's necessary to shield your eyes from the lights this world uses to disguise the blackness beyond."

"Not blackness this time," Hunt said. "In a way too much light, too much good light, like the sun."

"Be truthful to yourself," Tantemsapya said. "It's one thing to follow where the mind tells you to go, but the heart speaks as well. Perhaps you're closing a door that should best be kept open. Perhaps you need to open your heart to the truth, whatever that may be, to allow someone to touch your soul."

Hunt didn't answer. It was coming to an end, he thought, the wanderlust, the loneliness he had never defined before.

The general sat back, his hands on his knees. "My way isn't your way, Hunt. Perhaps you've been a stranger in a foreign land for too long."

"Could it be that simple?" Hunt asked.

Tantemsapya smiled. "I think you know the answer to that question."

WITHOUT A WORD Seth climbed a chair and pulled the postcard from the bulletin board in her office, where Jemma had stuck it. He examined the picture carefully, a traditional one of golden temples against a sky of iridescent blue, then discarded it.

"That's from Professor Gardner," Jemma said. "He's in Thailand." From under her desk came the soft movement of a half-grown puppy stirring. "Want to take Niko out for a walk?"

Seth shook his head, stalked out of the office without answering and went over to Jemma's new full-time employee, who was working the offset press. Niko, from the first, had become her dog, Seth playing with him in the evening merely as a device for staying up late. The animal was friendly, obliging and best of all, company through long quiet evenings.

Jemma picked up the postcard and read Hunt's brief comment. "Continuation of long hot summer. Work extremely satisfying." No return address, no love, no miss you. Why the postcard, then? She thought about throwing it away, heard her son's reedy voice through the office door and propped the card against her desk lamp with the picture facing forward. The card had arrived two weeks after Hunt's mailing it in mid-August.

Jemma returned to her bookkeeping, aware of a numbness in her soul. It was a numbness, however, that came not from the deep exhaustion brought on by too many cares, but from the realization that Hunt still occupied the dead center of her being.

She fell asleep late every night and woke sharply and too early in the morning, knowing that Hunt had been there with her every moment, moving like a shadow, touching her with light, remembered fingers.

Perhaps her memories and her dreams were the only order in her disordered life. Seth was restless, ready for school still a week away. And Walt had been true to his word about wanting custody of their son. The case was scheduled for Family Court a week after Labor Day, a week after Seth would begin school. Jemma was in full possession of two printing shops and, she congratulated herself, her senses. So much in control that she was determined to go into Family Court representing herself. She had profound belief in the integrity of the court. Walt had no case at all. She had never violated the divorce decree. She could prove, with Mrs. Lawson's deposition, that Seth wasn't at home the one time that Hunt had stayed with her through most of the night. Only one thing made her determined to go through with it: to stop Walt from believing he could call the shots.

There was a light knock on the office door and Sarah Crewes poked her head through. "Hi, can I come in?"

"What are you doing here? I thought you were in New York?"

"This is New York. I'm down for the weekend. It's Saturday, remember?"

"Saturday, right, I've been scribbling that date all morning. What the devil's happening to my brain? Sit down, Sarah. Want some coffee?"

"I'll help myself. Victor told me to stop by and shake some sense into you."

Jemma sighed wearily. "Both he and Celie tell me that a fool is someone who takes herself into Family Court without a lawyer. I don't need a lawyer, I don't want a lawyer, and I can't afford a lawyer. I'm chock full up to here with lawyers and debts, and I'm banking on the judge knowing how to read. One, that divorce decree, and two, Mrs. Lawson's deposition. People go unlawyered into Family Court all the time, Sarah."

Sarah came over with a mug of black coffee and sat down. "Your husband's a barracuda."

"Really?" Jemma smiled at her. "You mean it shows?"

"His wife's a Family Court judge. For all you know, everyone involved had dinner together last night. You need a lawyer, Jemma."

"Walt doesn't have a case."

"You aren't listening, Jemma. Celie, Victor and I—"

"Celie, Victor—strange how those two have ganged up against me. And you. I expect, Sarah Crewes, that you're the leader."

"Against you? Ganged up?" Sarah stared at her incredulously. "Has it ever occurred to you that you have friends who care about you? Who care about Seth, who think you're brave and terrific, and who'll never forgive you if you botch up because you think you need help from no one?"

"I accepted financial help from Victor," Jemma protested.

"The Bosworth Foundation gives away money, Victor doesn't. He didn't *give* you anything, Jemma. He helped you obtain financing for a business he knew was solvent. He isn't a fool. This custody fight with Walt is different. Victor pays his law firm a per annum fee. He wants you to agree to having a lawyer in court with you. You can argue your own case, but he'll be there if your ex pulls any tricks."

"I won't be able to pay Victor back until the Ramsey Falls' quadricentennial."

Sarah came over to Jemma and put an arm around her friend's shoulder. "My cousin does care what happens to you, but he understands about Hunt."

Jemma glanced at the postcard. "Everyone seems to know about Hunt," she said slowly, "except there's nothing to know."

"There's everything to know," Sarah said quietly. "Victor wanted to telex him in Bangkok—"

"Sarah, he wouldn't—"

"Celie and I told him you'd never forgive him."

Jemma turned in her chair and gazed out the window. The golden light of a late summer sun suffused Main Street. How beautiful it was, this quiet, hidden world of ordinary people going through their ordinary lives. "I can handle it," she told Sarah. "I don't want Hunt coming back because he feels sorry for me. And I don't want to intrude upon his life, his plans, because of a problem that has essentially nothing to do with him. Walt wants our son, and Hunt Gardner was an extremely useful peg to hang a custody battle on."

"Hunt Gardner loves you," Sarah said. "Isn't that enough?"

Jemma turned back and looked at her friend. "How do you know, Sarah? How do you really know?"

Sarah gazed at her for a long moment before speaking. "He's the man who came from a long way away and took your heart, that's how I know."

"OFF TO SCHOOL NOW." Jemma gave her son a pat on the fanny and saw him into the bus that would take him to the elementary school a mile out of town. Poor lamb, she thought, as the bus moved slowly down the street; he had no idea what was happening.

Earlier in the week she had taken her son into Merriman to be questioned by the Family Court judge handling the custody case and two psychiatrists, one representing Walt and Priscilla, and the other Jemma's interests. Later, at home, she asked Seth what had happened, but he merely dug his toe into the rug and said, "Nothing."

Nothing. Except the rest of their lives.

She was due in Family Court in Merriman at nine o'clock, and before she stepped into her car, Jemma glanced quickly at herself in the glass store front. Dressed in a trim black suit and white blouse with a soft print scarf, Jemma wanted to appear conservative, stylish, businesslike, attractive, strong, vulnerable, smart, the perfect mother. She was, in other words, counting on one lonely black suit to do the job.

She met the lawyer Victor had recommended, Bradford Kent, on the steps of the county courthouse. He was young, intense, with a trigger-quick mind, and she had liked and trusted him from the first.

"You look great," he said, enthusiastically shaking her hand. "Son get off to school all right?"

"He couldn't understand why Mommy wasn't wearing jeans. Brad," she said as they hurried into the courthouse, "I haven't slept a wink all night."

"I told you not to worry. It'll all work out. Your ex-husband doesn't have a case."

"My husband isn't a dummy, and he has a lot of friends in this town."

"Justice," the young man said with an acerbic smile, "may not be one of them."

Theirs was the first case to be heard; Walt would have seen to that. The hearing was held in a small, paneled room with the air-conditioning going full blast. It was empty of auditors but for three people in the front row, one of whom was the psychiatrist Jemma had hired to examine Seth. Sarah, Victor, and even Celie, had offered to come as support, but Jemma said no. She had no idea what punches Walt would pull and who he might involve. This was between her and her ex-husband, and one way or another she was determined to write *finis* to his hounding her.

Jemma had been in court before when her divorce became final, but she had almost no memory of the event. She was no longer the meek and stunned wife pushed through a divorce by someone who knew what he wanted and precisely how to go about getting it. She'd remember everything that happened this time, from the squeak of the court stenographer's shoes to the officer stationed at the door.

Walt was already seated, papers spread out on the table before him. He was, as usual, dressed impeccably. At his side was an equally well-dressed gentleman, his law partner she presumed. Priscilla wasn't there; as a judge in Family Court, her appearance would have been improper. It was, Jemma thought sardonically, the first *proper* thing Priscilla had done since she had met and married Walt Whiting.

Jemma was seated and conferring with Brad when the judge came in, a dark-haired man with a deeply lined face and an intelligent, curious glance that quickly took in everyone in the court.

"He's okay," Brad whispered. "Fair. Don't tighten up, Jemma. He runs a pretty informal court, and Walt's histrionics won't go down well with him."

The judge spent a few minutes studying the papers before him, his brow furrowed. "Whiting versus Whiting," he said, looking up. For the first time Jemma felt a long charge of fear rush through her. She had been busy, worried and entirely too cool. Now the reality of losing her son hit her with full force. Brad sensed it and put a hand on her arm.

"Relax, Jemma, you need your wits about you."

She took a deep swallow of air. "I'm all right."

"Let's see, change of venue for custody of son, Seth Whiting, six years old," the judge went on, "from his mother's care to his father's, is that it?" He looked at Walt, then at Jemma.

Hearing his easy tone, his unexpected lack of formality, Jemma let go the long breath she seemed to have been holding forever.

Walt stood up. "I believe circumstances have changed in the past few months and that my son's interests would be better served if he lived with my wife and me."

"What circumstances, Mr. Whiting?"

"In direct opposition to our divorce decree, which forbids it, my ex-wife has had her lover stay overnight with my son in the house."

Jemma started, but Brad shook his head, once more pressing her arm as a warning to stay calm.

"Let's see, where's that divorce decree?" The judge shifted through his papers.

"I have a copy," Brad offered.

"No, here it is. Now on what page?" He flipped through it quickly until he found what he was looking for. "Never mind." He spent several minutes reading and then with a quick glance at Jemma, said to Walt, "Go on."

"I have a deposition signed by Mr. Oliver Evans of the Evans Detective Agency, concerning some work I had him do for me."

He went up to the bench and handed the judge a file folder. "This is the log of a series of events that took place on the third weekend of July this year, between Mrs. Jemma Whiting and Dr. Hunter Gardner. In addition, I have some photographs—"

The judge looked up sharply. "Photographs? Just a minute. Is Mr. Evans here?"

"Here I am, your honor."

"Come on, let's hear you tell your story."

A small, slender man came forward and after a quick exchange of glances with Walt, told his story in a low, monotonous tone. The words raced passed Jemma; she could scarcely hear them for the thundering of her heart.

"Plaza Hotel...in each other's arms...fumbling for the door key...overnight. The ride back to Ramsey Falls...the door closing behind them on Main Street. Professor Gardner coming out at six the next morning, not a minute before."

Jemma knew one thing only, that she couldn't bear to hear Hunt's name used that way. Her expression of entreaty drew a faint shake of Brad's head, warning her to leave it alone. The battle was not over Hunt; he was in many ways an abstract issue.

When the detective finished his recitation, Walt, whose demeanor was one of a man not only wronged but humbled, held up a manila envelope.

"Photographs?" the judge said. "This isn't a divorce hearing, Mr. Whiting, merely a hearing over whether Mrs. Jemma Whiting has violated her divorce decree. I have Mr. Evans's sworn deposition as to the times involved. Mr. Kent?" he said, nodding at Jemma's lawyer.

"One question," Brad said. "Mr. Evans kept his eye on the front door of the Whiting apartment all night, from the time he saw Mrs. Whiting step out of the car."

"Just about," Evans said.

"You never slept, never left your post."

"I hopped over to the diner for a bite, back in about twenty minutes. That was about seven, a little after they returned to Ramsey Falls."

"Thank you, Mr. Evans. Let's get on with this," the judge said. "I have the reports of the psychiatrists who examined Seth. Both gentlemen are here today?"

The psychiatrist hired by Walt characterized Seth as shy, withdrawn, troubled and slow to learn. This was countered by Jemma's, who said that Seth was a sociable child, friendly, healthy, aware that he was loved by both parents and loved them in return. His feelings about his mother were especially warm.

"Checkmate," Jemma breathed to her attorney, but her throat was dry and chalky. She'd have her say soon. She had rehearsed it enough but suddenly found she couldn't remember any of the words.

"Mr. Whiting," the judge said, "is there anything else you want me to know?"

"Yes, your honor, I do." Walt stood and came around to the judge's bench. He held the manila envelope and used it to emphasize a point by tapping it against his left hand. "For three years my ex-wife lived according to our divorce arrangement."

"Oh yes," the judge interrupted. "That interesting stipulation that Mrs. Jemma Whiting may not have lovers overnight with your son present in the house. Go on."

"Lately my ex-wife has begun to change. For instance, she has accepted financing for her business, not from me when I offered it, but from someone who has been around her house at odd hours."

"That's not true," Jemma said, but Brad shook his head, and with his eyes, warned her to be silent.

"Early in the summer my ex-wife began an affair with Professor Hunter Gardner, knowing that it would end within a month of its beginning," Walt went on. "She was flagrant in her behavior, as I've been able to document, and has shown no remorse. I have no choice but to petition the court to award me custody of my son so that he can grow up in the proper environment."

The judge looked over at Jemma. "Mrs. Whiting?"

Jemma pushed her chair back, but the judge motioned her to remain seated. "Do you agree with your ex-husband that entertaining men overnight with your son in the house might be harmful to him?"

"I wouldn't be comfortable with it," Jemma said. "But I also don't want to be governed by my husband's narrow ideas. I have never had anyone stay overnight when my son was present in my apartment."

"Your honor." Brad handed a sheet of paper to the judge. "A sworn deposition by Mrs. Norma Lawson,

Seth's baby-sitter. Seth was at her house during the night in question, all night. He slept in the same room as her grandson, and the two boys were together for the entire weekend, until noon on Monday, in fact.''

"Let me see that," Walt said, hastening to the bench.

The judge, shaking his head, handed it to him. "Mr. Evans," he said to the private detective. "Do you have any proof at all that Seth Whiting was in the house during the time that you surveyed it?"

Evans shook his head. "I just assumed."

"Assumed Mrs. Whiting had left her son alone for the entire weekend while she cavorted at the Plaza Hotel."

"That he was brought back to the house by his baby-sitter when I went out for a bite to eat."

"Mr. Whiting," the judge said, giving a sigh of exasperation, "you're an able attorney. Your wife is a judge in this Family Court."

"Yes, your honor."

"Did you believe that you might have some influence in this court because of your standing and your wife's standing in this community?"

Walt hesitated a second before answering. "No, your honor."

"Then why in the world did you bring this case into court?"

Walt opened his mouth, but nothing issued forward. Jemma reached out and grasped Brad's hand and held on tight.

"I've examined your son and find him a perfectly normal, loving child who cares deeply about his mother, and you as well, Mr. Whiting. You want custody of your son for reasons of your own, and you believed that if you threatened your ex-wife with a court battle that would destroy her good name and her son's, she'd back down." He cast an admiring glance at Jemma. "She called you on it, and I might admonish her for taking up my time, not to mention the expense of running this session, when this whole business should have been settled out of court, but I believe I know why she did it. For one, the decree is repressive, and she never should have agreed to it. It's my recommendation that the decree be rewritten along more equitable lines. Mrs. Whiting?"

Jemma tried hard to repress what she was certain was a sparkle in her eyes. "Yes, your honor."

"If Mr. Whiting is inclined to fight the decree, I'll want to know about it. Now, Mr. Whiting, let me add something else. Your ex-wife would be perfectly within her rights if she hauled you into court for harassing her. The custody arrangements stand. I suggest you devote yourself to being a good father and that you don't take up the court's time with frivolous suits. Case dismissed."

Jemma sat immobile for a moment. She wasn't even aware of Walt hurrying out. Brad leaned over and put his arm around her shoulder. "A piece of cake," he said. "I told you not to worry."

"It's over? Just like that?"

"I don't think you'll have trouble with the formidable Mr. Whiting in the future. If you do, Jemma, just give me a call and we'll handle it."

"Brad, can I buy you lunch?"

"Jemma, with pleasure."

CHAPTER FIFTEEN

THE HOT SUMMER had eased gently into an early autumn. Days were cool and clear. The air bristled with the scent of pine and smoke. Piles of cut logs appeared in the yards of houses and baskets of apples at roadside stands, along with rashers of brussels sprouts and gigantic cabbages. There was hot apple cider mulled with cloves and cinnamon sitting on wood-burning stoves. Corn husks and deep red Indian corn were tied to porch posts, and fragrant and welcoming herb wreaths decorated front doors. Gardens grew rangy and late flowers neglected, as though they were already consigned to the compost heap, while fresh borders of proud mums seemed planted almost as afterthoughts. Gigantic pumpkins ripened in the fields as though by magic, puffing themselves up with importance. Halloween was more than a month away but witches and grinning skeletons began appearing in store windows.

By late September the leaves of ash trees and hickory had turned to pale yellow and dropped. A sudden overnight frost brought the first fall showing of red leafed maple and destroyed garden plants, leaving only the mums and a few brave roses. Fall leaves were raked by reluctant school kids, and one morning it snowed, fat flakes that melted when they hit the ground.

At night the sky was black and clear, the stars a bright game of match the dots.

Adriana began her classes at Pack College full-time, arriving at the shop twice a week breathless and distracted. She talked about philosophy and metaphysics and football with equal enthusiasm and decided in the space of three weeks to become an artist, a geologist and at last a teacher. "Education," she told Jemma. "I mean where will this country go without it?"

Jemma's new full-time assistant in the Ramsey Falls division of Whiting Printing was a lively retiree who was happy to be working again. He freed Jemma so she could handle the managerial duties that took up so much of her time.

Seth lost another front tooth and added an inch in height. The fact was even noted by Celie during that long-awaited and rather pleasant lunch Jemma had with her, at which Hunt's name was not mentioned. Although Victor's was, often and by Celie.

"I can tell Seth has grown," Jemma said, "by the condition of my wallet. New everything from sneakers on up."

"He's very handsome, your young man," Celie said. "Victor was saying so only the other day."

"Victor always had a soft spot for Seth," Jemma told her fondly.

"Pity the man never married," Celie remarked. "I wonder why."

"Look at us all," Jemma said. "You, Victor, Sarah, I, all single for a variety of reasons."

Celie shook her head. "Ah, but we weren't in control of our destinies, Jemma, you or I. We're single by default."

"We're in control now," Jemma reminded her. Then added when Celie gave her a skeptical smile, "More or less."

"Jemma, you know as well as I that you can set your cap for a man, and if he's not interested, you're plumb out of luck."

"Do I?" Jemma asked dreamily.

Celie was impatient. "He left. He went to Thailand, remember?"

"That was a tango we both had to dance, Celie, not just me and not just Hunt. Anyway, I don't think we're talking about Hunt and me, we're talking about you and Victor."

"Victor's a hard man to catch," Celie said with a smart little smile, "but you're right. I'm going to have to teach him to tango."

SETH RESEMBLED JEMMA in every way, except for the towhead, which was still a light, impish yellow.

He was fascinated with books and baseball and had given up dinosaurs for the time being. He found two new friends and forgot he owned a dog, except for feeding broccoli to him at dinnertime.

Niko grew at an alarming rate. Victor Bosworth guaranteed that the shepherd had attained almost full growth although Jemma didn't believe him. Niko barked at every provocation and some things that were not, but he decided were, and his bad habit added an extra measure of safety to the apartment over the store. Jemma enjoyed walking the animal; they became fast friends.

She had her life back on track and was truly truly happy, truly she was. Everything was for the best; a travelin' man and a stay-at-home would make odd companions at any time. She had done the right thing by not letting him know of the custody battle. There was only one way she wanted Hunt Gardner; he had to miss her, want her, love her with or without encumbrances.

He was the most glorious man she would ever know. He had left her a legacy of self-confidence, simply because he'd felt something special for her. She'd been no temporary fling; of that she was certain. He couldn't commit himself and understood that she couldn't either. There were simply too many obstacles way back then in that long-ago magic time when Ramsey Falls celebrated its birthday and Hunt held her in his arms.

There was a fresh dimension to her life for having loved him. And if through the long years he might become only a shadow in her mind, Jemma knew he had opened doors to hidden rooms in her, to a rich treasure chest of emotions. For that she'd be forever and profoundly grateful.

WEEKDAY MORNINGS were reserved for Merriman. Jemma used the pleasant, thirty-mile drive there in the morning and back in early afternoon, *not* to think of Hunt.

On the return trip from Merriman on warm, hazy fall days, she would turn off the road and drive to Ramsey Falls. She'd walk across the bridge at Painted Creek and along the grass to the lazy thrumming of late crickets and the last-minute foraging of sated bees amongst remnants of clover, until the noise of the falls drowned out everything but memory. She'd stand on Overlook Rock and gaze at the falls. The sun had lost its old, intense midafternoon heat, and way above a hawk might circle, drifting on air currents. Once a doe and two fawns came slowly out of the forest below and drank in short, tentative sips at the river's edge.

On the last day of the month Brad Kent called and told Jemma that her revised divorce decree was final; that she was her own woman.

"I'm going to have to get used to that idea," she said.

"It should take you all of five minutes, Jemma."

She exhaled a sigh. "Less than that, oh far less than that."

Jemma celebrated by taking Seth to a fast-food restaurant, letting him choose from the menu. He remembered liking dinosaur burgers.

Back home she called Victor and thanked him once again for sending her Bradford Kent. "He was nice, he was efficient, and best of all he was firm. It's all over now, and I'm free of Walt's interference in my life. Do you know how good that makes me feel?"

Victor laughed. "If you want, I'll take a guess."

"Of course," she went on, "we'll be sharing Seth, as always, but I never need dread the sound of his voice again or his footfall on the stairs."

"He's a somewhat chastened fellow from all accounts. One other thing," he added, "I've a little message from Cousin Sarah."

"A message from Sarah, indeed. Let's see, I don't need a lawyer or any new business. Do I dare listen?"

His voice held high good humor, the kind that told her he'd always be there if she needed him. "As a matter of fact, my young cousin decided that this news would please you. Walt and Priscilla are talking about adopting a child."

Jemma drew in a breath. "It does please me. Thank my darling Sarah and thank her grapevine. Do you know, I'm really sincere over it, too. One thing about Walt, he always loved Seth." Then she laughed. "Victor, did you hear what I just said? If after all Walt did to me, I can feel happy for him and Priscilla, I'd better keep on constant alert for signs of insanity. But I've a great idea, Victor, let's never discuss Walt again," Jemma said.

"Suits me fine. Actually, it's someone else I called about."

She gripped the receiver tightly and closed her eyes. "Go on."

"Jemma, I received a letter from Hunt," Victor began. "The program is going along splendidly."

I don't want to hear about it, she thought, *unless you tell me he's on his way home.*

"He has plenty of encomiums for Maxwell Tam, said my investment in the young man is going to pay off in a dozen different ways. Incidentally, it's hot in Thailand, and it's the monsoon season. He—he asked me to say hello to you and Seth."

"Fine," Jemma said. "If you write, tell him I say hello back and so does Seth." *Is that all,* she wanted to ask, *really all?* "Do you realize, Victor," she added hastily, sensing that he had somehow been waiting for more, "the best parts of the summer are over and also the worst." *And if only,* she told herself, *the winter isn't as cold as the summer was hot.*

THE FIRST WEEKEND of October saw Seth to his father's for the weekend. At Walt's ring, her son ran downstairs, carrying his usual weekend case and those things he could never bear to be without. Jemma had to restrain the dog from following him. She waited at the window to see Seth step into the car, waving up at her at the last minute. Walt couldn't be seen in the driver's seat and for that she was grateful.

It was Friday evening; there was still work waiting for her downstairs.

Sitting before the spreadsheet on her computer screen for ten minutes without adding or taking away a single digit, Jemma at last gave in to her restlessness. She couldn't keep herself from thinking about Hunt and now suddenly wanted to close her eyes and let the dream take over. She had no idea what to do with a love like that. Did one sit still and hope it would go up in smoke or grab a man, any man, and see if he turned into a reasonable facsimile of Hunt Gardner? Or sit and feed a computer facts and figures, the only reality? All of the above? None of the above? It didn't matter, really. Hunt was gone; she was in Ramsey Falls as ever and always with a lot of people dependent upon her.

She stopped, kicked some wrong figures out of the program and began again. After a while reality won and she was lost in the mechanics of her work. The minutes ticked away.

The sound of the cowbell suddenly punctured the night air as the front door was pushed open. The dog, sleeping at her feet, gave a short bark and sat up. Jemma glanced at her watch. It was late for customers.

"Jemma."

For a moment she sat frozen, then turned. "Hunt?"

"You still remember me."

"It was a wild guess."

Hunt came into the shop, leaned his hands on the counter and gave her a broad smile. He was tanned and fit, his hair windblown. He wore chinos and a leather bomber jacket, and she thought how handsome he was, how dear. But Jemma didn't move, didn't dare speak. She knew that her heart was doing something strange in her chest. The dog ran over to him, tail wagging. Hunt crouched for a minute and scratched its ears. "Just thought I'd check up, make sure the town survived it's tri-bi celebration."

"All the way from Thailand? You could've sent a telegram."

"Nothing like the personal touch. How's Seth?"

"Still losing his teeth and banking a fortune in the process. He had a dinosaur burger the other day. He's away for the weekend with his father and will be devastated you came by without seeing him. Are you really here, or have I dreamed you up?"

"I don't know. You could pinch me if you've a mind to."

"Perhaps I might. Did you walk out on Thailand and your adult education program?"

"I left Maxwell Tam where he belonged, administering a project absolutely suited to his talents. I decided what I needed lay elsewhere. This Niko?" The dog sat looking up at him, his mouth open, his tongue lolling.

"He seems to like you."

"I like him."

She couldn't move, nor did he. Instead they remained foolishly grinning at each other until Jemma at last jumped to her feet. "You've traveled a long way. Did you have any layovers on the way? I mean, have you eaten?" She made a face. "Oh, I can't believe I said that. Hunt, help me, tell me you're real. I haven't fallen asleep upstairs in front of the television, have I? In front of some crazy situation comedy followed by a commercial?'' She leaned back against the table, grabbing the edge and holding on for dear life.

"Jemma, I love you.'' He made no move toward her. His words rang clearly across the width and length of the shop, although they were spoken softly enough.

She was a long time answering. "Do you? Do you really?''

"Did I ever mention that Victor offered me a tenured position at Pack College?''

"No. I suppose it was an easy offer to refuse.''

He shook his head slowly. "It seemed far easier to run. I thought I'd forget you.''

"I hoped to forget you.''

"Looks like something far more powerful is making our gears turn. I've decided to hunker down for a while in one place, pass on what I know to the next generation of educators,'' he said and added, "You know, small-town living has its good points.''

"It gets boring sometimes.''

"Should be exciting with the tricentennial coming up.''

She laughed. "Oh, Hunt, you're real, you're so real. I love you.''

He came to her swiftly and gathered her in his arms. "These last two months were hell for me,'' he said, the smile gone from his face. "I didn't think I'd make it back here soon enough. I was sure someone else would find you, love you, marry you.''

"I've been blinded to the possibility.''

"Will you marry me?'' He put his finger to her lips. "I'll have to leave Ramsey Falls now and then, for distant lands. I'll want my wife and child to come with me.''

She took his hand and held it. "I think the word is compromise, Hunt. Shall we letter it on a card and hang it where we can both see it?"

Their shared kiss tasted sweet. He drew his hand along her hair. "We don't need cards to spell out Compromise or I Love You or any other damned thing. I went away and found out where I belong. And you," he said, "you stayed here in this rock-solid place, just waiting for me to show up."

Jemma laughed. She would tell him all in good time, but not now, certainly not how. He came back in spite of himself, in spite of all the troubles he perceived she still bore. Only they were all gone, and she was free to shout her love to all of Ramsey Falls.

"Oh, you're so right, Hunt," she said gaily. "I've been doing nothing these last two months but hanging around and watching the world go by and waiting for you to come back. You know, nothing much happens in Ramsey Falls."

"Nothing much happens in Ramsey Falls. The years go by, all two hundred and ninety-nine of them, and love lasts for all time."

"The kind of love," Jemma said, "that has happy forever written all over it."

Step into a world of pulsing adventure, gripping emotion and lush sensuality with these evocative love stories penned by today's best-selling authors in the highest romantic tradition. Pursuing their passionate dreams against a backdrop of the past's most colorful and dramatic moments, our vibrant heroines and dashing heroes will make history come alive for you.

Watch for two new Harlequin Historicals each month, available wherever Harlequin books are sold. History was never so much fun—you won't want to miss a single moment!

Harlequin Superromance

COMING NEXT MONTH